Dirk van den Boom

Emperor

DIRK VAN DEN BOOM
THE EMPEROR'S MEN

EMPEROR

ISBN 978-3-86402-670-6

Cover © Timo Kümmel
Editor: Rob Bignell

www.atlantis-verlag.de

1

Volkert had kept it to himself.

No one else had heard of it except him.

As he stepped on solid ground, left the wide gangplank, and stared up at the sky, he shaded his eyes with his right hand. He took a step aside to make way for the column of legionaries who, under the command of Secundus, began to leave the transport. There was a cheerful mood, almost hilarious. Not only had the nature of the Mediterranean been defeated, no, even a pirate fleet had been overcome. There were wonderful stories to tell once they set themselves up in their new camp on African soil.

Volkert brought the most wonderful story of all. And he had to keep it to himself, for although he thought that Rheinberg had to hear of it, he knew no way to communicate to him without endangering his hard-earned camouflage. No matter how he turned it around in his thoughts: Giving all the details he needed to be credible would seal his own fate.

So he kept it to himself and it triggered intense musings.

How did someone capable of the English language get into the pirates' slave chains? Volkert had had every pretext to interrogate the prisoners, but the result had been completely unsatisfactory. The man had been acquired on a slave market in the east of the Empire, quite legitimately. And where did this slave trader get him from? Nobody cared.

Volkert took a deep breath and sighed. One more thing he had to carry around with him. The loads he managed were not getting smaller. He moved his shoulders, trying to release the tension. As a Tribune, he enjoyed privileges. No one would blame him for taking a day off after the long sea voyage and getting some relaxation in the city's bathhouses. Except him blaming himself.

The city was the North African Hadrumentum. As far back as Volkert remembered the official nautical charts of the Mediterranean, the modern city of Sousse, in so far as he saw the future as "his" time, would be here, part of the French-dominated colonial territory. It was a very old city, he had learned, older than Carthage, and above all, unlike her more famous sister, she would outlive the millennia and survive until modern times.

Now it was a bustling port, an important transshipment point for the African goods, especially the grain that fed the entire Empire. The fact that Theodosius had chosen this port, in consultation with the local governors, to land his army added even more to the hustle and bustle of this place.

They had been expected. Officers advised Secundus. Volkert considered it necessary to stop looking at the city, although this was his very first visit to African soil. When he joined the men, he was greeted with respect.

"Centurion Rufus Argentius," one of the men introduced himself. "Sir, the troops must march on, I'm sorry. We are not opening the camp directly at Hadrumentum, as we don't want to affect trade. We go a little further south and have already started work there. In Hippo Regius, the African prefects unite their troops. Once they've finished, we'll unite all the armies and land back in Italy – or expect Maximus here, if he's so stupid as to follow us."

The self-assured arrogance that spoke from the words of the Centurion displeased Volkert. Maximus hadn't been a fool in the past, why should that have changed now? And if he transferred to Africa, then certainly with sufficient confidence to be able to win this attack. Who knew what von Klasewitz had been doing in the last few weeks and what he would do to make such an invasion feasible?

Volkert suppressed his need to correct the man. He preferred to save his strength for the march.

"Secundus, you organize that!" Volkert ordered his friend, who nodded eagerly. Then he turned back to the Centurion. "There was an incident at sea."

"Yes, I've already noticed that more ships have arrived than expected," Rufus replied with a smile. "I suppose they're pirates."

"Correctly. We have a pinch that I want to hand over to the harbor commander. In addition, I have prisoners whom I also want to get rid of."

"I will arrange everything."

"The prisoners are on the grain ship under guard of the Trierarch. He'll be glad if he can dispose of this load soon."

"Consider it done."

Volkert nodded, satisfied. He turned away with a greeting and walked back to the wharf. He wanted to perform one duty himself.

The liberated rudder slaves of the pirates were already led to shore. They looked a lot better now than at the time they had been released from their shackles. Their wounds had been treated as best as possible. From pirate holdings they had been given decent clothes and everyday items. All that remained now was the distribution of the money.

Volkert watched in silence as a man dragged the box of pirate coins ashore and opened it. Volkert had ordered to be generous with the money. The men came from all parts of the Empire and possibly had a long way home. That was the least he could do for them.

In the eyes of the liberated, Volkert saw gratitude and, moreover, a little surprise that the officer actually kept his generous promise – they were free, they had coins in their pockets, and a bundle for the journey. It was a turn of fate that everyone had thought impossible a few weeks ago.

One of the men approached Volkert after the money had been distributed. Nobody had complained about the sum. Everyone had received it with quiet, joyful humility.

"Sir, on behalf of my comrades, I would like to thank you again for your kindness. We will remember your name forever and ask God to protect and reward you in everything. We are all simple men, without influence and wealth. We can not offer more than God's blessing for you."

Volkert smiled, perhaps a little embarrassed but pleasantly touched, a feeling he had not felt for a long time.

"I accept your thanks," he said aloud. Any other word would have been disrespectful. "I send you all my best wishes on your journey and hope that you will see your families again. I gladly accept your good wishes, because the war is not yet over and I can use every good will that is offered to me."

There was still a bit of murmuring, and hands were shaken, forearm on forearm, as was Roman custom, leaving out the traditional kiss. Then, after a brief moment, while the men stood unsteadily against the quay wall, the group slowly broke up, almost hesitantly, as if some still didn't want to believe they could really leave.

Volkert remained standing until the last of the liberated had disappeared in the hustle and bustle of the harbor. Some would go home on the quickest way. Others would want to build a new existence here in Africa, uprooted as they were. And others would go to the nearest tavern or bathhouse and spend the money in the warm water of the baths, in the company of a soft bath girl's breasts, and with a lot of wine and food.

But that was their own decision now. They were free to fail and free to behave themselves and go their own way. Volkert hadn't been able to do more for them, and in a way he envied these men. They enjoyed, perhaps only for a short time, a freedom that he hadn't had for a long time.

Volkert's prison might seem gilded for these poor devils, and they wouldn't have understood his envy, smiling in disbelief, suspected a joke, if he had spoken accordingly.

So he kept it to himself.

He felt someone approach him. It was Bertius with their common luggage, modest as it was, on his back.

"Yes, Bertius," Volkert said, nodding at his factotum. "We carry on."

"You look worried, sir."

Bertius knew Volkert well, probably too well. He was extraordinarily secretive about certain details, but sometimes had something too maternal in his caring – not least because he wanted to distract him from the fact that he didn't always take his duties as seriously as he was expected to.

Volkert wasn't bothered. He had a serious debt to pay off, and this work would take a lifetime. It was certainly creditable to Bertius that he in turn didn't consistently remind him of this fact.

In fact, he never did.

Volkert sighed and looked at Bertius. "I'm always worried."

"That's just too true." The man raised the one hand he had left and wiggled his index finger in disapproval. "That doesn't improve your health, sir."

"That's why you're also a manifestation of vitality, my friend."

If the sentence was ironic, Bertius completely missed the message – or he had decided to ignore it. Instead, he dignifiedly raised one of his supervisor's large duffel bags signaling that he felt it necessary to leave. "We carry on," the legionary repeated, without pressing too hard.

Volkert looked back to the sea, as if a longing drove him back there.

Then he nodded to his factotum.

He had many yearnings.

His escape wasn't on the agenda by now.

2

Theodosius, Emperor of Rome, looked unhappy.

At any rate, Rheinberg hoped that had nothing to do with shaking hands with the Magister Militium and having to sit down with him in the narrow captain's cabin of the *Saarbrücken*.

But at least he guessed where the cause of the grief lay.

The plague.

The war.

Betrayal and intrigue.

The usual.

The cruiser had arrived in southern Italy just in time to protect the remnants of the army as they boarded ships and also set out to move to Africa. The Emperor himself insisted on residing on the *Saarbrücken*, if only to openly demonstrate his lasting reliance on the ability of the German commander.

The fact that he retired from his mission to gather a large army in the East and to lead it against Maximus seemed to necessitate this act of emphatic familiarity. The unimportant triviality of the pestilence raging in the east of the Empire and the lack of any army to deploy was not something that kept critical minds from nagging comments. All those who felt a bit pressed against the wall facing the seemingly insurmountable superiority of the time-wanderers now felt a bit better. The comments were subtle and pointed, always in well-spoken words, never offensive, at least not right away. But Rheinberg had learned by now to have an ear for nuances, and once he failed to grasp the deeper meaning of an incidentally thrown sentence, Aurelia was ready to offer him a comprehensive and exhaustive interpretation. The early pregnancy of his companion had a noticeable effect on her mood, and Rheinberg was not sure if that was a good thing. The latent, dangerous aggressiveness of the enchanting Aurelia now came to the fore, complemented by a radical protective instinct. Had she been given the opportunity, she would have marched against Maximus at the head of an army, only to be able to wade properly through the blood of her enemies.

Rheinberg was very happy that Aurelia counted him among her friends.

And he was glad that Theodosius was obviously prepared to continue to rely on him. In any case, the Spaniard was not one of those who indirectly blamed Rheinberg for the disaster in the East. He had received word of the plague from various sources, and one might blame witchcraft and the like for the time-wanderers, but that they would unleash the plague to destroy their own military power – no, the time-wanderers might be demonic sorcerers, but they haven't been notable for extraordinary stupidity, a fact accepted even by their worst critics.

Fortunately, these were at the court of Maximus. It was exhausting enough to endure the taunts and marginal notes of those who considered themselves loyal followers of Theodosius.

Rheinberg looked at the Emperor. He was visibly aged. Gray strands were discernible at his temples, more than before. His eyes were tired. He didn't sleep much, Rheinberg had heard, and so he was in the same situation as his general. He drove himself permanently. And the betrayal of Sedacius, of whom Rheinberg had been reported at once, had drained his strength. Less on the physical, but certainly on the emotional level. Who would be the next one willing to put the knife at the Emperor's throat? Rheinberg knew how the man felt. At least since Malobaudes, at least since Constantinople, he knew it exactly.

That didn't make it any easier for them both. The saying that shared suffering was only half suffering was utter nonsense. Sometimes it was even more potent.

"We should go on deck," Rheinberg suggested. "We're about to leave. It's a nice sight."

"He symbolizes movement. But is that also a step forward?"

Theodosius's remark, like nothing else, revealed his current state of mind. Rheinberg only nodded and led the Emperor into the open.

They stood at the bow, respectfully distant from the two sailors who had already started with the ropes. Rheinberg's gaze wandered over to the anchorage, where seven sailing ships of very different sizes were already heading for Africa, accompanied by the three steamers who would take over their escort. The *Saarbrücken* itself would pass by with half-strength, still much faster than the other ships, but the Emperor now wanted to get as quickly as possible to Africa to supervise the coordination and composition of his forces.

Rheinberg couldn't blame him for this restlessness. Miraculeously enough, Maximus' troops had not hunted them down here to prevent the crossing. The death of Andragathius by the hands of an ambitious young officer, of whom Rheinberg had heard, seemed to have kicked the usurper's strategy more out of balance than expected. Theodosius had promised to arrange a meeting with the young man. He considered him a rising star among the ranks of his officers, as he had also been instrumental for exposing the conspiracy of Sedacius. He was a lighthouse of loyalty, richly rewarded by his rapid rise in the military hierarchy.

Rheinberg was quite excited.

The hull of the cruiser trembled as the command was given to turn up the idling machines. At first imperceptibly slow, then clearly noticeable, the *Saarbrücken* broke away from the harbor wall. She drifted a bit sideways into the harbor basin before the helmsman turned gently at the helm and the bow began to itch toward the open sea.

Rheinberg's gaze fell back to the land he had barely entered. The civilian population had come to attend the spectacle. Still everywhere in Rome, where the *Saarbrücken* appeared, came big eyes, open mouths and this mixture of enthusiasm, curiosity and fear. It would take quite some time before the sight of the cruiser would be a normal thing, at least until the steamers became more widespread and people could possibly make the mental leap from these ships to *Saarbrücken* easier than before. In fact, the steamers had not been such a big attraction. In the end, they were too much like the types of ships people were used to – wood, sails, rigging, and that metal tube sticking out of the hull. The true quality was discernible only for the trained eye of the sailor, who suddenly had less to fear of high waves while the headwinds or currents no longer represented any danger.

Recently there had been news that someone in Alexandria had taken seriously to the generously distributed plans of the bronze steam engine. It was heard that one was built as a first prototype. Rheinberg was confident that in eight to ten years at the latest, the proportion of steam-powered ships – even if only as auxiliary propulsion – would be noticeably high on the Mediterranean.

Everything would be much faster, easier and more enjoyable, if not for the annoying triviality of the Civil War, a trifle that had dug these deep wrinkles into the Emperor's face.

Rheinberg himself didn't often look into the mirror. He enjoyed the critical scrutiny of Aurelia and the brief moments in which she looked very worried, whenever she believed herself unobserved.

Rheinberg suppressed a sigh. He now knew what it meant if someone aged early.

"I expect you to take command of the troops as soon as we are in Africa," Theodosius said. Rheinberg frowned. Of course, this was an expectation quite justified – he bore the title of Magister Militium and it was his job to lead the troops. But he knew as well that his experiences about warfare on land were very limited. Even in the decisive battle against Maximus he had to rely heavily on the advice of experienced generals. And they would have won if Gratian hadn't been murdered.

Theodosius knew that. He had to know.

The Emperor had apparently identified the doubt in Rheinberg's face. He allowed himself a thin smile. "We're not allowed to make mistakes, Magister," the Spaniard explained. "We've already lost an emperor and a battle. Our nimbus is scratched, loyalty questioned. Your failure in the East – not your fault, but nevertheless! – didn't help either."

Theodosius paused and looked at the water. The sun danced in the waves. It was far too idyllic for such a serious topic.

"There are many – and well-meaning – voices that advise me to appoint another commander. Someone who knows how to lead a

Roman legion. The voices have grown louder now that everyone knows that your own soldiers can only use their miracle-weapons sparingly. No one doubts the benefits of the *Saarbrücken*. Nobody wants to turn the clock back and put away the many innovations that you have brought. In fact, it is proposed to make you the top naval admiral and assign you full authority where you are best versed and have the greatest power. That's not completely illogical, is it?"

Rheinberg felt an itch in his throat and cleared it. Of course that wasn't illogical. It would take a big burden off his shoulder. Why did he now feel pain in the face of the discussion? "It's your decision, Theodosius," he replied calmly. "I won't cling to this office."

The Spaniard nodded as if he had expected this answer. "I won't do it. I won't replace you. Honestly, that's not because I do not know anyone better who could lead the troops. I have good generals. Men who would also listen to your advice but who know how to lead a war on land. But there is a very important reason for leaving you in office."

"Which one?" Rheinberg asked, knowing it was expected of him.

Theodosius held out a parchment that he had brought out from under his flowing cloak. It was a small scroll, typical of the messages that the Emperor reached by messenger every day from subordinates, spies or friends.

Rheinberg raised both hands. "I believe you, if you just tell me!"

Theodosius smiled knowingly. Rheinberg was able to talk very well in Latin as well as Greek, but reading was much harder. But the smile quickly disappeared from his face. Rheinberg immediately felt a sense of foreboding.

No doubt bad news.

"A message from Ravenna," Theodosius said measuredly.

"A new development with Maximus?"

"Oh yes. There's a new Magister Militium following poor old Andragathius." The Emperor looked at Rheinberg. Was there compassion in his eyes?

"Who?"

"Von Klasewitz." Theodosius lowered the parchment, said nothing further, just looked at the German.

Rheinberg tried not to stare too much, but he didn't succeed. Disbelief spread in him. That was … he didn't have the words. Was he angry? Was he disappointed? Or was he, after all, just amused at how it all happened that fate was constantly busy spitting him in the soup?

The Spaniard gave him a few moments, then spoke again. "It's a bit ironic, isn't it?"

"I didn't miss that," Rheinberg said. "I'm not happy about it."

Theodosius nodded thoughtfully. "Now the time-wanderers compete against each other as military leaders of their emperors. This has great symbolic power. And no one knows better how this man thinks, acts and plans. That's why you stay where you are, Rheinberg. Until the end."

"The end …" his counterpart echoed thoughtfully.

"Yes, the end," Theodosius affirmed, giving Rheinberg an intense look. "Make sure, Magister, that I'll like it."

Rheinberg lowered his head. Naturally. He had to work, he knew that. The Emperor was expecting a lot from him, especially now.

The end.

He didn't fancy even the beginning anymore.

3

Freiherr von Klasewitz was extremely satisfied with himself. He stood on the quarterdeck of the *Julius Caesar* and looked down at the long, massive ship's body in front of him. The view over the deck of the big transport was obstructed by the two masts and not least by the dark chimney that stretched out of the wooden floor and thus symbolized what this ship was.

It was a small revolution.

Von Klasewitz turned his head to the right. There was the *Octavian*, the sister ship of the *Caesar*, just as it was about to be completed. He turned his eyes to the left, and his eyes rested pleasantly on the almost finished construction of the *Traian*, the third new ship of this class. They were the largest ships Rome had ever built, even larger than the grain freighters that transported the precious food from Africa across the Mediterranean. There were also completely different ships, high-boarded, with a mighty keel and other sails and rigging. The classical square sailors of antiquity could neither cross against the wind nor perform a decent turn, these three leviathans were absolutely capable of doing so.

The steam engines built into the fuselage were far too weak for the big constructions. This was due to the haste with which Klasewitz had had to go about. Day and night work had been done on the transports, as well as on the three bronze machines. They wouldn't be able to power the ships on their own, but they would help with headwinds, maneuvers, and at least some movement if there was no wind. They made these three giants the most efficient ships of the Roman fleet. They were a great weapon in the hands of the right man.

Of course, he was the right man.

"When can we start shipping the legionaries?"

The voice tore the German out of his thoughts. Tribune Lucius Sempronus belonged to his staff, since the Emperor had already assigned the man, even before his appointment as master of the army, at his side. Von Klasewitz had secretly hoped to be freed from him after his promotion, but the Tribune clung to him like a burdock, always polite, even submissive, never contradictory, a faithfully caring assistant, but just there all the time. Just there. Von Klasewitz turned around, and there was Sempronus. When he opened a door, there was the Tribune, smiling, with a polite bow. He inspected a construction site, a maneuver, a building while Sempronus inspected him. He was his shadow, and he was good at it. The nobleman couldn't shake him off, because that would mean rejecting the Emperor himself, and that the newly appointed commander did not dare. Yet.

So it was the time to endure the Tribune.

And to answer his questions, because they were the questions of the Emperor.

"Each of the ships can transport a good 800 legionnaires, almost a legion," von Klasewitz said. "We can start the first transport in a week, maybe two. The ships are almost completed. It will take us about two weeks to reach the agreed landing point in Africa, then the return trip ... I think we will have the emperor's core force in Africa in two months. Until then, Maximus will have requisitioned enough other ships to let the rest of the army transfer in one swing, not to mention the ships the prefects from Africa will send him. We are on schedule. Everything works as agreed."

At least from their side, he thought silently. Maximus relied on the treacherous prefects of Africa, who acted as if they were supporting Theodosius, but in reality had sided with the usurper. Von Klasewitz had a healthy mistrust of traitors, and he was well-acquainted with the necessary traits. He himself had been one and he wanted to become one again. That's how he shaped his thoughts.

But none he intended to share with Sempronus.

The Tribune, in any case, listened to his Lord's words with respectful devotion and was very pleased with everything. How much of it was sincere and how much was pretense von Klasewitz couldn't guess. In the end, it didn't matter because the Tribune himself was of no importance. He was the loyal follower of the Emperor, his ear, his voice, nothing more than an extended arm, a puppet. Von Klasewitz had to watch out for him, because he had to watch out for Maximus, but Sempronus himself was ... nothing.

Nobody.

Annoying.

Von Klasewitz took a deep breath. Of course, there were many lies. From the outside, the ships looked pretty neat, but in fact it would take some time before they were really operational. In late summer, maybe. But that didn't hurt. Until then, Theodosius' troops would feel so safe and spoiled by the African prefects that the sudden change in loyalty and the emergence of Maximus' army would completely disconcert them. Until the end, they would believe that victory was assured. And then their fate would be sealed. Von Klasewitz looked forward to this moment, especially since it would be the starting point for the sealing of his own fate. With a loyal force at hand, he should be able to overthrow Maximus and make himself the Emperor. Maybe there would be another little civil war after that. But the situation helped him. The East groaned under the plague; with luck the illness would spread to other parts of the Empire. He just had to wait until enough people died that his government would be seen as an anchor of stability, a source of confidence. He didn't expect serious problems once the deed was done, which would ensure him the purple.

Sempronus, he had decided, would also be one of the victims. A little revenge, actually not worthy of him, unnecessary, but pleasing. As an emperor, he was allowed to treat himself to these little pleasures, the nobleman considered. Why else to hold the power in your hands?

He smiled at Sempronus. "Shall we inspect the ships together?"

The Tribune waved. "If you order so, immediately, of course. But I'm not a specialist, and I do not understand most of it."

The German smiled wider and patted the officer's shoulder. "That's okay."

Von Klasewitz knew perfectly well that Sempronus had tried to avoid these endless inspections that were done wherever possible. The German himself didn't do this to control everyone continuously, but rather to chat with all the workers, foremen, and the guards, to listen to their silly worries and hardships, to pretend that he was actually interested in the chatter, and then applying himself regularly to exactly one of the little grievances and to put an end to the problem. Such a thing got around and did well for more loyalty and trust in his person. And it was not a big effort. The mob had problems that matched his mental horizon. Maybe the wine tasted too watery or lunch break had been too short yesterday, and after someone injured himself at work, there was no one around to put on a bandage. This and that. Von Klasewitz then made sure that the next day one or two amphoras of really good wine were delivered or that the break for the workers who so suffered was extended the following day or that a doctor walked the site and treated every ailment with great sympathy.

This made von Klasewitz popular.

And that was a capital he could use well.

Sempronus left the ship, entered the quay, and marched toward the canteen.

Von Klasewitz's smile changed. It wasn't false anymore, it was now full of sincere and honest arrogance. This eternal acting certainly took its toll and for a moment to be allowed to be quite the old certainly served his mental health. And the price he paid for this effort was nothing compared to the price he would once receive as a reward.

How well, he thought to himself before he began his inspection, *that the world consists mostly of idiots, and I don't belong to them.*

How good, how wonderful.

4

"At some point you'll have to decide," the old man explained as he watched Godegisel brush his fingertips gently over the newly healed scar.

"Decide what, Clodius?" the Goth asked softly.

"Whether you want to be happy about being alive or appalled for carrying the scars of your illness with you."

Godegisel nodded slowly and looked down at himself. He felt weak and looked like it; the bumps of the plague were clearly visible on his now emaciated-looking body. They were on the way to healing, the pain had subsided. For some days, Godegisel had been eating three meals a day again, carefully prepared by old Clodius, and he was able to wash himself carefully, wear fresh clothes, and occasionally got up to take some shaky steps. It was best when he sat with his benefactor on the bench in front of the hut and let the summer sun shine on his aching limbs.

Clodius used this time to tell him about his life. He also read to him from the scriptures, of which he possessed versions of varying quality, the greatest treasure in this modest dwelling. Godegisel was sure that at no time in his life had he been more intensively and comprehensively engaged in the Lord's words than in the past few weeks. Clodius took care not to tire his patient. Godegisel slept a lot. And the nightmares subsided, they faded with the receding fever.

When Godegisel looked at the old man, he felt great warmth and affection. When he woke for the first time from delirium, completely disoriented, burning with hot fever, fainting and fainting again, he had seen the smiling face of Clodius, which was covered with fine wrinkles. And then there had been the cool, damp refreshment of a cloth on his forehead, and the gentle voice that calmed him, assuring him that everything was alright and that he was beyond through the worst part soon. He remembered with pleasure the strong taste of the chicken broth Clodius administered to him, the pleasant, invigorating warmth in his stomach, the animation of his spirits, and the almost euphoric joy of being alive.

Old Clodius was like an anchor and constant companion, the embodiment of the feeling of security and concern. The old man had taken care of the infected bumps, endured the unbearable stench, calmed the suffering of the sick if he threatened to despair of his fate. He had been by his side, by day and by night, and Godegisel could only guess what powers the old body had needed to mobilize to accomplish this task.

Godegisel had thanked Clodius many times, and he had accepted it with a refreshingly natural modesty. But the Goth felt every day that he hadn't yet adequately addressed his debt, and promised Clodius a house and honors and money when he had returned to serving his Roman masters.

Clodius always made a wide movement of both arms and shook his head. "What else do I need? Live your life, young Goth, that's enough for me."

Godegisel then accepted these words in apparent humility, yet he could not shake off the thought of being indebted.

And he looked at himself, the slowly healing wounds, with emerging scars that would be visible forever at the joints, in the area of his loins, something that would accompany him for life. A sign that he was blessed, a survivor, tougher than most, not even a blemish.

But, Godegisel kept asking himself touching one of the healing bumps with careful fingers, what would Pina say?

Maybe it would actually be better to banish the woman from his thoughts. He had left her, secretive, and would not return to her as a radiant young man of nobility, as honored hero, in office and dignity, with salary and wealth, but as someone exhausted, aged by the plague, and whether still in honor, that alone would be decided by the outcome of the civil war. And that perspective didn't look good at the moment. The East couldn't help Rheinberg and Theodosius. The West was in the hands of Maximus, who cornered his opponents. Help was not to be expected from anywhere.

Godegisel thought he wasn't doing a very good job at this time.

Clodius seemed to at least partially guess his thoughts. The old man looked at his charge with a mixture of pity and indignation. Godegisel sensed that Clodius would have little sympathy for his whining, and it took a few queries from the old man before he was finally ready to say a few words in regard to his state of mind.

"I'm glad I'm still alive," Godegisel said finally, answering the old man's question. "But I'm not sure what kind of life that will be."

Clodius raised his eyebrows before shaking his head indulgently.

"The weakness that came from the disease damages your soul," he explained, casting a searching glance at the hearth, where a pot of his excellent chicken soup simmered. "If the body feels bad, we get sad and expect the worst. It isn't different with you. Once you have fully recovered, you will think differently about it. There must be things in your life that please and make you rejoice. Dedicate your thoughts to these."

Godegisel hadn't told the old man much about himself, and his caretaker hadn't asked. But surely enough Clodius has gathered that the young Goth wasn't just any traveler who was just unlucky.

He had already considered telling Clodius a lot more about himself. But who would believe such an adventurous story? First captured the Emperor of the East, then killed a time-wanderer, Valens then, whom everyone had considered dead, brought to Britain. There, first part of the conspiracy of Maximus, then the flight to Gaul, then the death of Valens, the journey south, Pina, the admission by Rheinberg, special envoy to the Goths and now a plague sufferer in the hut of an old freed slave – all this within a little over a year.

Such a life wasn't led by any normal man. He had experienced more than old Clodius during his entire existence, and he was still young. Now he had even survived the plague, something many don't, and now ... by God, what now?

"I hope the Lord has had enough of my adventures," Godegisel said quietly. "I've done my part, I guess."

Clodius didn't know what his patient was alluding to, but he probably guessed that he was not just talking about the epidemic. The old man seemed to want to suppress another shaking of his head – he managed to do so halfheartedly – and then he sighed softly. It was hard to give hope and confidence to someone who was tired and suffering from a serious illness.

He got up and looked down at Godegisel.

"I'll bring you some chicken soup and bake fresh bread. Tomorrow, I go to the market and buy a roast."

Godegisel shook his head. "No, it costs way too much money, my friend. I can't pay you back until further notice."

Clodius made a derogatory gesture. "I have my livelihood, my pension from my former master, I can't spend all that. Or how else could I have afforded the scrolls, in your opinion? I'll buy a roast, a decent piece of meat, and we'll see if we wouldn't get you a long way along the road to recovery."

Godegisel didn't object again. His appetite grew. And he wanted to get stronger. He still had a long way to go and, as life had taken everything from him, there was no alternative to choose from. That wasn't a prospect that pleased him. But the restlessness, which became stronger with each passing day, was difficult to control. As soon as he was reasonably able to travel, he would set off, and then certainly to Clodius' displeasure, who enjoyed the young man's company despite all the work.

"What's the situation in the surrounding villages?" he asked the old man. "How are they keeping up?"

"I'm pretty surprised," Clodius replied. "The authorities reacted with expedience and apparently took the right measures. Sick people are quickly isolated. Everywhere people are hunting for rats. Purifying fires are kindled. The movements of travelers are closely controlled. In my time, the plague has spread faster and more extensively. Everyone is not half as panicky as we were then. I wouldn't have thought it possible, but there are actually these moments that I want to be grateful for the Imperial administration. Anyway, the plague seems to stay here in the area. But I heard that the eastern army was badly affected. The men were isolated in time, but they suffer."

He examined Godegisel scrutinizingly. "We must make sure that you don't embark on your journey until your bumps have healed well and visibly, my friend. Otherwise, you will be mistaken for an ill person and immediately picked up and isolated. It's better if you keep your impatience in check and stay with me." He smiled understandingly at Godegisel. "I'm getting boring, right?"

The Goth shook his head. "Clodius, I love you like my father."

The old man looked at the patient strangely. Then he turned his head quickly, wiping something from his eyes and concentrated on filling a plate with chicken soup.

5

Charamadoye felt that it was too early to deal with these issues. He had the cape plucked by his body slave, then sighed softly. Aira withdrew her hands from the royal figure and smiled. She was, like her overlord, not even seventeen, and last night she had served him in a different way than helping him dress. Charamadoye's gaze rested with pleasure on the slender and tall figure of the slave girl, who had evidently been chosen with great care by his elders. She wasn't just any girl qualified solely by the external beauty and docility of spirit to serve the King of Nobatia. She was also a daughter of the King of Alwa, and the campaign Charamadoye's father had waged against the distant neighbor, with the tacit and silent support of Makuria in between, had not only led Charamadoye to ascend the throne, but also brought plenty of booty.

The young ruler of Nobatia looked at himself in the richly decorated Roman mirror in front of which he stood. This item had also been part of the spoils of war. He wasn't sure if his father's death on the return trip from Alwa had been worth it, although after last night he was almost ready to believe it.

The young king had to get up early. At night, the Aksumite delegation had arrived. The wars between the three Nubian successor states, which had divided the remains of the once mighty Kush, were one thing. The mighty Aksum was a completely different one. Ezana had once conquered Meroe, the ancient capital of Kush, and thus killed the once mighty empire. But Aksum had renounced a permanent conquest – their territorial interests were more in the Arab world, and there was nothing against three beautiful buffer states between themselves and Rome. That didn't mean that Aksum wasn't interested in what was happening in Nobatia, Makuria and Alwa, and Charamadoye's father's campaign didn't necessarily bring joy to Aksum. The elders suspected that the delegation, which had now arrived in the capital of Pharas, graciously indicated to the young king, who had just risen to the throne, that the Emperor had a watchful eye on the Nubian developments, and therefore a rambunctious man like Charamadoye would prefer to think twice before he sets out on new deeds.

The king of Nobatia had absolutely no problem with that notion.

He would use the presence of the Aksumite delegation to announce his engagement with Aira and her release from the status of a slave. This wouldn't only bring peace but also sent a strong signal to Aksum that the new Lord in Pharas had the intention to conduct his foreign policy through his bed and not his sword. The Aksumites, who were dependent on a complex marriage policy within their Empire, mostly between the rival family clans, would understand that well. And if they gave him his blessing, that would surely cement his position in Nobatia.

That was only right for the King, especially in the face of the confusion that threatened to develop in the Roman Empire north of Nobatia. Aegyptus was close – too close to Charamadoye's taste – and above all, his spies heard no good.

The King sighed. It was too early for him. And diplomacy was exhausting when one had just spent the whole night exploring a beautiful woman in all subtleties. With fervor. It was tiring a bit. Charamadoye wasn't looking forward to the duties that lay ahead of him. He wouldn't be happy again until he had performed all of them.

"Then we don't want to keep our guests waiting," he murmured more to himself, but Aira saw this as an invitation to pluck at his robe one last time and then quietly retire.

The King of Nobatia left his personal apartments. At the door, the four men of his personal bodyguard joined him; they would accompany him today. They were all no older than him, sometimes playmates, sons of influential personalities, good friends. In their presence, he felt as sure as a king could feel these days.

Soon they had reached the courtyard of the modest palace. It was built in Roman style. For a true Roman, it might be nothing more than a sprawling mansion of a wealthy knight, but Charamadoye was not so vain as to overestimate his place in history. Young indeed, since his earliest childhood he had been prepared for his function with the best teachers. When Kush collapsed about thirty years before, Charamadoye's family had been an important aristocratic powerhouse, provincial princes only, but still important. That his father would then become a king himself had been rather unforeseen. But he quickly got into the role and died the death of a ruler.

Charamadoye respected and even loved his father, but had planned to die of old age. In the arms of young girl like Aira, preferably. After all, he was the King.

He should have the power to arrange that.

His equally modest entourage had already assembled, and there, opposite the slightly raised armchair that the King claimed as his throne, stood three Aksumites, well recognizable by their dress as well as their posture. Not rude or even arrogant, but not too submissive either.

One of his advisors joined the King's side and whispered to him, "The leader of the group is Wazeba, Ouezeba's brother."

Charamadoye stiffened involuntarily. Wazeba was a high nobleman and officer of the Aksumite forces, and thus certainly a worthy envoy. But above all, he was the brother of the future Aksumite Emperor, and that was remarkable. It symbolized the importance that the Emperor gave to this embassy, and it also meant that Charamadoye had to be extra careful.

He sat down on his throne chair and looked kindly down at the gathering. Then he raised his hands.

"I want to greet our guests. Come forward!"

The three Aksumites moved forward, keeping a respectful distance and bowing.

"I'm Wazeba," a particularly tall man said in a deep voice. "I represent Mehadeyis, the Emperor of the great Aksum. I bring the friendly greetings of my overlord, and I look forward to see the King of Nobatia in good health."

Charamadoye nodded majestically, but as condescendingly as possible. "I greet you, Wazeba. Please, sit by my side."

Seating next to the throne chair was reserved for the counselors and elders, or particularly important guests of honor. Wazeba and his companions took their seats and were immediately served with refreshments, which they consumed more out of courtesy.

"What message did my fatherly friend, the Emperor of Aksum, give you?"

Wazeba smiled. It seemed to him quite pleasing that the young king came straight to the point. "My Emperor was worried about the death of your honored father and the process of your accession to the throne. He wanted to make sure everything was fine in Nobatia." He made a sweeping gesture. "I see that my master's concern was unfounded."

"Not at all," Charamadoye said. "It's always a risk when someone without much experience suddenly succeeds a ruler. Your Emperor is so wise to prepare your brother for this high office. My father didn't have much time for that and was often busy with … other things."

Wazeba inclined his head. "My Emperor is not sure if the campaign against Alwa was a wise decision."

"Ah, I assure you, noble Wazeba, that I'm absolutely convinced that my father's decision was at least premature."

The Aksumite nodded interestedly. Charamadoye leaned forward.

"Please tell the Lord of Aksum that I have no intention of continuing my father's martial activities, at least not offensively. Kush only vanished a few decades ago and many nobles from that time have a deep desire to revive the Empire. I would like to assume that my father also had thoughts in this direction."

"You do not?"

"Not at all. There are reasons why Kush fell apart. We had lost all inner unity."

"Aksum conquered Meroe."

"That was a symptom but not the cause of the disease."

"You are kind."

"I'm realistic enough. I'm less worried about what's going on in the south than what's happening in the north."

Wazeba's eyes narrowed, his face curious with tension. "You speak of the Roman civil war."

"Yes, that is true. I understand you got a visit from the time-wanderers."

"You are well-informed."

"Every friend of Aksum is well-informed about what's happening at court."

Wazeba grinned. "It's common among good friends, isn't it?"

Charamadoye grinned back but became serious again as he continued. "Warn your guests, Wazeba. The Egyptian Prefect knows that the time-wanderers are in Aksum, and it seems to me that he expects to welcome them back in Egypt soon."

"Is that so?" Wazeba frowned. "Why?"

"Why? Because he has exposed a bounty on men named Neumann and Köhler as well as on a Roman officer named Africanus – 200 gold denars, old coinage, for each one of them. But this message was only for military units and was not publicly proclaimed."

"You are well-informed," Wazeba repeated.

"Some young men of my people are in Roman service. Some already a bit longer. Some voluntarily, others as slaves. But they haven't forgotten their homeland. I ... learn things."

"How useful."

"Useful also for your master, noble Wazeba."

The Aksumite leaned back and looked thoughtfully at the dusty floor of the palace courtyard. "My lord will be grateful if you keep him informed. In fact, I indeed want to send him a messenger today."

"Before you do, pay attention to a second piece of news I want to give you," Charamadoye warned.

"I hear."

"The prefect gathers troops and sends them west."

"Civil war. The African prefects support Theodosius, I've heard." Charamadoye smiled bitterly.

"Yes, that's what *you* hear. But what did I?"

Wazeba's gaze seemed alarmed.

Charamadoye, King of Nobatia, told him one or the other detail that his informers had leaked to him. Then he told Wazeba his marriage plans and asked for Aksum's blessing, so that the king of

Alwa could approve of the connection and Charamadoye could take care of other things than to repair his father's mistakes.

Wazeba, brother of the future emperor, assured him of all this. His words spoke of gratitude. And respect, almost reluctant respect for a seventeen-year-old king, who already proved more capable than his predecessor.

The day turned out, as this particular king mused, to be quite pleasant.

6

"Well, that's a camp!"

Secundus was satisfied, and that was remarkable, for although the Centurion had gone through so much in his life and had suffered so many hardships, he was somebody who actually set high standards for his life. Patience distinguished him: if, through promotions and small "business," he could accumulate the riches that would enable him to change his life in a few years, he would endure less enjoyable circumstances for some time.

But that he would be satisfied at once with a camp, Volkert felt to be quite remarkable.

And his friend was right.

The workers, who had been assigned by the prefects of the African provinces to set up the camp for Theodosius' men, had achieved two things. First, they made it possible for the legionaries, who otherwise would have borne the brunt of the work, to relax a little. Secondly, they built with a little more attention to detail than the soldiers focused on drill and practicability. The fact that the camp was built around a deserted village helped: Not only were old stone buildings refitted, there was also a beautiful little bathhouse, which was repaired very quickly. When the first wagons arrived with supplies – fruits, fresh cereals, amphorae with wine, and barrels of beer –, the mood didn't only lift inside critical Centurion Secundus. Nobody had anything against the usual cereal porridge, but the variety was welcome.

Volkert let his people relax a bit, but not too much. He continued to report his unit regularly to night and guard services, much to the displeasure of his legionaries. The subliminal criticism he endured. There was nothing wrong with some holiday and rest, but they were at war, and nobody should forget that. Sometimes fate loudly reminded you of such facts, and then it was good to not be too surprised.

Secundus was satisfied, Volkert wasn't.

He was looking for an excuse, but he found none.

He had to comply to a duty he really wanted to avoid. This consisted of a staff meeting with the Emperor, who had arrived the previous day in camp. The *Saarbrücken* was near, too close for Volkert's taste. But as an ascending star in the military hierarchy, he was invited to the Emperor's meetings, as of now. The problem was that not only Captain von Geeren would be present but also Rheinberg and Engineer Dahms, both men who knew him well. The question was if the beard, the attire of a Roman officer, and the signs of the hardships of the past few months that had made him age visibly – he himself preferred the term "matured," but that was ultimately a matter of opinion – were enough to conceal his true identity.

And was that still necessary?

It was a war, and Volkert was an officer, a most respected one, a man whom everyone foretold a great career, even greater than the one he had completed in the past. Everyone was very interested in him. Volkert felt his former comrades might be merciful. Should he reveal himself to Rheinberg?

This inner turmoil and uncertainty made him look for an excuse not to attend the meeting. If he could avoid it, he only would delay the confrontation, Volkert was well aware of that. But sometimes that was enough.

But his search for a reason to abscond had been unsuccessful. Secundus hadn't helped him much. When Volkert had suggested that he would rather not attend the meeting, his friend and companion had stared at him in disbelief. "Are you crazy?" had been his spontaneous reaction. "The Emperor is waiting for you! You will be presented to the Germans! They want to hear your opinion! You have to go there! Think of you and your career! And think of mine!"

Secundus had sounded like his mother to the last sentence, Volkert thought. But the very last remark had put things right. Of course, his good friend was quite interested in profiting from Volkert's rise. It was reassuring, though, that he made no big secret of it. That made Secundus reliable in his own way.

And so Volkert had no choice.

The meeting took place in a large building that used to be the main mansion of a squire and was still being worked on. But part of the roof was restored and a large room so clean and equipped that it was well-suited for the gathering.

There were twenty-five officers in all, a selected group, and this made the fact that Volkert belonged to it particularly problematic. When he entered the room, most of the invited guests were already present, but Theodosius and Rheinberg were still missing. Small groups had formed and talked, but Volkert didn't want to join any of them. He knew most of the men only superficially. Richomer, the youngest general in the room, was most likely someone he could talk to. He had made the preparations that led to the imprisonment of Sedacius – and his subsequent suicide, all triggered by Volkert's betrayal.

He shook his head, trying to get rid of these depressive thoughts quickly.

"Ah, Thomasius!"

The heads lifted as the Emperor's loud voice boomed through the room. He walked next to Rheinberg and hadn't been announced. Theodosius appreciated being as informal as possible at such meetings.

Volkert tensed, forced a smile, lowered his head submissively. Maybe that helped.

"Here, Rheinberg, this is the young man I told you about."

Volkert looked Rheinberg in the eye, presented his forearm to the Roman handshake. For a moment he relaxed. There was no sudden recognition in the eyes of the man, only friendly curiosity. Volkert looked too different, older, with lines on his face, a beard, a Roman uniform – probably not even his own mother would have recognized him. He even managed a smile.

"I've heard a lot about you, Tribune," Rheinberg said in greeting and took his arm. "You have unmasked a traitor, killed Maximus' best general, conquered a pirate fleet, rescued a barbarian heir, and thus brought us an ally – did I forget something?"

"Thank you, sir," Volkert muttered softly. He wanted to say as little as possible. His voice could still betray him; it was well-known to Rheinberg. To play the intimidated young man was easy, one, who preferred not to speak too much in the presence of his elders. Modesty was also a good thing for a steadily rising officer. In the background, he discovered Engineer Dahms, who apparently examined him only casually. From him, in all probability, he couldn't expect any real danger.

"Even the suggestion to go to Africa to plan the reconquest of the entire empire came from you," added Rheinberg, putting a hand on Volkert's shoulder. "Keep up the good work, Tribune. We can only win this war with men like you!"

Applause and approving noises were heard. Volkert felt for a brief moment the strong, almost overwhelming urge to drop the mask, to explain himself to Rheinberg now and at that moment, but he couldn't manage more than a narrow, seemingly timid, but actually rather tense smile. He lowered his head humbly and accepted the applause.

He hoped that all of this would pass quickly. He wanted to disappear faceless in the crowd of others.

"Enough, enough," Theodosius shouted, laughing. "The good Thomasius might vanish into the ground right now! We want to begin with our deliberations!"

Gratefully, Volkert took his assigned seat at the table, while the Emperor and Rheinberg positioned themselves before a large map of the Empire, which would serve as an orientation for all of them. All attention now focused solely on the Emperor, for which Volkert was extremely grateful.

"First, may I introduce you to all our esteemed guests," Theodosius raised his voice as they all sat down and stared forward silently. "This is Lucius Gaudentius, the Comes Africae, and at the same time the supreme coordinator of the troops of the African provinces, who will join us shortly. Together we will muster a force of more than 35,000 men, enough to seek the final decision against Maximus."

Gaudentius took a step forward, bowed and then waved. Applause greeted him. He was well-known to most men here, and came from an old and respected aristocratic family, as Volkert had been told in advance. He looked confident and sympathetic, someone who knew what he wanted, and who was willing to risk it. So he was in the right company now.

"Noble Gaudentius will now explain to us the preparations of the African prefects," said Theodosius, "and then we will set a timetable."

He paused for a moment.

"A schedule to destroy our enemy, the traitor and murderer Maximus!"

Cheers came up. Volkert cheered, but he had no heart for it. Then Gaudentius began to explain all the details. Volkert initially only listened with half an ear.

Traitors and murderers?

Something was ringing in him.

7

After the long meeting, Rheinberg and Dahms wandered through the balmy African night toward the large, well-equipped tent that they occupied together. Behind them, almost hidden in the dark, four men from Rheinberg's bodyguard followed. Memories were awakened in regard to the assassination attempt, and involuntarily Rheinberg touched where the sword had pierced him. The wound had healed superbly and was visible only through her scar – and sometimes a bit of pain that reminded him of caution.

Even if an attempt in the middle of one's own camp was unlikely.

Nevertheless, Rheinberg now groped for the butt of his pistol, which he wore under his robe, and felt the reassuring hardness of the handgun. He led a life, despite all of his power and high office, in which he had to fear for his life daily. That left marks, as Aurelia had told him once or twice before. He looked older than his years suggested, and that wouldn't get any better.

Maybe after all this was over, he could just take a vacation.

"And what do you say?" Dahms asked after a few minutes of silence. "We seem to have a real chance to end it once and for all."

"That's true. Once we have the African troops assembled, we will land in Italy and defeat Maximus!" Rheinberg was convinced of his words. The meeting had been very successful. The plans were as watertight as they could be.

"And if the rumors are true that Maximus wants to follow us to Africa and attack us here?"

"Same way. It will be even easier for us. He's just welcome to try."

Dahms nodded, but Rheinberg could only guess what he really thought. When they reached their tent, both their faces were illuminated by the fires burning before them. They stood in front of the canopy of the entrance and looked at the flickering flames.

"What happens after that, Jan?" Dahms asked softly. "If Theodosius governs the whole Empire – as it has been in our past –, what shall we do then?"

"The Huns," Rheinberg reminded him.

"Is that so? On the one hand, there was this report of ill-fated Sedacius, according to which the Huns operate farther west, much closer to our frontiers than expected."

Rheinberg stated in silence that Dahms spoke of "our" borders. Like all of them, over time he had begun to perceive himself no longer as a foreign body in this epoch and to feel a certain loyalty to the circumstances here. Whether this was based on reciprocity, Rheinberg couldn't say with equal certainty. He doubted it.

"On the other hand," the engineer continued, "more and more reports have arrived in recent weeks that the activity of the Huns has diminished. Lastly, a letter from our new allies, the Quadian King, who said that he could no longer find Huns in his territory and beyond, though he sent many scouts."

"Perhaps the victory of Sedacius intimidated the Huns?"

Dahms made a doubtful face. "Huns are not so easily intimidated. They put away defeats easier than we do. I can not believe that. But maybe they have become a bit more careful. Allow their approach some more time. But if that makes them better prepared, there's still a lot to come."

Rheinberg put a hand on Dahms' shoulder.

"We should cross that bridge once we reach it."

"I'm sure you're right. But there is still another question left."

"Which?"

"Von Klasewitz."

Rheinberg let out a snort. "What should be with him? He made his decisions. That he is on the other side can't surprise us. He will pay for his betrayal. If the developments allow for it, it'll be my pleasure to do it personally."

Dahms surely felt the cold anger and determination in Rheinberg's words and nodded in satisfaction. That was probably exactly what he wanted to hear. And if Rheinberg wouldn't find the opportunity, Dahms was obviously quite ready to relieve him of that burden.

They stood still for a few moments in the cool night air, before they went inside the tent, which was more like a small house. Servants were waiting for them. One told Rheinberg that Aurelia was already sleeping in her part of the tent. The hardships of the journey, combined with the physical effects of her pregnancy, showed their effects.

Rheinberg was still struggling to get used to the idea of fatherhood. It was now an incentive for him to create conditions that would allow his child to grow up in peace and security.

"Bring tea!" Dahms said, and they sat down on the couches provided to round off the evening. However, "tea" was by no means to be understood as Rheinberg and Dahms knew it from their time. The tea plant had come to Europe only in the 17th century. The Romans knew hot potions from different herbs, which resembled in taste and application rather classic healing teas. Thyme, chamomile and other plants were well-known, including their medicinal effects. It was better than nothing, but not what the two men really wanted to drink.

"I'm not allowed to tell you," Dahms mumbled, "but the men of the *Saarbrücken* are busy making you a very special crib out of old metal parts. With chimney and so on. It will look awfully silly, and Aurelia will accept it with iron politeness then banish it from her eyes as quickly as possible. But that's why you should prepare her for it. The men mean well, they just ... well, just don't know."

Rheinberg grinned. "I will be pleasantly surprised and pleased. Aurelia is an outstanding actress. I wouldn't be astonished if you'd even see tears in her eyes. It will be heart-wrenching."

"Then all will be well."

The servants brought the tea, the usual herbal mixture, sweetened with honey. It didn't taste too bad and was probably horribly healthy. For a moment, the two men silently dedicated themselves to the drink. In contrast to the "real" tea, this one didn't stimulate but was rather relaxing, which should be conducive to the subsequent bedtime.

"Jan ..."

"Yes?"

"It is him, isn't it?"

Rheinberg looked at Dahms, not asking, but with a slight, knowing smile. He nodded.

"Without doubt. I didn't recognize him at first, but it gnawed at me all evening, and when he spoke once or twice, it became clear to me. It's Volkert, no doubt."

The engineer set down the cup. "What do we do with him?"

"Nothing. He has established himself well. I'm pretty proud of him."

"A great guy," Dahms confirmed. "Who would have thought that? Shall we not tell him?"

"On a private occasion, if it fits. He shouldn't be afraid. He should decide for himself whether others should know. It's his life. He went through a lot and paid enough for his mistake – which was possibly my fault as well. He is now master of his destiny, as far as we all are."

Dahms nodded. "A good idea. I agree. He didn't fall on his head and accomplished amazing things. He will throw himself into battle with all his strength."

"What about Julia? She's also in the camp, along with her father."

"And her daughter. Volkert's daughter, as you have told me. Shouldn't he know about that?"

"I'm sure he knows or will soon find out. Then he will find a way to get in touch with her. This is a family affair. We only interfere when it gets loud."

"Hm?"

"Theodosius can solve the problem with a simple decree if he wants. But I think we should not interfere from the outside. They are both safe here, as much as they can be. We leave her alone. They are no longer the same young people we separated a year ago. They've become far more self-confident and mature, if you ask me. "

"I think so. The Volkert at the meeting was a very different man from the Ensign of our day." Rheinberg emptied his cup and set it down. "I'll talk to the Emperor soon enough. He should know. Maybe he will settle things quickly and calmly. He thinks a lot of Volkert."

Dahms shook his head. "We're both older and wiser, aren't we?"

Rheinberg looked into the empty cup in front of him and sighed. He recalled his thoughts from some time ago, about his appearance, the burden of the office, the marks they left behind, and the almost heretical desire for relaxation and idleness. Then he looked at Dahms, who was already much older than Rheinberg anyway and on whom all the excitement of the past few months had also not passed without a trace. He smiled at him, almost forgiving. "Older, my friend. And more determined."

8

Helpful to be a hardworking legionary.

Centurion Salius, who was no longer performing as a centurion but the odd decurion, had made a great effort not only to be industrious but also to be obedient – as well as the other comrades of the special troop founded by military prefect Renna, who joined the army of Maximus.

Nice, hardworking and competent. And once he had indicated that he had experiences with the open sea, he had risen immediately in the eyes of his superiors. The number of marines available to Maximus was limited. The bulk of the Roman fleet was either in Constantinople, which had once again declared open opposition to the usurper, or had joined Theodosius. When Salius could state credibly to have a little sea experience, he was immediately a little bit closer to Magister Militium von Klasewitz. Salius was commissioned to train willing legionaries as marines to defend the ships in the unlikely event of an attack during their passage to Africa. Since von Klasewitz inspected the three large transports almost daily, Salius was given several opportunities to talk to the traitor and prove his qualities.

Fortunately, von Klasewitz didn't remember him anymore. Back then, when the nobleman had instigated a mutiny on the *Saarbrücken*, it had been Salius and his men who had turned the matter in the direction of Rheinberg. Von Klasewitz and his assistant Tennberg had fled in the confusion, and since then Salius had made it his personal duty to make up for this mistake. When Renna had assigned him the delicate mission of infiltration, he had said good-bye to him with the phrase, "Salius, you must do what you have to do!"

Both had understood exactly what was meant by that.

But so far von Klasewitz had always been accompanied by his bodyguards. Being assigned to serve in this bodyguard was the most important milestone for Salius and his few unidentified comrades. If you were in the immediate vicinity of the man and enjoyed his trust – as far as anyone in the world enjoyed the confidence of the traitor anyway –, then it could be done what one had to do.

Salius would try to survive that occasion and then escape.

But that wasn't his priority. The time-wanderer and as many men as possible from his close staff with him had to die. It had to be a deep cut and then best at a time that was considered ideal. Not now as Maximus' loss was easily offset.

Salius had to strike once the German's decisions were of real importance. Just before the battle. During the battle. His death not only had to tear a vulnerable gap, it had to lead to a deep, festering and crippling wound.

So it wasn't time yet for murder.

Now it was time for dinner.

Salius had a busy day behind him. As an instructor, he enjoyed the privilege of being provided with food in the officers' kitchen tent instead of cooking for himself or having to hire a simple legionary to serve him. The chefs in the large kitchen tent understood their craft better, and the choice of food was excellent. Von Klasewitz had decreed that good food was extremely important for morale and that everything had to be done to ensure its steady supply.

Salius didn't disagree.

He was a little early and the large tent with its numerous benches and tables was still relatively empty. A buffet of considerable proportions had been set up, and all sorts of servants were ready to fill the bowls and plates of the hungry. Amphorae with wine had been lined up and there was also beer for the friends of a rougher taste. Salius grabbed a wooden plate and looked at the food presented with an appreciative look.

"Noble lord, may I serve you?"

Salius looked up and looked into the submissive eyes of a young, plump woman with rough hands and equally crude features. Her reddened skin spoke of hard kitchen work. Her clumsy body was stuck in a baggy working gear that made her already unfavorable body even uglier. Her expression spoke, Salius thought, of a lack of intelligence, a staid woman with no prospect of ever being able to escape from this existence. Having been hired as a kitchen helper here in the camp was probably already the best thing that would ever happen to her. With great luck, one night she would be nailed by a drunken legionary who valued so much soft meat.

Salius forced a smile. "Thanks, I'll take a look at the selection. You have all done a good job. One doesn't know where to start."

The woman grinned a little stupidly, but apparently touched pleasantly by the simple praise. "Thank you, noble sir. Call me if you need anything!"

Salius shivered when he remembered that for a simple kitchen aid "anything" included services that he didn't even want to think about. He kept his smile and turned away.

He was about to open a sweet cake for starters when he felt a new presence next to him. He looked up and saw Lucius Screpius, one of his own men who had recently made it to decurion. Screpius, a gifted artisan, had also been promoted to instructor and shared the privileges of his co-conspirator.

"All is well?"

"Everything is great. The cake looks good."

"Yes …" Screpius grabbed a piece of biscuit and looked up as the kitchen assistant approached him.

"Sir …"

"No, no, thanks!" the man protested, and the woman lowered her eyes sadly, then withdrew. The eyes of Screpius lingered for a long moment on the waddling figure.

"Do not tell her you like her," Salius said with a faint joke, as they looked for a seat.

Screpius didn't return the smile but seemed more thoughtful. He watched the woman with searching interest, how she served the other guests, how she submissively accepted orders, received insults without further emotion, suffered ridicule, or was simply ignored as if she did not exist. She carried food from the kitchen and cleared away leftovers.

Salius couldn't gauge what caused Screpius to pay so much attention to this subject. He was about to open his mouth and ask again when his mate was already speaking.

"I know this woman," Screpius said, shaking his head. "That is quite unexpected."

"You know her?"

"Only too well. And not how you think. I arrested her once when we helped Ravenna's city guard on Renna's orders."

Salius looked at Screpius in alarm. "Tell me!"

"Her name is Flavia. Don't let her appearance fool you. She deliberately uses her modest shell to keep everyone in the dark about her true intentions and abilities. That's worked fine with you just now, or am I wrong?"

"Go on."

Screpius took a sip of wine. "She's a shrewd and intelligent cheater, blackmailer and thief, and probably a murderer, they say. And she has escaped every time. When we captured her, we found her carrying bags of gold stolen from a senator. Two weeks later, shortly before her execution, she disappeared again. We had overlooked gold, enough to bribe the guards and cheat herself to the freedom. Then she went underground. And now she is here." Screpius bit into the cake and moaned appreciatively.

"Then she fits in well with this company," Salius said thoughtfully.

Screpius looked at him inquiringly and asked with his mouth full, "I don't like your expression, my friend. I don't like it at all."

Salius grinned. His mind developed a spontaneous plan. "I think I've always underestimated the attractiveness of fat women," he mumbled. He ignored Screpius' moan again – this one out of sheer despair – and turned around. His searching gaze found Flavia, who was just putting a jug of wine on the table of some dining officers. "Hey, you there! Woman!"

Flavia came out of the gloom, the attitude full of dumbfounded zeal to serve the gentlemen at once. She shuffled in quickly, anxious not to let the noble gentleman wait unnecessarily for even a second.

Damn, Salius thought to himself. *She is good! She is really good!*

"Greetings, Flavia," Screpius said in a measured tone.

"The Lord knows my name? I am honored, sir. What can I bring you?"

"Tell me where you went to after your escape. Evidently you didn't do too badly."

A remarkable transformation took place before Salius' eyes. While she seemed submissive and stupid, now her body stretched. She was no less plump than she had been before, but there was an alert intelligence in her eyes, an unexpected hardness about her mouth. The thick, raw hands, just like wet rags dangling at her side, suddenly seemed strong, gripping ... almost menacing. Her posture betrayed inner tension and strength. Her eyes were calculating, careful, but without fear. "I must know you, sir," she said, now carefully articulated, with a lurid sharpness of tone.

"You don't remember me, Flavia. But you are well.known to me. I once had the pleasure of arresting you. You relieved the honorable Marcus Tullius Praetonius of a large bag of glittering denarii. Ah, I remember – were not you also employed as a kitchen helper in his urban mansion?"

Flavia's eyes narrowed. "I do not remember."

That sounded sincere, really honest. Salius was very impressed.

Screpius chuckled. "Of course not. That would've been too much to ask."

Salius looked around. Nobody paid attention to their conversation. He smiled at Flavia, not warm, but with the cold calculation of a predator. "Sit down, Flavia. I want to talk to you."

Interest and expectation sparkled in her eyes, as she followed his request. She folded her hands on the table and looked at Salius calmly. If she was afraid of imminent arrest, she didn't show it.

Salius developed enthusiasm for this woman.

He liked to work with professionals. That made everything much easier.

9

"I don't think you can travel."

"And I think you just miss not being able to mother me anymore."

Godegisel took Clodius in his arms and hugged the old man for a moment.

"Thank you for everything you've done for me. I won't forget you, and I mean that. As soon as this war comes to an end and I know what has become of me, you will enjoy my gratitude."

Clodius shook his head, smiling. "You keep saying that, my boy. But it's still not necessary. See that you go your way. Hurry to the west and escape the plague as best you can."

Godegisel nodded. He wore scuffed but clean clothes from Clodius's supply. The old man had given the Goth goodbye gifts that shamed him. A new pair of laced sandals purchased on the market, a great foundation for the long hike that was about to dawn. A travel bag that Godegisel could throw over his shoulder, filled with other clothes, bread and cheese and a small amphora with diluted wine. And finally, a wallet with some smaller coins, a very modest sum, but enough to keep Godegisel alive for a few days.

Godegisel's goal was to reach Dyrrhachium and from there find a sea passage to southern Italy to join Theodosius. From what Clodius had told him, access to Constantinople was heavily regulated, and the plague was also spreading in that direction. It was a kind of race he might not win. Once he had found Theodosius' army in southern Italy, the Emperor might find a suitable use for him. Rheinberg was probably there by now, so he could tell the German about the failure of his mission.

For a few moments, the Goth had considered returning to the settlement of his people, but he immediately rejected that idea. There was no future for him with them. And even in the event that he could still persuade them to intervene, the plague had quite destroyed all these considerations.

Godegisel had failed, both due to his fellow Goths and to the external circumstances. He accepted that. It wasn't possible to do more than to try something else at this time. By now, he was able to assess his position well enough that he knew he wouldn't be the cause of much adversity. He hoped for a position from which he could keep watching things and play a role without being too much in the foreground.

It was nothing to worry about.

"We'll meet again, Clodius," he said again, and the old man just nodded. They both didn't know what the future would bring. And after all what Godegisel had told his savior, the old man surely realized that humans like the Goth had a completely unpredictable life path. It may be that this path led him back to his hut. But it could just as well happen that they saw each other for the last time despite all their good intentions.

It would happen as it should, Clodius had said many times.

At some point, both men had enough of saying goodbye and Godegisel started walking. He had meant his promise quite seriously, although he didn't even know if he would achieve his goal unscathed. But he felt filled with great optimism. He had survived one of the worst scourges of humanity, something not many people could claim. He felt a little weak at times and was still a bit emaciated despite the good care of Clodius, but he was tired of waiting. There were so many things happening, and Godegisel no longer wanted to watch, but most of all, not be considered a coward who had waited until the storm subsided.

His good spirits rose, as he met a small caravan bringing goods to Dyrrhachium. With a coin he bought a place on the large barrels, which were transported by a cart pulled by two powerful oxen. Godegisel stretched out his legs, squinting in the sun, and relaxing under the gentle movement of the cart, which carried him toward his destination without any further effort needed by himself. They would be underway for another two weeks, as the coachman had told him, but it was two weeks Godegisel didn't have to march.

The carters were friendly men. They shared their supplies with their guest when it was time for supper. The Goth ate modestly, didn't want to appear excessive, and compensated his benefactors with exciting stories of his flight from the Huns, which eventually led him to Rome with his people. The carters themselves came from all parts of the Empire and traveled everywhere, and they found the history of the Great Migration exciting and asked many questions. When they all went to sleep on the first night, they were all aware that they had received adequate compensation for every effort made, whether in the form of porridge and bread or in the form of enjoyable and interesting entertainment.

The journey passed without incident. Godegisel knew about oxen and wagons, for he had witnessed the long trek of his people fleeing from the Huns. He helped where he could, earned food, and, when it rained, a corner in one of the tents spanned over the goods. He didn't annoy anyone and wasn't a nuisance. When, after a good two weeks, they saw the walls of Dyrrhachium and Godegisel left, the master of the caravan shoved the coin back into his hand, which he had previously demanded as a transport fee.

"You'll need it, my friend. The city is expensive."

The Goth thanked him, a little touched, but glad that he had come this far without any great expenses.

The following day, he arrived in the big harbor town. He knew that his money wouldn't be enough for a crossing, so he looked a job. To his displeasure, he found that the travel opportunities to that part of Italy, which seemed to be in the hands of Theodosius, were rather limited. The directly accessible cities were controlled by Maximus. He had confined any trade to the territories under control, so direct passage to southern Italy was not possible, at least not at present. Rumors persisted that Theodosius had fled to Africa, and there were only ships allowed whose passengers had been thoroughly interviewed by the city guards before departure. Godegisel didn't have an increased interest in such attention at this time, although he didn't expect to be regarded as particularly famous or even notorious.

In addition, the city authorities passed strict quarantine regulations to prevent the spread of the plague. Godegisel had been investigated before entering the city. The healed plague scars had prolonged this investigation, but at the same time aroused admiration and respect. He had finally been allowed to pass through the gates.

Even those who left the port by sea were thoroughly scrutinized. The plague was everyone's enemy, whether loyal to Theodosius or Maximus, and no matter how much the parties wished to fight, no one dared risk spreading the terrible scourge on purpose or even by negligence. If it would spread unhindered throughout the Empire, the victor of the civil war might not have much left to rule over, and the barbarians were already waiting in the East to exploit this weakness with great joy.

Nobody was that stupid. Godegisel accepted the delays and thoroughness of the multiple controls. He didn't wish anyone to go through what he had endured and survived only because of the intense care of an old man and a robust constitution. Nobody should suffer that way. Nobody should die like that.

He didn't spend too much time waiting, which was very helpful given his financial limitations. When faced with the prospect of spending the night outdoors, he witnessed a conversation between two sailors who put him on the right track. A coastal sailor would leave for Italy with the destination Ravenna and the captain was still looking for some extra hands.

Godegisel was modest in regard to the pay, and he was allowed aboard.

He had mixed feelings about returning to this city. But at least it was going in the right direction, and the controls were not half as stringent as when traveling to Africa. Godegisel didn't want to be discovered. He was well-known to Maximus, to many of his henchmen as well. He was sure that the escape of Valens still bothered the Emperor until today. It would indeed be a great pleasure for everyone to capture those responsible. At that moment, Godegisel was extremely grateful for the scars of the plague. They didn't disfigure him very much – he hoped it anyway, and still nurtured that little doubt of how young women, especially a certain one, would react to his altered appearance –, but they changed him. His narrowed, almost thin stature helped to make him recognizable only for someone who knew him very well.

Would Pina recognize him?

No, Godegisel thought to himself as he entered the ship with his bundle and volunteered for duty as cook for crew and passengers, armed with the recipes of Clodius.

At first, it was not about whether Pina would recognize him.

The question was more if she wanted to recognize him at all.

10

"There's no doubt about it," Gaudentius uttered, looking seriously at Rheinberg.

"Well, we suppose so, anyway," the German said, looking thoughtfully at the map of North Africa they had spread on the table in front of them. "If the spies are right, it's no surprise. It just requires sufficient preparation."

"So the decision will be made in Africa," von Geeren mumbled. "Maximus is pursuing a daring game. We should just sail out with the *Saarbrücken* and sink the ships with the troops he sends us on. That would be the end of his attempted attack."

Theodosius looked at the Captain in astonishment, then shook his head. "That would be mass murder."

Von Geeren calmly returned the Emperor's gaze. "It would protect the lives of your men and end the war."

"Thousands of legionaries would drown miserably, and at the behest of the Emperor claiming to be their master," Richomer defended Theodosius' horror. "How shall the Emperor ever gain legitimacy for his rule, if he secures his victory by such means? It's a horrible idea."

"They'd have no chance," Rheinberg replied softly. "We'd approach the transport ships at maximum range, just blow them away, and they'd sink quickly and take all the men to their deaths. They wouldn't even know what hit them, if we fire from far enough away."

He shook his head. "No, I don't accept such a slaughter on my watch."

The Captain didn't know for a moment how to react. Rheinberg was certainly different from him in regard to decisions like this. Von Geeren thought of the immediate military advantage. Rheinberg didn't disregard this argument, but it became clear that he also considered other things that went further into the future and had a different, perhaps greater, significance than a simple victory.

Von Geeren sighed. "Once Maximus lands his troops, there will be a great land battle, during which many men will die."

"In a proper battle. Everyone will have a chance to sell their lives as dear as possible," Richomer insisted. "They are Romans, not animals. They have the right to use their weapons in their defense."

"There will be cannons. Guns. The weapon ..."

"On both sides. Everyone knows it. I'm not saying that everyone will survive. But they get a fighting chance. You may surrender. You may escape. You may fight. But once we send them crammed together in the body of a transport ship to the bottom of the Mediterranean, they have no choice. We just can't do that."

Rheinberg continued, "It's also about what this means for our reputation as time-wanderers, Captain. If we do this, any conflict thereafter will be more terrible. How can we reach out to achieve reconciliation if we've just massacred our opponents?"

"This is not uncommon among the Romans," von Geeren said. "They always waged their wars with the utmost brutality."

"And they sowed wind that became too many storms," Rheinberg answered. "By force, you can not reach a lasting political solution. If you are lucky, you can create a basis for resolving the conflict differently. But in the end, it only provokes another chain of violence." Rheinberg's voice became insistent. "The real enemies are outside the Empire. There are the real challenges. We can not mercilessly slaughter our own people and then expect their friends, relatives and companions to fight with us against those who really threaten the borders. That's just absurd!"

Theodosius stepped forward and laid a hand on the Captain's shoulder. "Another Theodosius, maybe in your past, might have acted differently. This other Theodosius has caused thousands of defiant citizens to be rounded up and massacred, and only because he was an irascible man. He then regretted it bitterly. I don't want to be this man. If the arrival of the time-wanderers gave me the chance to become a better emperor, then I should take advantage of this opportunity. I'm not a berserker and no barbarian. I don't want to be, but especially not against Romans who think they fight for a just cause. That's not only not possible, Captain von Geeren. It simply doesn't work that way."

The infantryman nodded hesitantly. "You are the Emperor. If it is your order ..."

"It is. May Maximus land his troops. We should find out where he wants to do that. Then we offer him the decisive battle he seeks. The African troops at our side, we will throw everything in the balance. We have a material superiority against which even the cannons of your traitor can't do much. It's going to be bloody and it's not going to be easy, but we have every chance of winning this contest." He looked at von Geeren. "In a decent way."

The Captain nodded again, gesturing that the discussion came to an end. Rheinberg understood the reasons for the man's proposal. It would've been a quick and effective solution, a clear demonstration of the power of the time-wanderers. And it would have further strengthened all the prejudices against them, provoked indignation and fear, promoted their image as savage, brutal slaughterers, as dishonorable barbarians. Their victory would've been stale. Their life in the Roman Empire would've become one of constant caution, mistrust, rejection. Rheinberg didn't want to do that to anyone. They needed to be accepted here, both by the winners and by the losers alike.

The fast, clear solution was not always the best and certainly not in this case. Theodosius had recognized this in his own way, and his respect for the Emperor grew. This was indeed a different man from the one he had read about. Theodosius the Great, it seemed to Rheinberg, was on the way to earn his surname with justice and dignity.

"So let's allow the men of Maximus to reach the coast. We have to assume that they know exactly where we are. Are they going to land close by or further away?"

"We have to make it easy for them!" Richomer explained. He stepped next to Gaudentius. "It'll be better if we do this – you get in touch with Maximus and tell him you want to change sides. You are communicating a favorable landing place for him, which we choose – and we keep the troops on standby. To reduce his mistrust, you will receive and take care of the landed soldiers yourself. It's not about surprising them, it's about determining the time of landing and then the exact location of the battle. "

Gaudentius looked at Richomer with an almost startled bewilderment. Rheinberg had the impression that the Prefect had not considered this kind of betrayal by itself.

"I ... I'm supposed to pretend I'm a traitor to Theodosius?" Gaudentius said with an incredulous tone.

"That's the way it would work. You should succeed, because this idea is not completely outlandish. Demand something – a higher post, a payment, or just a favor that the Emperor has to grant you in the future. Maximus will trust you."

Gaudentius nodded thoughtfully. He seemed to be pleased with the thought. "It could work out. A daring game. I can't be near Maximus at the wrong time, especially when he realizes that the African troops are marching alongside Theodosius, and not with his side as promised."

"There are always risks. But once the battle begins, you can rightly say that you must command your troops in order to change sides at the right time. With this excuse, you'll be out of his reach and under our protection. Nobody requires you to lead the assault on Maximus himself. Everyone is doing his part. It doesn't have to be yours."

Theodosius clapped his hands and nodded pleased toward Richomer. "An excellent thought – if our friend Gaudentius takes on the burden of this special task. It's not without risks, you said that yourself. But it could bring us victory, much easier than expected."

The Prefect seemed to consider the proposal for a few more minutes, asked a few questions, but Richomer seemed to have planned well in advance. In the end, they came to the understanding that they would do as discussed. They even had a suitable battlefield with good positions for the remaining riflemen from von Geeren's infantry company. When Gaudentius said goodbye, they were all confident. The Prefect promised to reach out to Italy and see if he could get in touch with Maximus quickly.

After the Prefect had gone, von Geeren looked compellingly at Richomer. "Sinking Maximus' troops out to sea would be dishonorable. To defeat the army by betrayal and vice, wouldn't?"

Richomer smiled indulgently. "Betrayal or not, every one of the Maximus side fighters would have the same chance – fight, give up, run away. We're only increasing the likelihood of choosing one of the last two alternatives."

"The legionaries of Maximus are not as disciplined as they should be?"

Richomer shook his head, this time rather sadly. "No, I don't think so. On the contrary. They will begin with full confidence. And yet, they have a choice. They even have the chance to win the battle with superhuman effort and great steadfastness. Would they have this chance in your proposal?"

"No." Von Geeren sighed again and looked at Rheinberg. He didn't give the impression that it was particularly important to him that this opportunity would be granted to the enemy. On the other hand, he would faithfully carry out his orders and not keep an endless discussion alive.

"But?" Rheinberg asked anyway, noticing von Geeren's discomfort.

The Captain shrugged. "But it would be over quickly and we could take care of the really important things."

11

Quintus Virilius was a simple legionary without great ambition. He shared the fate of so many of his comrades, whose voluntary involvement in the armed forces was at least questionable. His father had been a soldier, and his grandfather too, and while elsewhere it was a venerable tradition that had filled all offspring with pride, it had always been a burden to Quintus. His grandfather had voluntarily joined the Legion and had been promoted to decurion. His father had already been compelled by law to join, a law according to which sons should take up the profession of the father, and this law was enforced particularly zealously in the case of legions always striving for new personnel. His father had not come far, but he had not shamed his profession either. He had survived, had been dismissed honorably, had settled down, fathered three children, and had fallen down to the ground dead at the age of 51 when attending his fields.

Quintus had nothing against the Legion.

But it seemed the Legion had something against him.

He always met the wrong people – the wrong comrades who turned out to be drunken rogues and involved Quintus, who was not looking for that kind of distraction, in things he was not responsible for but still was held accountable ... the wrong superiors who saw a victim in the lanky, pale-faced young man, someone who could be made a bad example for other lanky young pale men. But since Quintus was thoroughly committed to duty, followed orders faithfully and kept discipline, one had to look very much for lapses to make a bad example of him. Some of his superiors seemed to have made this a life's work.

And so Quintus Virilius kept watch all week on a distant frontier post, a wooden lookout built on four trunks, with a very rickety staircase leading up to him and his two comrades. The lookout had a roof – which was leaking – and a horse whose rider had to be ready to rush to command with an important observation while the other two legionaries had to see how they got along. All three men were in a bad mood, and with each passing day in the airy, not always dry height, with the monotonous meals of porridge and rock-hard bread and the duty to stare constantly to the east, should the hordes of Huns come from that direction, this mood became constantly worse.

And so they got on each other's nerves.

Quintus tried to say as little as possible.

That alone seemed to irritate his two comrades, of whom he knew little more than their names.

No matter what he did or did not, it was wrong.

When he had time, Quintus was daydreaming. He didn't see himself as an emperor or knight, as a glorious general or the like. He had loved his youth on his father's farm, the freedom he had enjoyed there. His father hadn't been a bossy man, had been tired of roaring and commanding after being discharged, a gentle, fast-aging man who had loved his wife and children very much. Quintus wished to return to the yard, dreaming to do something with the neighbor's daughter, sweet Sabina, as he had never dared. Now he would never see her again, he was quite sure of that. He dreamed of completing the extension buildings his father always talked about but never started, and a stable for a few cows, if he could afford it.

These were modest dreams. They consoled him in the night when he was cheated once more by his comrades with the dices, when they laid sleeping and snoring, as he stared through the murky fog toward the wooded area barely lit by the starlight, guarding his post somewhere on the edge from Moesia Inferior, about 200 miles from Noviodunum, where Roman civilization and comfort beckoned.

Quintus sighed. This was his third year in the Legion. He had turned 20 two weeks ago, which didn't interest anyone, and nobody noticed. The prospect of spending another 17 years serving such as this – or suffering an early death by the barbarian blade – didn't lift his spirits. Then he was 37. With luck, he would afterwards enjoy ten or fifteen good years before his life ended.

That was not what Quintus had imagined.

At least it was relatively quiet.

It was also annoyingly boring. It was cool. Damp. The feet in his boots felt clammy, and now and then he stepped on the spot to get some feeling into them. The fog was dancing. Sometimes Virilius thought he could see shadowy figures in it. He heard the sounds of the night, and it was not always to assign the cause clearly. Animals, yes. But there … weren't these steps?

Of course, nothing happened. The snoring of his comrades was the only sound that clearly came from a human being. And it was at the same time the one who strained his nerves most during the night. The sawing sound reminded him that he would hardly sleep that night, and that the coming day would only be full of leaden fatigue and hardships.

Virilius expected nothing from this guard except a continuation of his frustrating and sad existence as a Roman soldier.

At least until the time the figure appeared in the fog of the night.

The guard post had been built on the edge of a forest. To the east stretched a thinly wooded area with a lot of open grassland, a position that allowed a good view especially during the day. At night, visibility was limited, and though the sky was starry, a kind of fog billowed in which an entire army could be hidden. At the same time the fog carried sounds, so that the cacophony of nocturnal animals made itself heard easily. The footsteps, the clatter of metal and the snorting of a horse were therefore good to discern, much sooner than Quintus' strained eyes could see anything.

Out of the mist a dark, barely recognizable figure peeled with a horse on its leash. That was not exactly what was called a surprise attack, and yet Quintus felt a certain satisfaction when he could shake his two comrades from sleep.

The silent cursing of the awestruck and dumbfounded men ended once they also spotted the figure who had stopped about fifteen feet from the guard post and seemed to be waiting for something.

"He wants something from us," Quintus muttered.

"One of us should go downstairs and talk to him," one of his comrades said.

"Shouldn't we all go?" Quintus asked, already suspecting what that was all about.

"We'll give you backing from up here," came the expected, far from reassuring answer.

Quintus thought for a moment about how he could defend himself, but nothing clever came to mind. He sighed – which his comrades acknowledged with a hypocritical grin –, grabbed his weapons and climbed down the ladder, emphasizing slow and loud movements, so as not to be misinterpreted as an attacker.

When he stood on the ground, he adjusted his sword in the scabbard and leaned the spear after a brief reflection on the scaffolding of the watchtower. He preferred to fight with only one weapon, and the spear only obstructed him. He replaced his shield with a torch, of which a supply at the bottom of the high stand was waiting to be ignited. The flame promised the illusion of security. Then he took a deep breath and strode toward the patiently waiting figure.

As soon as he approached, he realized that he was dealing with a man and an old one for that. The weather-beaten, wrinkled face and white-gray hair spoke a clear language. Still, the man, a little shorter than Quintus, stood remarkably straight and upright. Attentive eyes met the legionary. The horse was one of the ponies that the Huns liked to ride, and the man himself, as far as Quintus could judge, was also a representative of this people, and to look out for them his most important assignment.

Quintus felt a little bit how anxiety took possession of him. The old man was completely motionless, and he carried no weapons, especially not the dreaded bow of the Huns. Quintus could not see a blade either. And wild warrior or not, he should be able to deal with the old man in case of doubt. Quintus didn't like being a soldier, but he quite mastered his craft. He had a strong intention to stay alive, and the ability to effectively use a weapon was quite helpful to a legionary.

He stopped a few paces from the man, held out his torch, and nodded to him. "I greet you. Why are you approaching our post?"

Quintus did not even know if the man understood Latin or Greek, but it didn't seem to matter. The old man slowly and visibly pushed forward a bag, which he had worn behind his shoulder, and opened it. Quintus remained watchful, but the Hun didn't produce a weapon, just a scroll, carefully wrapped in a tubular leather bag, which he opened briefly for the legionary to peek inside.

Quintus nodded. A message from the Huns?

The old man laid the leather tube on the floor, nodded encouragingly to the legionary, then turned and mounted his horse. Without making any utterance, he turned the animal and rode away slowly. It only took a few moments, then the fog had swallowed him.

Quintus took the container and looked closely at it. Characters had been carefully burned into the leather. It was unmistakable that there was a name there: Rheinberg, Magister Militium.

The Huns sent word to the Commander-in-Chief of Theodosius.

Quintus pocketed the tube and returned to his post. With luck, a little luck, the cowardice of his comrades would now be of use to him.

Fate had thrown him a few new dice, a little bit weighed in his favor.

Quintus would take the chance.

He only had that one, he knew.

12

"If it's not his own goal, it has to be ours."

Ambrosius leaned down and smoothed his long, articulated fingers gently over the herbs that grew in the garden through which he wandered with Petronius. It was warm, sunny, and the air was dry, too dry, actually. When they entered the small church garden, greeted by the priest living here, he had first complained of his suffering – it was generally too cold and too dry this year, and he had great difficulty in stimulating the plant's herbs and vegetables to grow.

Petronius stopped beside the Bishop and waited.

"Your objections are justified, my friend," Ambrosius went on. "Of course, it's dangerous to question Maximus at the moment. But he is ambitious and too independent for me. God's fear alone is not enough. If Theodosius is defeated, much more work is required. I want to make sure that someone is Emperor whom I can trust to enforce the necessary orders on a permanent basis. Nobody should get tired. Never let up. Do not waver – and above all, never should the interests of the state be more important than those of the Church. That's exactly what, Petronius, is at the heart of the matter. The Church has priority in everything."

"I don't contradict you, Bishop," Petronius knew only to say, and Ambrosius nodded as if he had expected nothing else.

"And yet?" he asked when the priest didn't say another word.

"And yet … we can be glad someone like Maximus rules. To make von Klasewitz Emperor is very dangerous. He is a stranger, one of the time-wanderers, and if we kill Rheinberg, he will be very alone, too, surrounded only by those who fundamentally distrust him."

"Very wise, my friend." Ambrosius stretched and clapped his hands. "And that's the point! An Emperor whose only friend is the Church, whose only support is the Hierarchy of the Church. Who must inseparably link a program to enforce our orthodoxy with his own political survival in order to stay in power and be alive. He would be a man of our graces, Petronius, who would receive consolation and help only from us, would find protection and encouragement in the faith and in the arms of the Church, nowhere else. Precisely because he has no supporters on his own in the administration – unlike Maximus. Precisely because he has no supporters on his own in the army – unlike Maximus. Because none of the senators will work for him – unlike for Maximus. One, who can't show his own victories to gain legitimacy, no great deeds, no brilliant successes – unlike Maximus. The perfect puppet in the hands of the Church, constantly pursued by the fear of falling victim to an assassination attempt or rebellion, if he doesn't devote himself completely to our cause in order to maintain his position. We will speak, and he will hear. Even if he doesn't like what we have to say, he will have no choice but to enforce it. Would we withdraw our support, even in public, not a month would pass and his body would drift in the Tiber."

Petronius nodded, an excited sparkle in his eyes. They both took a few more steps, watching the insects dance in the sunlight, and enjoyed the wonderfully peaceful silence of this secluded place not far from Ravenna. "Then it's wise to wait until Maximus has prevailed over Theodosius," Petronius finally said. "It must be the victory of Maximus, not of von Klasewitz, so that he can not obtain his own additional legitimacy."

"You think well," Ambrosius said, taking a deep breath. "That's exactly what we have to do. But that doesn't change the necessity to take the right steps to initiate the change of power after a victory against Theodosius, and as soon thereafter as possible. In fact, I don't think there should much time between the triumph of the battle and the abdication of Maximus."

"That sounds very challenging."

"It'll be. Above all, it requires a person who is close to the Emperor and is prepared to do the things to be done at the given hour, regardless of his own safety, without hesitation and in full trust in God – and without too much blemish falling on the church."

"So von Klasewitz himself. Or someone from whom one can ... distance himself when it happened. A ... crazy man, who acted of his own initiative, by no means on higher orders. Someone who took the message of his superiors too literally. Someone of ... a simple mind."

Ambrosius nodded his approval.

"Very good, brother. Your thoughts are clearly going in the right direction. But of course we have to talk to von Klasewitz. He is an important part of our plan, even if he himself should not make the final blow. We have to make our goals his own. It would be even better if he had similar plans, and we could help him realize them, putting his fate into our hands."

"I can talk to him," Petronius offered, scraping the sandal tip of his right foot in the dry floor. Dust-dry the earth was here, crumbly, almost indistinguishable from sand. No wonder it was a great challenge to grow plants here.

"That would be helpful."

"What can we offer him help with?"

"You."

Petronius looked up and stared at Ambrosius. "If I raise my hand against the Emperor, it falls back to the Church. And you. Everyone knows that I'm your confidant."

"Thou shalt kill no one. This feat should be done, as you have just suggested. Let us find a suitable tool. Among the young priests are some who know nothing but the Church and are willing to give their lives immediately for their salvation. A good candidate should be available. But your task is a different one, my dear Petronius."

"Tell me."

"It's about the time immediately after such an act. It causes turmoil, and all too loyal henchmen of Maximus might be compelled exercise judgment on von Klasewitz. Someone must be there who moderates the excitement. Someone who speaks reasonably and is able to demonstrate the benefits of the new power structure, who expresses the Church's regret over the sudden death of the Emperor, but at the same time suggests that the new emperor is quite one with whom we intend to cooperate. It's a difficult task, Petronius, but ultimately you don't have to do anything except save von Klasewitz's life so he can do what we expect of him. Once the first excitement is over, I take over and make sure that everybody makes friends with the situation in the long term. I have senators who eat out of my hand. I have administrative officials who do what I say. Bishops will follow me, the Pope as the supreme man of our church as well. But that takes some time, preparation, it takes a lot of talking and more or less gentle pressure here and there. You are responsible for the first days, the first weeks. I lay a big burden on your shoulders, my friend. I want to prepare you well, but you must quickly proceed for Ravenna and be close to the Emperor. I trust that the Lord will give you inspiration at the right time to do your work properly."

Petronius remained anxious, concerned about meeting this major challenge. "The Emperor knows me, I've often accompanied you," the priest muttered. "Von Klasewitz has given me his trust for a long time. But the most important obstacle is the others, the officers, above all."

"They're all Trinitarians, friends of the Church," Ambrosius said. "I talked to everyone, and my word has weight there. Just take care of the first days. As soon as I have news of the deed being done, I rush to your side. Then everything should go its course, as we have imagined."

Petronius sighed.

"I want to do it. But first, the traitor must be persuaded to become our tool."

Ambrosius smiled pensively. "I feel that you won't have to do much persuading. I'm even sure that this will be the easiest part of your assignment."

Petronius nodded. "I don't contradict you, Bishop. But first, I'm looking for a suitable candidate … someone ready to execute the will of the Lord without much thought."

Ambrosius put a hand on the man's shoulder. "And when all this is done, we should ensure that a certain Petronius becomes bishop of Ravenna?"

64

The friend smiled in flattery and bowed his head.

"I serve the church."

The bishop of Milan nodded affirmatively. "Indeed, Petronius. You do just that."

13

"This is where the battle is supposed to take place. It's the perfect location."

Gaudentius made a sweeping gesture. From the city walls of Mactaris, one could see far. The surrounding landscape with its green hills looked peaceful and fertile. Rheinberg shaded his eyes. It was warm but not uncomfortably hot; the sky was almost cloudless. Mactaris lay far in the interior of Africa Byzacena, about a hundred Roman miles from Hadrumentum, nearly 150 kilometers. The way from the port city there was relatively easy to cover, although no road led directly to Mactaris. They had ridden over Sufetula and from there north to this location, but the detour was not significant because of the good condition of the roads. In Sufetula, they had rested briefly to look at the bow of the tetrarch, a building that glorified the rule of Diocletian and his co-rulers. They had also been invited to the Three Temples, although these were barely used, as the Christian Church had taken over spiritual supremacy here as well. Instead of building a common temple to the central deities of the traditional Roman pantheon as usual, Jupiter, Juno and Minerva each had their own building in Sufetula. Rheinberg once again regretted not having time for proper sightseeing, which was by far more interesting than planning a battle.

Mactaris was an ancient city, already built as an outpost of the Numidians against Carthage and then settled by Roman colonists. Here Rheinberg had been convinced after their arrival to a visit the inevitable bathhouse. He had been glad to shake off the dust of the journey. Afterwards, Gaudentius had led him and Langenhagen to climb the city walls, since one could well recognize from here the place of battle suggested to him.

The location had been well selected. The hills provided ideal hiding places for the infantrymen, and there were points from which one could have an excellent view of the battlefield. Of course, this advantage also applied to Maximus, but Rheinberg would be there first and able to choose his position very carefully. He could see nothing wrong with the suggestion of Gaudentius, but in the end he wasn't the expert. For this reason, the newly-minted General Richomer accompanied the small expedition.

"Of course, a battlefield within the reach of the *Saarbrücken's* guns would be a lot more suitable," Rheinberg said, looking at Langenhagen, who had accompanied him to the interior on this journey, because he had wanted to see "something else."

"Since von Klasewitz, a former artillery officer, knows the capabilities of our guns better than anybody else, he would never accept such a battle," the officer said with a regretful undertone. "The Romans alone, maybe. But with the traitor and his knowledge at their disposal – never. We have to offer them a battlefield out of the reach of our cannons, even if we prefer otherwise."

Rheinberg nodded and looked inquiringly at Richomer, who had been silent so far. "What does the General want to add?"

"I'd like to have a closer look at the area."

"We can ride there anytime," Gaudentius suggested. "It's just an idea, I myself follow the suggestions of my officers. I'm always ready to be persuaded of the benefits of a better place. Only we should know the selected area soon. The African troops gather at Hippo Regius. I want to set them up and unite them with your legions, so that we can unite the command structure as well as quickly as possible. A few joint maneuvers shouldn't hurt either."

"Absolutely correct," Rheinberg confirmed.

"I see that need as well," Richomer said. "The location isn't bad. Over there, on the hill, we can position the signals and horns, from there we have a nice overview. The valley is gentle and does not form a cauldron, there is room for maneuver, yet at the same time it is well visible. The traitor will appreciate it likewise."

Rheinberg smiled sourly. "Where will he put his cannons?"

Langenhagen looked around. Before Richomer could say anything, he pointed to a ridge of hills. "If we choose this side of the battlefield, he'll probably position himself over there. Anyway, that's what I would do."

"Never count on the predictability of the enemy," Richomer advised. "There's a good chance he'll disappoint you."

"We will not commit that mistake," Gaudentius said. "But if our plan succeeds, it's not just about predictability, it's about factual preparation. Once I have credited Maximus with changing to his side during the battle, he will accept that I need your trust in return. So if I get Maximus to accept a prepared battlefield, he'll be sure that his opponent will trust me and the planned betrayal will work. He will be very surprised if, at the agreed time, the African troops by no means change sides but faithfully continue to serve Theodosius. But then it will be too late for him."

Rheinberg nodded. He couldn't deny this logic. And since Richomer apparently also agreed with the conditions of the battlefield, there was no reason to delay the decision any further. Not only the African legions had to be relocated here, also the units of Theodosius had to leave soon from Hadrumentum to be able to prepare properly.

"You're in contact with Maximus?" Richomer asked the Prefect.

"He accepted my messages, and we'll meet in southern Italy. Everything else will be discussed there. I'll leave as soon as I am back at the coast. When I return, the battle will not be long in coming."

Gaudentius looked seriously at Rheinberg. "All is coming to an end, Magister. Soon we will know who rules Rome."

"I can't wait," the German muttered. "I'm tired of this war. There are so many things to do, which are much more important. I want to build, not to destroy and kill."

"I feel Maximus would say something similar if asked," Richomer said. "With the small problem that he desperately wants to ensure that Catholic Orthodoxy becomes a state church and infidels either abjure or die."

"Yes, a marginalia," Rheinberg said with bitter irony. "Oh, that stupidity."

"This verdict is useless," Gaudentius said. "When it comes to God, God should decide. This is the battlefield where the Lord will announce His judgment, written with the blood of the vanquished. What should we be worried about? Everything will happen, as the Lord has predestined. We are nothing more than his tools."

Rheinberg decided to forego a religious-philosophical discussion of this topic. He still vividly remembered his futile attempt to come to a common denominator with Ambrosius. If it was true that this decision would be made on the battlefield alone, he wouldn't be able to do anything about it anyway.

It comforted him little to know that even without the arrival of the *Saarbrücken* in this time, this civil war would've commenced. And it was sobering to see that his intervention had only accelerated the outbreak of the conflict. Maybe Gaudentius was right in his own way. The fateful power behind history seemed to have an interest in starting certain developments, no matter what plans Jan Rheinberg had. *God laughs at plans*, he thought grimly. *What a pity that I find it so hard to laugh at God's plans.*

Nevertheless, he would continue to prepare events and ensure that projects were put into action. Maybe he would fail. But what kind of life would it be to remain in complete passivity and just let everything happen? Rheinberg was certain that as a human being he was only capable of a meaningful existence if he intervened creatively in the course of the world. This didn't always lead to the desired result. But not to try, that would be, in his eyes, nothing but complete self-abandonment. Such a life, he was sure, could only be called completely meaningless.

He felt that he unconsciously clenched his fists and forced himself to open them again.

"Good," he said then. "Richomer, we ride through the area and make sure this is the place. Langenhagen here is free for the rest of the day. He should look around the city and forget the *Saarbrücken* for a moment. He deserves it."

"Actually, it's the good Joergensen who really deserves it," the officer said, grinning. "But he isn't here."

"So don't complain," Rheinberg said in German.

"Never, sir. I'm off!"

With that, Langenhagen turned on his heel and disappeared. Rheinberg sighed.

He was back on horseback now, inspecting hills and groves to prepare everything for thousands of men to die here soon.

It was not an enjoyable view.

14

In Hadrumentum, there was everything. Goods were traded that found their way from Africa to the port city, one of the important trading places for further transport to the rest of the Empire. And here those goods from the Empire arrived that were not made in Africa, or whose nimbus as import goods from distant lands was important enough for the upper classes to spend a lot of money on them. Julia and Claudia strolled over the bustling market square, which extended across the whole forum. Here was nothing foreshadowing the approaching war or fear of the plague from the East, here was trade and haggle, and everyone was looking for opportunities. The poor who offered their services along the road were as much a part of it as wealthy Romans – civil servants mostly, or merchants, their wives and slaves, many on foot, some on litters, and all with loose purses. Julia was certainly one of the wealthy, had suffered no lack since their return to her father, not least because the family of Michellus had always had commercial interests in Africa and possessed assets. Her father had been happy to welcome her and his granddaughter, and the absence of Lucia, the dreaded wife and mother, helped Julia to wrap her father around her little finger in a tried and tested way. However, she had written a long letter to Lucia describing the circumstances of her separation from Martinus Caius. No matter how traditional and narrow-minded her mother might think and act, this violent approach, even the threat to her granddaughter's life, would never be tolerated by Lucia. Civil war or not, Julia was pretty sure that her mother was already thinking about which means would be appropriate to humiliate Martinus Caius in a permanently satisfying way.

Julia was fine.

Her daughter she had tied her around the chest. The little girl watched the market with sleepy serenity, having only recently been breastfed. She had already made some travels and seen much of the world in her early years, so Hadrumentum's market seemed to be of little interest. She yawned and gave a satisfied chuckle before her eyes closed completely. Julia gently stroked her head.

At a stand, guarded by two beefy slaves with powerful clubs in their hands, goblets of glass and special works of art, all sinfully expensive, were sold. They stood on velvet towels that had been spread on the table. There was a heavy, soft carpet in front of the sales table, should a customer be careless and drop one of the precious pieces. Julia's glance went expertedly through the goods. She had no home or house, no place that was her's to stay. This restlessness of her life forbade her to think of such an expensive outfit, but that didn't stop her from pausing for a moment, imagining herself having dinner with her husband and invited friends in her house, looking at the wine in those glittering glass caskets.

Maybe one day.

Claudia had only a passing eye for the goblets. Her lodging, provided by the city authorities, was not far from the Forum, and if she wanted, she could go shopping every day. Her trip today had therefore less to do with the joy of shopping – although this joy was consistent and permanent, especially a welcome distraction from the thought of the approaching, final confrontation – but more with Claudia's appointment.

The freed woman stopped at a stall selling candied fruit. Since her arrival in North Africa, Claudia had discovered her enthusiasm for these delicacies, which were heavy and sweet enough without adding sugar. In the candied form, the sweetness exploded in waves, so to speak, and Claudia valued these explosions with fervor. Besides, she said, she must put on a few pounds in the right places. Although Julia doubted whether the strategy chosen by her friend was the right one, she knew that the goal was by no means just an end in itself. For the eyes of Claudia had rested for some days with pleasure on the figure of a young centurion, who for a while had organized the watch-duty for the civilians brought along, and had often, by chance and only in fulfillment of his duties, appeared in their quarters, being polite to Julia, but almost charming to Claudia – at least with the degree of charm to which a raw soldier was capable. It was probably just what made him attractive to Claudia. Anyway, he had told her that he wanted to organize supplies for the legions with his superiors on the market today, as the troops had built a camp near the city and would soon, the rumor said, set out to prepare for the battle against Maximus, either here in Africa or back in Italy.

Claudia was not the youngest anymore. The fact that she hadn't been forcibly impregnated in her time as a slave was primarily related to the custom that slaves were generally not subjected to such practices in the house of Michellus. There were issues in which the senator and his wife showed rare concord. To use young slaves as producers of more slaves was something they both didn't approve of. On the other hand, if nature took its course, they had nothing to object. But sometimes that also meant that nothing of that kind had happened.

It was by no means that Claudia wasn't attractive to the male eye. And she hadn't taken any chastity vows either. Still, she had been very choosy in her partners, especially as her goal had always been to bewitch a free man who would then be willing to marry and free her from the status of a slave.

One she never had found.

But she was no slave anymore. A free woman, however limited that freedom might be in the society of the Empire, where everything depended on the man and only a few women – those with charisma, power or who were simply very attractive – reached the highest positions. Claudia's ambition didn't reach that far. Her goals were more modest, and she seemed within reach of an important milestone on her way to the life she dreamed of.

Therefore, now that Claudia was free, her interest in men had increased abruptly. Instead of giving birth to slaves as a slave, there was now a good chance that her offspring would be born in freedom – and in honor, which presupposed a marriage. One was as important as the other. Both meant a lot for a former slave. And if it was possible to bet on the right man – and a successful centurion was not a bad match, especially if he looked reasonably good and didn't behave like a Martinus Caius –, then everything was perfect.

Claudia was clever. The experiences of her mistress with her husband had made her very attentive and critical. She paid attention to the important things and informed herself. Her chosen one was obviously not a blank slate, but neither a womanizer nor anyone inclined to unnecessary brutality aside from the battlefield. Claudia had therefore decided to put her bets on him, hoping that he would survive the war.

Julia sighed softly. She had this hope in common with her friend. The difference was that she didn't know where Volkert was and how he was doing. Claudia had something ahead of her, but she didn't react with envy. She had learned that in these times one must be grateful for every moment of happiness, as it had the habit of passing away very quickly.

She looked at her daughter, who pushed her lips back and forth in her sleep, as if she were thinking about something important.

Grateful for every moment.

"He's over there!" Claudia said vaguely. The sticky sweets in her mouth didn't contribute to a clear pronunciation. She noticed this herself and chewed bravely to keep her mouth free for the upcoming conversation. She quickly stowed away the small sack of remaining candies she had just picked up in the bag she carried with her.

"He's not alone," Julia observed. "That must be his superior."

"A chaperone," Claudia chuckled. "Sweet!"

Julia showed mild interest as the two men, who were still far from her, strolling slowly in their direction. The Centurion pointed to a large stall with bags of corn while his companion made a note on a long list.

"Come on, we'll go to meet them!" Claudia said excitedly, pulling at Julia's robe. She allowed herself to be pulled along, but she renounced unreasonable speed. One should not make it too easy for men. Show interest too clearly, one was considered easy prey. It was always necessary to hang the fruits a bit higher.

74

Claudia adjusted her dress, which, as Julia noted critically, seemed to be a little too close up. It seemed as if Claudia wanted to present at least some of the fruits appropriately. Without doubt, this display would attract the Centurion's attention, Julia was sure of that.

Then they were approached.

"Secundus!" Claudia shouted. The Centurion looked up, then looked where he was supposed to, and his friendly smile became even friendlier.

The other man raised his head, also shortly fascinated by Claudia's breasts, and then ...

Then there was this moment.

There were sometimes moments you wanted swim in.

Seemingly, it lasted forever, dragged on by sheer focus. It truly was the culmination of long-cherished desires and came so suddenly that it could only be described as sacred.

Julia and Volkert looked at each other. None uttered a word.

He looks old, Julia noted with concern. There were wrinkles that she hadn't noticed before. The skin was tanned by the weather. The expression in his eyes was ... so tired.

And then the tiredness disappeared and gave way to fear.

It could have worked out this way – they would have bowed down, preserved formal distance, supported the facade for mutual protection, perhaps, or even because they didn't know how to deal with this moment.

But then her daughter opened her eyes, turned her head, saw her father for the first time in her life.

Tears came to his eyes.

Secundus and Claudia stared at each other, stunned, as Volkert spread his arms, pulling daughter and mother close to him, infinitely gentle. They watched the Tribune stare down at the small face with stunned fascination, which in turn looked rather puzzled, as if the little one didn't know if this mighty, bearded shadow represented something good or disturbing.

Secundus and Claudia exchanged a look. Secundus knew nothing; Claudia was informed. It was dawning on her now. Then she too started crying.

Centurion Secundus was helpless for the first time in his life. His superior howled. The woman with the child howled. His girlfriend – he had justified hopes! – howled. Then the baby started it too.

He stood there for a moment, perplexed, confused and felt the other visitors to the market watching the strange spectacle with a mixture of emotion and incomprehension.

He cleared his throat, glimpsed toward the small tavern he had actually chosen for a cozy meeting with Claudia, with its winding taproom, where one could sit well unobserved. The landlord was waiting for him, keeping a particularly nice spot free.

It would be tight sitting, more than expected.

Secundus thought practically. He pushed the weeping band ahead of him, and everyone allowed him to.

Good to have a cool-headed centurion around, Secundus thought amused, and was pleased to see Claudia cling to him and offering everything she had to show.

A centurion took care of things.

And he did.

15

Ravenna was a hectic city. Soldiers were everywhere, and there was a lot of tension tangible in the metropolis. Despite this situation, the coastal sailor from the east was able to proceed without problems. The legionaries who entered the ship were mostly looking for people who had symptoms of the plague. No one was found on this ship, although Godegisel was subjected to a particularly intensive assessment. His scars, however, were easily recognizable as such – far too obvious, as the young man still found – and finally left undisturbed.

The crossing had been quiet and uneventful. Godegisel had to work hard, was one of the first to get up in the morning and was one of the last to find rest He had been in the small kitchen all day, preparing food for the crew, as well as serving the passengers who had paid for it. The coastal sailor was a larger ship with a crew of twelve men and again so many passengers. Even those who initially preferred to eat their supplies had, over time, joined the queue of those who wanted to enjoy Godegisel's preparations. They were simple meals, but Clodius had taught the Goth a few things about seasoning and the right balance of ingredients that now proved extremely helpful.

Godegisel was very busy, and that was a good thing. It scared away the troubling thoughts, focused his mind. He lay down to rest after sunset, when the sailor had anchored somewhere close to the coast, and he fell asleep immediately, so very tired. The work and the fresh air also strengthened his body. The weakness was gone, he felt invigorated and as strong as before.

When they reached Ravenna, the Captain offered him another wage for the rest of the summer and a subsequent employment in his brother's tavern, where he also worked during the winter months.

Godegisel thankfully declined the friendly offer, cashed his narrow pay and left the ship with the best wishes of a well-fed crew.

Strange how things sometimes evolved, the Goth thought. He had lived his life as a nobleman, as a warrior, then had become an assassin, a bodyguard, a charcoal worker, an ambassador, a carter and a cook. It seemed that fate wasn't yet ready to decide in which direction his life had to develop. And with every step Godegisel understood that, in spite of all the dangers and setbacks, a great variety of possibilities opened up to him, and that there were many ways that promised happiness and contentment. In almost everything he had done, there was joy and satisfaction, even in his failed mission as a diplomat by his own people. Understanding did not help him make a conscious decision about his future path, but it filled him with great curiosity as to what further opportunities he would have. He was aware that he would eventually get tired, and the need to find peace sometimes felt overpowering. Restlessness was not something he had been born with; it was the product of his previous destiny, to which he had often reluctantly surrendered.

As he entered the grounds of Ravenna and his eyes wandered along the moored ships, at once looking for another passage, this time toward Africa, he sensed that he was free.

Here and now, he thought, he was free to decide where to go. He could accept another job offer. He was able to travel to Gaul and convince a certain woman that he wasn't a liar. He was able to return to the Goths and begin a life of honor. He was able to travel to Africa and join Rheinberg and the Emperor again.

He closed his eyes.

Freedom was good. But sometimes it was a burden, too. Making decisions was so much easier when God pushed you one way. But here, in the port of Ravenna, Godegisel was abandoned by the feeling of predestination, and for the first time he really felt what it was like to be free.

He opened his eyes.

Of course that wasn't true. He had imposed rules on himself, a morality, an obligation, several even. He wouldn't be himself anymore if he wiped them off like a dirty tunic. Godegisel took a deep breath.

Therefore ...

He found lodging in a tavern frequented by sailors looking for a new assignment. The price was acceptable, and Godegisel had little personal belongings, apart from his clothes and a modest supply of cash, so he didn't mind sharing the dorm with three other men. When he entered the room and the innkeeper showed him his bed, a bad stench of alcohol came to meet him. Two of the other residents were snoring in their beds and had obviously spent the last night turning the remains of their cash into liquid. The innkeeper looked relaxed, not only because everyone paid for the accommodation in advance, but also because the said fluid surely came from his amphorae.

Even otherwise, the innkeeper was a helpful man. When Godegisel asked him about the possibilities to travel to Africa, he shook his head sadly. "Most ships are at sea, young man. The grain sails from Africa are on the way, but only a few come here. However, there is a way to make the passage, if that's not too much for you. Maximus builds his fleet, also here in Ravenna, and they are looking for seamen to help to carry the legions to Africa. You can sign up for the armed forces or hire as a civilian; they are currently taking everyone. I can tell you where to report. But hurry up. The rumors say the departure is imminent. The time-wanderer is gone with his magic ships, now they wait only for the rest of the fleet to be available. Maximus confiscates every suitable vessel. One more reason why you currently can't get a civilian salary. The war fleet is your only chance when you're in a hurry."

Godegisel thanked for the information and marched this same evening to the specified address. The recruiters were still operating, evidently in the urge to hold out as long as possible, to catch every willing one that could be put into service. Godegisel had heard that the ban on forced recruitment, which had still been issued under Gratian, was maintained by Maximus. It was interesting that apparently not everything was seemed to be evil what Rheinberg had introduced, even in the eyes of those who had made it their mission to destroy him.

The Goth didn't feel well at the thought of hiring into the fleet that was sailing against those whose supporter he was. It was unlikely that anyone would spot him – the scars and his still emaciated form camouflaged him far better than any disguise could do –, but the feeling was strange. He would have to settle quickly after their arrival in Africa and to seek contact with Rheinberg's troops. Maybe he even learned something worth reporting, then the trip was not such a disturbing move and could bring benefits.

Godegisel frowned. The thought had something. Cook last, before that producing charcoal – and now a spy?

He was obviously on it again. Godegisel was pretty sure the Lord was having a good time with this young man. He hoped that at some point it would all make sense to him.

It didn't take half an hour until he had the job. The next morning, he had to report to the port, where he was expected to work on a requisitioned transport galley, as oarsman and cook primarily, but to be ready to work as a loader and for any other activity for which the foreman would see him fit. The reward was scanty – there was food, lodging and a ridiculously small sum –, but with that he bought his passage. The contract was for the crossing and a subsequent return to relocate troops to Italy, but given the meager wages, Godegisel had absolutely no guilty conscience about abandoning the task after the first half of the contract.

Well, since he had made the contract with the enemy, that wasn't a moral issue anyway. He would like to work again if it came to bringing back the victorious legionaries of Theodosius. Godegisel, however, secretly hoped that it would no longer be necessary for him to row.

A small reward, he found, he had already earned.

Godegisel went back to the tavern, ate a simple but affordable dinner, declined the offer of beer or even time-wanderer-brandy thankfully – to the apparent displeasure of the tavern's master, who probably, with his mixed calculation, didn't make the expected profit out of Godegisel – and went to bed early.

The conversations he listened to in the tavern while eating were a reflection of a rather depressed mood. Obviously, not everyone was happy that the time-wanderers had left Ravenna. Many missed the new economic opportunities offered by the city's strange visitors. Those who considered the future had some hopes for the reforms that Gratian would begin and which Maximus would only partially pursue. The civil war also met with fear and displeasure. The times were hard enough. The crops have been bad for years. The supply situation, especially for the major cities, was tense. And now the divided Empire had to feed two armies, which in the course of their battles brought trade and agriculture to a standstill. Everyone wanted an end to the war. The problem was that many hoped for peace at any price. If Maximus won, there would be a kind of peace too.

Godegisel had a slightly more differentiated view. But he was careful not to get involved in one of the conversations. He finished his meal and retired early.

At night, he was awakened only briefly by his roommates, with whom the landlord apparently had more luck.

After his meager breakfast the next morning, Godegisel left the tavern early. As he walked along the harbor, he saw a great coastal sailor, not unlike the ship on which he himself had traveled, entering the basin. It had to either have anchored nearby during the night, or the captain had actually used the starry night to orient themselves along the coastal beacons to Ravenna. Usually, captains preferred to interrupt the journey at night, but some daredevils – and those who knew waters and shores from years of experience – continued their trip even in the dark. The authorities knew this, they didn't like it, not least because a ship that maneuvered during the night was able to transport smuggled goods without any problem. Fees and taxes were high, especially in times of war, and for many too high.

The ship reached the quay. Dockers, not used to the early bustle, began to line up on the wharf with grumpy faces, ready to unload the newcomer.

Then shouting, a different kind of hustle and bustle.

"Leave me alone! Let me go!"

The loud shouting of a man from the deck of the ship. Everyone was curiously focused on the spectacle. In the corner of his eyes, Godegisel noticed two harbor guards approaching, swords on their belts. He decided to take a few steps back. It smelled like trouble, and he couldn't use any now.

"I have ... keep away! Asshole!"

A man wriggled himself out of the grip of two sailors, knocking one of the henchmen against his chest, then leaped over the railing to the nearby shore, a mighty jump. The dockers backed away and made rude remarks.

The man looked around hurriedly.

The two harbor guards were approaching.

"Take him!" the Captain roared from the railing of his ship. "Don't let him escape!"

The two harbor guards attacked with courage. There was a fight. The man resisted doggedly. A worker, a mountain of a man, now approached to put an end to the matter. He grabbed the furious one by the collar, but the clothes didn't do what was expected of them. There was an ugly scratching, then the tunic was only in shreds in his fists.

Suddenly, it was very quiet.

The fight was as soon over as it had begun.

Godegisel leaned forward, feeling sudden sweat on his forehead.

The man, now shirtless, stood trembling, trying to cover the evidence with his hands.

"It's just a mistake," he sobbed. "It's just a mistake!" He looked around him imploringly. "I'm fine!"

Then silence.

Godegisel saw the workers and soldiers gain distance, forming a circle around the miserable bundle of a human. He heard shouts and orders and remarks full of fear.

There was no doubt.

The plague had arrived in Italy.

82

16

Von Klasewitz poured another cup of wine. This wasn't the thin piss drunk by the ordinary citizen, the legionary, and all the others who were no longer disturbed by the acetic taste. This was an excellent drop delivered from Greece, a treat that lived up to the highest standards. Von Klasewitz had never been a true wine connoisseur, but since he had arrived in this time, he had taken a liking to this drink. And since he was Magister Militium, he made sure that only the best wines found their way into his throat. He was not always able to gauge whether the promised quality was really that outstanding; he simply had never developed the palate for it. So he relied on the one criterion that remained at the end for any ignoramus – the price. The wine couldn't be expensive enough. Based on the reaction of his guests, which he sometimes invited to his assigned villa, this strategy was consistently successful.

Petronius, the priest, was by no means averse to this form of pleasure. He ate in moderation, as von Klasewitz had already discovered, although the meals the new Magister served met the highest standards. Whatever they needed, the German went by the motto that everything good also had to be expensive. But drinking was the passion of Petronius, and here it was specifically wine. In contrast to the German, who occasionally tasted strong liquor, now that it was widely available, the priest continued to favor the Roman's traditional favorite drink. Even today, on this warm summer evening, he softly clicked his tongue as he put down the goblet and closed his eyes dreamily.

"Really a wonderful treat, Magister. You maintain a good cellar."

"No effort is too great for my honorable guests," von Klasewitz lied convincingly and raised the little decanter that stood between them on the side table. They lay at table alone, even the ever-present servants had been sent away at the request of Petronius. Von Klasewitz was curious. By then he had guessed that this wasn't a courtesy visit. Wine might enhance Petronius' joy in his task, but it wasn't the reason for his presence.

"Another cup?"

"I can hardly refuse," Petronius replied, watching with satisfaction, as the red liquid filled his goblet with a gentle gurgling sound.

"How is the venerable Ambrosius? I've heard that he's back in Milan," von Klasewitz continued the conversation.

Petronius sighed. "He's here and there, always on the move, entrusted with the highest tasks. A restless man, workaholic, I mean. He sleeps little, doesn't eat well, works late into the night."

"These are hard times that demand the utmost from every Roman."

"That's just too true. We all need to reach our limits to serve the Empire and secure its future." Petronius raised the goblet. "All the more precious are those few minutes of retreat and relaxation. A rare refreshment and one from which Ambrosius refrains too often."

"If all this is over, there should be opportunity to rest."

"Yes? Are you sure?" Petronius pursed his lips before continuing. "Securing the Empire is a big task, which certainly involves more than just getting Theodosius out of the way."

"Many challenges are imminent," von Klasewitz replied vaguely.

"Not everyone will see it that way," Petronius said now, straightening himself up slightly. "The Church is still worried about the future. There are many problems. Not only must the Empire be strong, but above all strong in its union with the true faith."

Von Klasewitz nodded thoughtfully. It was the same story that Petronius and the Bishop kept popping up with, and as far as he could follow that line of argument, he didn't mind Ambrosius' plans to eradicate Arians and make Catholic Orthodoxy a state church. But the constant repetition of the issue became annoying. Maximus was a convinced Trinitarian and allowed the orthodoxy free reign in their ever stronger pursuit of heresy. What did Petronius want more?

84

"The Magister Militium is a key player in this struggle," Petronius went on. "Your word has weight. Your power is considerable. "

"I serve the Emperor with all faith and conscientiousness," von Klasewitz intoned, which he had so often repeated that he had to pull himself together each time so that it didn't sound stale and empty. That was probably because it was with him as with any person with ambition: Once you have reached a position, the satisfaction was short-lived. Soon one glances at the next step on the ladder. And if there was no higher position – in this case it was Emperor in the end –, then all that remained was to seek greater fame, greater fortune, each time a little more, more satisfying, even more liberating but then again only to represent a position from which one strove for even more.

Von Klasewitz was quite aware of this fact. He had become accustomed to the position of the Magister Militium. And he was aware that he was still only a servant. An exalted servant, sure, but no more than that.

To admit this was nothing that pleased him.

"Of course, of course," the priest hurried to reply, and it didn't sound more convincing. "Nevertheless, we want to be prepared for the emergency. The Empire needs continuity at its peak, stability, but also willpower, a clear political direction both internally and externally. Assertiveness, a clear line based on the unbreakable and sacred alliance between state and church. That's how we're going to fulfill God's will, I'm sure of that."

This time, according to von Klasewitz, the man was indeed passionate about it. He came to his point now. The German smiled and nodded in agreement. Petronius should talk. This promised to be very interesting.

"You've come a long way, dear friend," the priest said.

"Not least with the help of the Church."

"It's good that you remember that."

"You yourself do not tire to emphasize this fact."

Petronius narrowed his eyes slightly but then nodded. "There is a reason, Magister. We have big plans for you."

"*We?*"

"The Bishop and myself. The community of true believers and patriots."

Von Klasewitz looked at his empty goblet and decided against another drink. He was pretty sure it would be better to refrain from alcohol until this conversation ended.

"Big, Petronius?" he said slowly. "I'm supreme commander of the legions. The Empire doesn't offer much more power to a mortal. Any further reward is otherworldly, and here you may be able to make promises, but it will ultimately remain in the hands of the Lord."

"That reward is more than certain to you," Petronius hastened to say. "You should not worry about that."

"Very kind," von Klasewitz muttered. "What are we talking about then?"

"The purple, what else?"

The German showed surprisingly great self-restraint. The emotion he felt was a mixture of joy, surprise and disbelief. It couldn't be that the plans of others were so wonderfully aligned to his own! One almost wanted to speak of divine providence! Von Klasewitz sighed softly. That's how you felt when you were a Chosen One.

Damn, he could get used to that!

He looked at Petronius and formulated his words with great care. "Maximus is a respectable man full of godliness. He will certainly look for a suitable successor when things have developed as desired. I'm not sure his choice will affect me."

Petronius waved his hand. "Maybe his election is not the key here."

"So what?"

"Your choice, Magister. How will you decide?"

That was indeed the central question, and the answer would determine whether the priest's implicit offer was serious or a trap to test his loyalty. The sudden distrust that von Klasewitz now felt was in sharp contrast to the brief euphoria he had just enjoyed.

But he hadn't come this far without taking risks.

"If the church sees me as a worthy tool to achieve its highest goals, I will never refuse to heed the call," he replied, and was very pleased with himself. He had put the problem back in Petronius's lap.

The priest smiled again, this time deep and showing a tiny trace of relief. He seemed to be hoping for that answer, actually counted on it.

"It's good. We understand each other. The time will come when the call will be made to all men who are strong in faith and in the Church."

"That's where I belong to," the German insisted.

"I agree with that. For some, following the call will mean little effort and hardly a personal risk. Others, however, will have to come forward to write history."

The traitor understood very well what that meant. He tried not to look too triumphant. Etiquette demanded humility, that was part of the game.

Petronius nodded toward von Klasewitz. "And now, dear friend, I'd like to have another cup of your excellent wine."

17

Rheinberg had to get used to many things throughout his life. The exhausting and sometimes degrading training in the Navy. The cramped living conditions on a ship. The constant conceit of his noble comrades, the implications of the life his sister chose. A childhood that had suffered greatly under rigidity and discipline, the inability to fulfill his true dream of life. In any case, Rheinberg had become tougher, at least insofar as he was now in a position to meet challenges without being overwhelmed by them. There were always situations that he encountered with perplexity, sometimes with desperation, but never for long. Rheinberg, as he saw himself, was someone who in the end always landed on his feet.

On the basis of this philosophy, he also calmly accepted that Aurelia, the lady of his heart, vomited with devotion every morning, and then had an angry thunderstorm inflicted on her husband, who was ultimately responsible for all this.

Aurelia's accusing eloquence targeted at him was mostly about the fact that he was putting the good of the Empire above her private happiness. She didn't mention the fact that his cautious stalling tactics regarding his own offspring had been thwarted by producing facts by herself – a task in which Aurelia had been at least as passionately involved as himself, of course including a good deal of calculation.

Forgotten was also the small but very beautiful ceremony with which Rheinberg and Aurelia had officially joined into the marriage a few days ago, with the Emperor as witness, the presence of numerous other notables, with a long-lasting and chosen meal followed by many congratulations and gifts. Rheinberg remembered that moment when Aurelia leaned over the container next to her bedstead to empty the contents of her stomach with loud moans interrupted by still louder curses. He remembered her cheeks, flushed with excitement and pride, and the pleased, honored gleam of her eyes as Theodosius presented her with a wonderful tiara, studded with jewels, carefully chiseled by an artisan hand, a jewel in whose presence other women showed all recognizable signs of burning envy – a reaction that, as Rheinberg found, only furthered Aurelia's enjoyment.

Well, all of this, lively as it was that morning in front of Jan Rheinberg's mental eye, seemed to have been forgotten, at least by his wife, and he couldn't even blame her. Of course, there were also experienced midwives here in Africa, who described the circumstances of a pregnancy to Aurelia in not a few details, but these descriptions didn't really help. Of course, Aurelia was quite of the opinion that her husband had to stay by her side at this time, where other women in this state subtly retreated into their own rooms – especially when the said husband was involved in planning a decisive battle for the continuity of the Empire and the rule of his Emperor, the same who had presented her with this beautiful jewelry ...

No, Aurelia didn't tend to be too subtle.

Rheinberg watched her take a clean cloth and wipe her mouth before sitting up in bed, groaning and looking at him. The pungent odor of the vomit spread – as every morning – in the warm air of the dawning sun day and spoiled, as every morning, Rheinberg's appetite for breakfast. That was quite befitting, because Aurelia couldn't eat anything anyway after such an attack and considered every attempt by her husband to take in food with about the same joy as Rheinberg watched Aurelia giving it back to the Gods.

After all, he was sure, as he smiled affably at his wife and patted her hand, there was something like divine justice. He was ready to endure this, not least because of his affection for the stinking suffragette beside him, but nevertheless, he allowed himself the hope that this stage of child production would soon be over. After all, he had asserted himself that Aurelia would not accompany him to the battlefield. Instead, she remained in Hadrumentum, living in the captain's cabin of the *Saarbrücken*, undoubtedly the safest place in the entire Empire.

Today he would leave for Mactaris again, and this time he would stay there. Many of the troops had already been transferred. In Hadrumentum, there was nothing left for him to do.

"Honey, how are you?" Rheinberg asked the most superfluous question in the world. The look in response only confirmed the quality of his inquiry, and he decided, perhaps for the better, to say nothing more.

An hour later, they sat on a balcony of their residence at a richly covered breakfast table. There was the usual food – baked bread with cheese, honey and eggs, milk as a drink. Rheinberg had developed a special passion for *moretum*, a herbal curd, with which he covered the flatbread generously, then stuffed the resulting composition half-curled into his mouth. Wheat bread was also abundant, but Rheinberg preferred the bakery products made from spelt, since together with the curd the bread produced a very pleasant flavor. Aurelia, too, seemed by now to be anxious to resupply, and with the slaves clearing the bowl of vomit and the air on the balcony fresh in the morning, her husband's appetite returned.

The breakfast was conducted in complete silence. Both knew that the goodbyes were coming, and also knew that there was a good chance that they would never meet again.

Rheinberg sighed and put the half-eaten bread patties aside. He looked at his wife until she noticed his glance. She also stopped and looked her husband in the eye. There was no snippy remark on her lips. She knew Rheinberg well enough to know that he had a serious topic on his mind.

"Jan?"

"Aurelia, I made arrangements," he said. He didn't want to sound too depressing, so full of ominous forebodings, but it surely came out like that. Aurelia didn't seem to be alarmed, but the worry in her expression was unmistakable.

"Which kind of?"

"If the luck of war turns against me and I should either be captured or killed, you need not worry."

That sounded a bit awkward, as Rheinberg considered.

Aurelia frowned at him. That any imprisonment would lead to his death only with some delay was a safe assumption. He had become a symbolic figure, an incarnation of those aspects of the time-wanderers that Maximus was opposed to. And von Klasewitz would also have great pleasure in a proper execution. Rheinberg wasn't sure if he would muster the courage to throw himself into a sword. He probably lacked that discipline. Someone would have to help.

The gloomy thoughts were undoubtedly visible on his face.

"What arrangements?" she asked softly.

"The *Saarbrücken* will run immediately, should they receive information about our defeat. The cruiser will try to find a safe haven in the East. Modestus will help you to disappear, maybe somewhere in Greece. There is money available, even loyal servants. You mustn't reveal yourself, but you will not lack anything."

Aurelia looked a little surprised, as if she had not expected her husband to plan so far ahead and calculate with this kind of eventuality. She was silent for a few minutes, swallowing several times – more often than the food in her mouth made necessary –, and finally said, "Just come back alive. If we have to hide together, I'm fine."

Rheinberg nodded. "I want to do my best. I'm not anxious to find an early end."

"I'd like you to wake up at night and clean our child when it's full of shit. It would be annoying to have to take care of it alone."

"Aren't there nannies?" Rheinberg asked, quite aware that this argument, even in the event that he would return safe, wouldn't count.

Aurelia shook her head indulgently.

"No, beloved man. I think parents should take care of these things. And not just the mother. Once you have won, maybe there is more time for such unimportant matters ... however annoying they may be for you."

Rheinberg grinned. "I think if that's the prize for my victory, I'll gladly pay it."

"Let's wait and see."

They finished the breakfast. Rheinberg rose when Richomer entered her quarters.

"Magister, we have to leave."

"One more moment, General."

"I'll wait outside."

Aurelia looked after the man, then she could no longer suppress a sigh. She let herself be engulfed by Rheinberg's arms, hugged him for a moment with almost desperate effort, and then released him abruptly. "Go. Victory. Stay in one piece. Come back."

With that she turned around, paid no further attention to him, and disappeared in the adjacent bathroom. Rheinberg looked at her for a moment and wanted to say something else, but it seemed his wife had decided that it was enough for him to simply carry out her instructions.

He thought about it for a moment, then took his helmet and cloak.

Those orders didn't sound so bad.

That's the way he would do it.

18

The plan was simple.

When Salius and his men – both official and unofficial – entered the big steamship to embark for Africa, he looked around contentedly. At the edge of his vision, he had seen a clumsy woman help the last of the food on board. Salius controlled himself. A smile would have betrayed him, as currently the mood was generally rather depressed. To be forced to live cramped for days on the narrow ship was not something the legionaries greatly appreciated. The weather conditions might also hurt many a soldier who had never gone to sea before. Although they were happy to be transported on one of the three giants of the Mediterranean – the shipwrights of the time-wanderers had a far better reputation than the latter –, that only made the prospect marginally better.

Salius didn't blame the men. But if all went well, their suffering would become even more unbearable than they had imagined, and an absolutely weakened and incapacitated force would arrive in Africa. Since these were the elite troops of the Maximus – his bodyguard, the artillery crews, and their security forces –, this would be a heavy blow to the usurper, which would not be easy to deal with. Once they arrived in Africa, Salius would see how he could send a message to Theodosius informing them of this not inconsiderable tactical advantage. Then all that remained was to kill von Klasewitz, to finally sow confusion and fear into the ranks of the enemy. In fact, Salius found that the crossing itself might have been an opportunity to do so, especially since he and Screpius had landed on the same ship as the new Magister Militium.

Salius stood by the rail and pretended to be critical of the soldiers' embarkation. In fact, his gaze sought the figure of Flavia, who now stood with many other servants on the shore with nothing to do but attend the departure. Apart from a number of sailors who were not in the direct service of the military, no civilians would be taken along, and no one cared. Salius saw Flavia looking at the railing herself with a searching look, then she recognized him, and she waved furtively. Salius ignored it. But it was clear that Flavia had brought the poisoned food aboard.

Not everything had been poisoned. About three quarters of the supplies on the three large steamers had been provided with the special additions provided by Flavia, and Salius knew the markings in order to locate them very well. He wouldn't suffer from severe nausea, vomiting diarrhea, and persistent weakness, like some others who were just lucky. Many would initially think of the symptoms as effects of seasickness, but very soon, the realization that it was something far worse would prevail. The few legionaries who were unaffected would be just enough to supply their comrades and keep the ships on course.

Salius braced himself. Gold had changed hands, a promise of amnesty, a prospect of further missions to be conducted in those spheres that, even with forbearance, could only be described as "gray." Flavia had proved to be very willing, especially as the alternative would have been to be extradited to the authorities by Screpius. Which he would've never done, because it would endanger his own camouflage – which again was not what they'd told Flavia. Ultimately, they were dependent on each other. And Flavia had done a great job.

Salius, too, if everything worked out.

He had originally intended to put everything in the balance, as he and Screpius, as well as two other of his "unofficial" men, had all been stationed on the ship, where the Magister Militium would also make the journey. It had been his plan to make an attack on the man in order to bring unrest to the troops and cut off an important head. But Flavia's emergence had opened other possibilities for them, and only once was the effect of this attack was to be fully realized was he prepared to think of any further steps.

The first coup was a sure thing, and with some luck von Klasewitz would also consume the poisoned food and endure a thoroughly horrible trip. Maybe he puked himself to death. That would be a very elegant solution to their problem.

The three big transport ships set off. There were already about twenty other galleys and sailors waiting for them at the anchorage off Ravenna, at least as long as the weather was helpful. Should there be headwinds or rough seas, the three big vehicles would quickly leave the escorts behind.

The steam engines were an attraction. As a pastime, the Trierarch let spectators into the engine room, only five at a time, and for no longer than ten minutes. This offer was very interesting. Salius also pretended to be inspired by the bronze monster in the heart of the ship. He had to stay in the role. No one could even guess that he had once rescued the iron cruiser from mutineers lead by von Klasewitz, fighting aboard the *Saarbrücken*. He knew the strange ship almost as well as the Roman crew members who had subsequently been hired to fill vacancies.

The weather was fine, a peaceful, sunny day, with a light breeze. The mood on board was good, better than expected. The outbreak of the plague in Ravenna had been a major deterrent, and Salius had to admit that he also had to deal with some worry. It was one thing to fight an opponent with a weapon in the hand. Although this opponent might be feared and of great skill, there was a chance, always at least a small chance, to win. It was much larger than fighting an unseen enemy one could only surrender to without the ability to really measure his powers. Salius didn't mind putting himself into the hands of God – he would in the end anyway –, but this helplessness over a serious, deadly illness also took its toll on his self-confidence. All the soldiers had been thoroughly searched, all had to shave their hair so as not to provide nesting grounds for fleas; any kind of animal, especially dogs, had been banished from the jetty, the already stringent hygiene measures were once again tightened. Patrols had intensively hunted for rats. The crew of the coastal sailor who had brought the infected man to Ravenna was immediately arrested and isolated. Salius didn't know what had become of them. If there were infections there too, the authorities would keep them secret in order to avoid a mass panic. The mood was irritable enough.

On board the transporter was, according to human discretion, not a single rat and not a single infected man. But everyone knew that it was only a matter of time before the epidemic spilled over to Africa. Despite all efforts, complete containment wasn't possible. With luck, the development wouldn't be as severe and comprehensive as comparable outbreaks in the past.

Salius watched as the food rations were distributed. On large, iron ovens, pots with grain porridge were heated. There was flatbread and fresh fruit, and for drink, diluted wine. Salius hovered near the open-plan kitchen, as if he didn't want to miss the distribution of food, and studied exactly which sacks of cereal and other ingredients were being brought up and opened by the legionaries who had been ordered to cook. A good half wore the markings Flavia had placed. So it would start immediately.

Salius then withdrew unobtrusively, sitting down next to his luggage, rummaging about aimlessly. He had an extra bag filled with his own food, cheese, bread, nuts, dried fruits. Enough to feed him for three or four days without relying on official rations. Flavia had expressly refrained from poisoning the drinks – water and wine. That would have put the assassins themselves in dire straits.

Salius grabbed a handful of nuts and began to nibble them. The first queues formed before the cooking place. Flavia had said that the effect of the poison would not be immediate, but with a delay – eight to twelve hours had been her estimate, enough time to finish breakfast the next day, and thus to secure the spread of the poison all over the galley, albeit in different dosage. Especially those with a strong constitution could possibly survive a lower dose of the poison with mild discomfort.

Salius leaned back. He heard the men joking, as they fetched their hot porridge.

He almost pitied them.

The calming sway of the waves and the murmur of the eating legionaries lulled him into a gentle slumber. When he awoke, it was already pitch-dark. He felt cold, rummaged for his coat and wrapped himself in it. He could have gone below, but warmth there was mixed with the stench of sleeping men, while up here the fresh sea air was very pleasant. Salius stared for a moment into the clear starry sky, enjoying the sight to the fullest before his eyes closed again.

The next morning, he woke up at sunrise, watching again casually the tired meal of the tired legionaries. Again the porridge was prepared, again bread distributed. The food was monotonous, but usually well digestible and fortifying. That would, Salius was now sure, change in the course of the day. Once again, bags of flavia-labeled food had been brought to the deck. The poison was definitely going around, and the first effects were soon to come.

There was not much to do on board. Everybody tried most of the time to avoid the seafarers, so as not to disturb them at work. Dice games helped to pass time, and some of the more educated legionaries began to read from works of poets and historians but found a mostly rather bored audience. Many were just dozing or taking care of their equipment. It was mended, whited, cleaned, although the latter only with salt water and coarse soap. Everyone was busy, and an almost peaceful mood descended on the sun-lit deck. The officers largely left the men alone, as long as there were no problems. It was a rest before an important battle, the last for a long time. Since a drill on the cramped decks made little sense, there was no other pastime than to take care of them-selves.

Salius, however, became restless. It was approaching noon, the sun was at its zenith, and it was warm, almost hot. Many men sought shade, either below deck or by pitching tarpaulins and squatting underneath. Some were sweating. Amphorae with chilled, thin wine made the rounds.

But everyone seemed to be just fine.

Too fine indeed.

Salius frowned at the scene, his eyes searching for the signs of the poison, as Flavia had predicted. He was so engrossed in his activity that he almost didn't notice the Trierarch of the ship joining him, accompanied by two squat legionaries, sweating but still wearing helmets.

Salius looked at the man and felt the agitation rise in him.

"Have a nice day, Decurio," the man murmured in greeting. "But you look worried. May I know your concern?"

"Do not worry, Trierarch. Maybe I feel a little uncomfortable. I'm not used to the sea."

The man nodded thoughtfully and gave Salius a sympathetic smile.

"Yes, that's a problem for a lot of people. All in all, however, the men behave well, and the complaints are rare. We must endure."

"That's probably true."

"How fortunate that the plan to make our crossing a cruel ordeal by providing poisoned supplies to us has failed so terribly, isn't it?"

Salius froze. He was struggling for composure. The Trierarch had said the sentence so casually that the true meaning of his words was beginning to trickle in slowly.

Treason.

He had been betrayed.

The image of the maliciously smiling Flavia was right in front of his eyes, as real as if she were actually on board.

Salius felt the hands of the two soldiers closing around his own wrists, as the Trierarch took his sword away, again in an almost casual gesture. The action caught the eye of everyone, especially as two more legionaries took red-headed Screpius to the deck, hands tied behind their backs, disarmed, betrayed. And then came the other two men who had also been unmasked by Flavia.

Screpius' gaze towards Salius was fatalistic and reproachful.

Salius couldn't blame him.

"What's going to happen to us?" he asked the Trierarch firmly. To deny anything now would have been meaningless. Besides, the question was ultimately of a rhetorical nature. They were traitors to Maximus' men, and there was only one fate for them. The only question was whether he would suffer death quickly and painlessly, or whether its end was only the conclusion of prolonged agony.

The Trierarch scratched his beard thoughtfully. "I'll have you and your friend tortured until we know all the details of your job. I suppose you are acting on behalf of Theodosius."

It did no harm to admit this, because it was so obvious that it didn't need any discussion at all. Salius nodded.

"I understand. Well, torture is a good approach, as we want to know everything. Maximus is not happy about this development. We have you people, but I suppose there are more of your kind. We would like to know where."

Salius frowned. Flavia had unmasked them all. But she didn't know that, and the Trierarch had to assume that there might be other traitors. For him, the interrogation was the logical consequence of this situation. Salius couldn't even blame him. He probably would have done the same in his place.

Salius feared torture like every sensible man did. He could endure pain, and probably quite a long time. But he knew the methods, and he knew the perseverance of those in charge – either men who enjoyed what they were doing, or those who just exercised meticulous precision and care in the task.

Salius would speak if he didn't die before. Masters of their craft made sure that the latter only came about if intended. Screpius would talk as well, finally. That wasn't an expression of lack of trust in the comrade, it was a simple fact.

Salius met Screpius's eyes. He noticed the imperceptible nod. Regret filled Salius. It was so sad it had to end now. After all, he would die at the side of an old companion. This thought comforted him for a moment.

He lowered his head. He couldn't look at the other two of his companions without arousing suspicion. They had to take care of themselves now. It was bitter to see that.

Very bitter. It hurt more than what he was about to do.

"I ... I don't want to be tortured ... I will talk."

The Trierarch smiled. "Naturally. But you'll understand we want to make sure."

Screpius sobbed aloud and dropped his shoulders forward.

One of the legionaries laughed sardonically.

Then the two men sprang forward, twisting in a sliding motion out of the hands of their captors, who had let down in their care. And they were surprised that the two men didn't turn against them, didn't seek weapons, didn't strive to fight.

Salius and Screpius dove headfirst over the rail and splashed into the water.

There was shouting, angry screams.

"I'll loosen your shackles," Salius said, as he appeared beside the struggling comrade.

He shook his head. "Leave them. That's how it will be faster."

Salius saw Screpius submerge, gasping up again, driven by the creature's fear of death, only to go down again.

Ropes fell into the water. Legionaries, only in their tunic, began to climb down.

Screpius didn't reappear.

Salius glanced at the Trierarch's face, still angry, and waved to him, then descended, deeper, deeper, deeper and deeper, reaching the body of Screpius, who still twitched softly, clutching at him.

It was a painful death, a torture of its own, but short, very short.

And nobody heard him give any names to anyone.

19

Godegisel had only noticed some of the excitement on the other ship, heard rumors spreading about betrayal and a planned attack, and how it had all collapsed. He saw worried faces in some men, as he helped prepare the food for the legionaries, heard some inquiring questions as to whether the grain was still good or the cheese wasn't too old. Godegisel responded to the best of his knowledge and belief but was relieved when the Trierarch turned to the passengers and crew alike. Thus, all learned of the dark plans of the adversaries, of their insidiousness, and of the intelligence of their own military leadership, which had succeeded in thwarting them, whereby the traitors, the scum, had found their deserved death in the waves of the Mediterranean. The food on board, it was assured, was impeccable and everyone should calmly return to their duties, if they had any. The fact that they got some duties was quickly ensured by shouting NCOs, and everywhere already cleaned and sharpened swords became even cleaner and sharper, and helmets and shields even more brilliant. Godegisel knew that this sudden wave of work was primarily designed to direct the men's attention elsewhere.

He was both happy and unhappy about the course of events. Happy because such a poison attack wouldn't only have hit him – and he couldn't afford another illness, just having recovered from the plague –, and actually he'd also be suspected as part of the kitchen staff immediately, either for being sloppy or to have acted deliberately. His scars didn't make things easier. But he was unhappy, because a successful attack would have significantly weakened the power of Maximus' troops, especially in the artillery. That would've surely helped in the upcoming battle.

So, however, all legionaries – aside from those with a strong tendency to seasickness – would arrive well-fed and relaxed in Africa, ready – yes, angry and eager – to show the enemy that his treacherous plans hadn't been successful. Thus, the failure of the infiltrators had led to an increase in morale of the troops and their combat readiness. Godegisel had once listened to a German officer say using a phrase that he wasn't aware of before – the idea had "backfired," a phrase that suddenly made sense with the time-wanderer's firearms and described very well what had obviously happened here.

Therefore, Godegisel simply fulfilled his duty, remained inconspicuous, calm, sought no personal interaction, but didn't reject it either, was submissive where appropriate, and affable, where he could afford it, all in all a wonderful strategy to settle on board and not stand out in any way negative. Even the searching glances that had initially struck him when his scars were visible diminished. This was a very welcome development for him.

In the evening after Trierarch's speech and at the end of endless rehearsal drills, the ship's command let the amphorae with the proper wine circulate – not the watery vinegar that was served as a regular drink, and from which nobody brought down so much that he could get drunk, but the real wine, not mixed with water, not of the highest quality, but especially in its form as a red wine with a certain effect, at least to those who were not completely dulled by constant drinking and needed several amphorae to feel the effect. In any case, this action led to general relaxation and below deck, when the sun was slowly setting, there was finally an almost happy mood on the ship. Since Godegisel was commissioned to walk around and refill with a large decanter in hand, while making sure no one consumed more than three cups, he quickly became a welcome guest among the joking and celebrating men.

He always half-listened to the legionaries when they talked, which became easier as the evening progressed, as the volume of talking increased. Even as the released ration slowly came to an end, the mood remained stimulated and relaxed at the same time.

At a rather late time, Godegisel, with his newly-filled carafe, passed a group of senior NCOs gathered in a corner of the hold around a flickering oil lamp. Reddened cheeks and a slightly blurred look showed that the fixed ration had not been respected by every-one, especially those who had the authority to override such silly limitations.

They waved Godegisel to come closer. He rushed in, which was enough to get the men's attention back to their conversation. As a servant, the young Goth had not much higher priority than a piece of furniture; basically, he didn't exist for the drinkers at least not as long as he pleasingly and efficiently refilled their cups.

"I hope I'll be with the troop storming the commander's tent," a man with gray hair in the carefully groomed whiskers said, as he set his mug down. "I just want to see Theodosius' face when he realizes his time has run out."

"Boring," another said, causing protest. He raised a hand. "I want to see his face when he realizes that his African allies are turning in the middle of the battle and going for his throat!"

Godegisel pretended he hadn't heard.

"Yes, but then we'll be too close to victory," the first lamented. "I'll take what I can get."

"If the Spaniard is clever, he plunges himself into his sword first."

"Ah, damn it, yes. He could be trusted to do that. Honest man, that's what he is. Ha, I would have liked the fun so much. But that won't work."

"His face," a third now said, reverently suppressing a burp. "His face is one thing, but the other one ... I want to see that from this time-wanderer, Rheinberg. He won't kill himself, I don't think so. All the cowards, these time-wanderers. No guts. They hide behind their weapons and are afraid of the hard reality of the blade. I want to see Rheinberg how he trembles and moans."

"That won't be so exciting. He will think up until the end that the Africans wouldn't betray him, but only try to lure Maximus to safety and then give him the death-blow," the first explained. "He wouldn't want to realize until the end that he was really betrayed. That's how it's supposed to go, as planned from the beginning!"

All three of the men giggled and ignored Godegisel, who poured with a submissive expression in his face until the decanter was empty, then withdrew quietly.

His heart pounded his throat.

He brought the empty container back to the amphorae, where he was told there was nothing left and he could go to sleep. Godegisel was grateful for that. His thoughts were racing. His return to Africa had suddenly taken on a whole new meaning, a special quality. There was more to it now than just finding the way back; it was now a matter of hurrying to the troops of Rheinberg and telling him what he had just heard.

Time was suddenly burning on his nails. He wished for a strong wind that would increase the speed of the ships, even though this would allow the enemy to arrive faster in Africa. The words of the men dominated his thoughts and he rolled them restlessly in his head, trying to think of a way out, a reaction, a strategy that could make this betrayal ineffective. He hoped and prayed that Rheinberg would come up with something.

Godegisel stared into the clear starry sky as he made himself comfortable on deck in a corner. He found no sleep, felt the thoughts circling in his head; he kept turning, but sleep didn't come. As the snoring of the wine-lovers reached his ear from all over the ship, he cowered restlessly on the rail and felt his hands clench into fists.

Ah, his fate, he thought with a touch of desperation.

Slowly, it became a bit too much to bare.

20

Volkert didn't look back when he left the camp at Hadrumentum with the rear guard. He felt light this morning, almost elated. Julia's words were still ringing in his ears. Her description of the separation from Martinus Caius had filled him with both joy and anger. On the one hand, it meant that, as he wasn't too good for marrying an outcast, he had a good chance of still living with Julia. Since he lacked the arrogance of the Roman upper classes, although he might become a member slowly due to his steep career, this was no problem. He had felt great anger when he heard Caius almost murdered his daughter. His thanks to Claudia had been sincere and long, and the young woman was almost ashamed that a Roman officer had known such nice things to say about her. But since Secundus had overheard everything and was informed by this way that Claudia was a thoroughly respectable and caring young woman, she had endorsed the hymn of praise with dignity and side glances toward the Centurion. Secundus, for whom respectability and caring were not as important as the abundance of Claudia's bust and her willingness – in principle – to let him partake of it, knew what was expected of him. Above all, he knew that a victory over Maximus would also start a new chapter for him. As a Centurion, he was already a man of great standing, and if Volkert continued to ascend – which he didn't doubt for a moment –, a loyal friend was needed, which would certainly promote his own career. Officer's position for Secundus, the crook – an interesting perspective, especially one that required to reconsider one's lifestyle, at least outwardly. Marriage was an important option, and if he married the best friend of his patron's wife, there couldn't be a better combination.

So Secundus had mastered himself exemplary, wrinkled his forehead with sorrow wit perfect timing, looked admiringly and appreciatively if needed, and held Claudia's hand at the climax of the drama. He had behaved so politely and decently that Volkert had not failed to give him one or the other slightly surprised look.

It was therefore not surprising that a few days before their departure for the final battle Claudia was ready to fulfill the true wishes of Secundus, of whom she was well aware, and so exhaustive that the Centurion's resolve to ask for the lady's hand after his safe return had only intensified.

Claudia was happy. Julia was happy. Secundus was happy. Volkert was happy.

It was hard to believe.

Volkert looked at the column of the last 2000 men who had stayed in the camp in front of the port city and now began the march inland. He firmly believed that his luck was short-lived. Something would go wrong. Someone would die. A misfortune would happen. It had been so good and so bad at the same time lately that Volkert couldn't believe that everything would come to a happy ending. This dark foreboding plagued him. He wanted to strip it off, forget it, and laugh at it. But once he was not busy with other things, his thoughts wandered back to the subject and his head was covered in dark clouds, as if the threatening evil was already clearly visible.

Bertius, sitting on a horse next to his superior, noticed that. Unfortunately he was in a bad position to cheer Volkert up. The German himself had his doubts and fears. It was the decisive battle, and Bertius was no one who valued decisions. He preferred to move in the dimness of indifference, in the shadow of indecision, was a man of the vague. As soon as things began to pinpoint and threaten to turn black or white, provoke a yes or a no, he felt uncomfortable. And that's where everything went at the moment.

Bertius therefore was not happy.

Of course, he didn't miss any opportunity to express his emotional state. Since Volkert was used to that, he usually didn't pay any attention to it. This time, however, there was a new quality in the man's constant lamentation, the hint of fear. Of course, Bertius was always afraid of things, not least of all having to work too hard or not getting enough food. His current fear, however, was fundamental, almost creaturely. He was torn between his loyalty to Volkert and his need to maintain as close a distance as possible between himself and the battlefield.

"That's okay, Bertius," Volkert said, as they rode slowly along the marching column.

"I'm just ..."

"Me too. But we can't run away. Things develop without our help, but we are caught up in them, can't pretend that they'd never affect us."

"It must be the last battle," his servant said hopefully. "I don't think my weak mind can handle another 'decision.' I mean, someday *something* has to be decided."

Volkert smiled indulgently. He had given up this belief some time ago, whether he wanted to call it cynicism or not.

Had to give up.

"No, I'm afraid not. Whatever happens, it only triggers another change. Hopefully one that we think is right, but don't expect any rest afterwards. One decision triggers the next. Always."

"But we need to be satisfied at times," Bertius complained. "We have achieved something and are satisfied. This may make us more frugal, and we won't have to look for a new quarrel."

"A little less conflict would be in my own interest. But the hope that we will ever be satisfied with something permanently – you can't expect that. Once we have achieved something, a goal, a wish, a stage, we pause for a moment, then look up or forward again. Then we see something glittering on the horizon, we have a new, even better idea, the house is getting too small, the horse is getting too old, the food is monotonous, and we want to do more, something new, the next step. There are no final decisions, no final events, no end of something. As soon as we have something, we strive for the next. Only when we are very old can we look back and rest, and leave the effort to others."

Volkert looked at Bertius almost apologetically. It wasn't that he himself cherished this realization very much. The problem was not always to strive for something new. It only started when people were striving for very different things and these desires contradicted each other. Unfortunately, a particular ambition sometimes lead to the assumption that every means could be considered appropriate to reach the goal. The consequences of such a consideration is what they experienced currently. An experience that gave Volkert, like Bertius, only very limited enjoyment.

He looked at the stump of his factotum's arm.

Very, very limited joy.

"If this continues, I won't get very old," Bertius said. "Otherwise, I don't believe you, noble Tribune. I know myself quite well. A beautiful house, a nice woman, a peaceful life. This is me. No further desires, ever."

Volkert grinned. "That's why you wanted to stay in the Legion after your injury, rather than retire with your bonus?"

"I regret this decision now."

"If you continue to complain, then so will I."

Bertius looked a little offended for a moment. Then he regained his composure, sighed with little enthusiasm – it was still necessary for the master to be fully informed about his suffering –, and focused on opposing the next development. They couldn't continue their conversation anyway, because Volkert realized that Secundus was riding toward him, turning his horse, and joining them. He had just ridden at the top of the column.

"It's all right," said Secundus, wiping the sweat from his forehead. The helmet rested tethered on his saddle. Although the day was still young, Africa's sun was already burning from the sky. Volkert had ordered a break every two hours and made sure his men got enough to drink. His intention was to bring the troops safe and sound to their new camp.

"A tearful farewell?"

Secundus frowned.

"A centurion never cries," Volkert said.

"But maybe his fiancée."

"A centurion's fiancée never cries."

"But a fiancée she is?"

Volkert watched with a grin as Secundus' forehead clouded even further.

"I think that's what it amounts to," Secundus said a little awkwardly. He didn't seem to have developed comfort with this thought yet.

"Well, it'll be fine," Volkert assured him soothingly.

Secundus sighed.

Silently, they continued on their way, everyone busy with his own thoughts. The march went without incident, was calm, almost too calm. It was as if destiny wanted to give them one last rest before entering Armageddon.

Secundus joked. Bertius complained. They drank. They ate.

Volkert wasn't emotionally involved in any of it. He joked listlessly. He only half-heartedly advised Bertius. He drank out of duty and let the meal go.

He knew he was waiting for something, but it was more than just the onset of the decisive battle.

Something was brewing.

And whatever it was, it robbed him of more than just his appetite.

21

The passage from Ravenna to Hippo Regius lasted a good twelve days, and von Klasewitz enjoyed the time at sea very much. The incident with the agents of Theodosius was forgotten shortly after it had occurred, the fact that two of the traitors had killed themselves was an unfortunate mishap that had ultimately not affected his feeling of triumph. The other two hadn't been fast enough and had been extensively tortured. When the torturers had fed their leftovers to the fish, two findings had been made – who was responsible for some of the attacks of the last few weeks and that in all likelihood only those four had belonged to the group of culprits.

When von Klasewitz learned that the leader of the gang was responsible for his failed mutiny on the *Saarbrücken*, his mood had been raised quite considerably. This was, if anything, an act of divine providence. Fate wanted him to succeed, there was no doubt about that. The German burst with confidence.

Slowly he took pleasure in this game of betrayal and conspiracy, especially when things developed in his favor. When Hippo Regius appeared in the mist of the morning sun on the horizon, the Magister Militium felt refreshed despite the relatively short period of sleep he got. Everything was now approaching toward his final triumph. He hadn't allowed the last few days to pass unused. He had many conversations, sometimes subtle, sometimes less restrained. It was about preparing the activities that would lead to him seizing the purple. The Church had also laid a good foundation here, Petronius and some other priests had begun in their own way to influence especially the artillery legionaries, so that no matter what would happen, von Klasewitz always had a loyal force at his disposal – the "divine providence" that had saved everyone from the poisonous attack came just in time.

The German grinned into himself. That this "divine providence" had consisted of a fat and ugly kitchen helper who had been ready to blurt everything out for a bag of *denarii*, no one but the already informed had to know. The German supported every rumor that helped him to get close to be regarded as a divinely chosen being, because especially for the simpler minds this was a helpful bridge over which the sheep would walk.

He needed the shepherds to help him, he was quite aware of that.

He stiffened involuntarily as Magnus Maximus stepped at his side. The Emperor had spent the entire journey relatively withdrawn, brooding over plans and tactics, and following up with briefings of his inner circle. It all depended on whether the African prefects would fulfill their promise to flip to their side at the crucial moment. Sure, Maximus had collected hostages, but the Emperor had no illusions about the merciless ruthlessness of many Roman dignitaries, for whom the family was no more than a resource that had to be used in the struggle for power. And, as with any resource, their use was sometimes synonymous with their destruction to serve a higher purpose. So there remained a small risk. Thus, the Emperor and his officers also planned for the case that the African legions would betray the wrong side. Von Klasewitz had no problems with that. His artillery would ensure that they won in any case, especially since the opponents apparently had no intention to sink their fleet, as it had been his greatest fear.

There seemed to be something like chivalry in the enemy's considerations. The German didn't know if he should admire it or laugh about it. It had no major impact on morale, because most legionaries didn't understand how easy it would've been for the *Saarbrücken* to send their entire fleet to the bottom of the Mediterranean.

He would have given this order without hesitation. A clean end without any losses on his side. A gigantic massacre, sure – but that's the way it was.

Maximus watched the passage into the harbor. No cheering crowd greeted them. They hadn't expected any. Hippo Regius lived off trade with the rest of the Empire. Most of the people here preferred the Pax Romana instead of constantly having to deal with changing emperors. Peace was good for business. War was a disruption, a threat, an interruption that could cause huge losses. Maximus had no intention of staying here long. He was thirsty for the moment of decision.

The docking procedure took a while, although the three transport giants were dealt with right away. When Maximus, accompanied by his officers and secured by his personal guard, entered firm ground, an emissary of Gaudentius was already waiting for him, as agreed. It was not long before they had moved into a larger room in the harbor administration, again sealed off by the legionaries and thus a place where they could talk undisturbed.

"Mactaris is the place of battle," the officer had immediately told the two men. "We chose it, and Theodosius agreed, because the location also benefits him. We have already had a precise map made – a copy of the one used by the time-wanderers. Gaudentius has taken an officer to the meetings, who has a keen eye and an excellent memory, and a wonderful gift for drawing."

Maximus and von Klasewitz leaned over the unrolled parchment.

The German nodded in satisfaction. "There are good positions for my guns. This time we have to strengthen the artillery's protection so that the men of von Geeren don't get too close to me. But from here, we will clearly dominate the battlefield."

"Which would not do much good for us if the African legions don't switch sides," Maximus remarked, watching the officer lurking. He bowed.

"Gaudentius has agreed signals with his commanders, as proposed by you, my Lord. As soon as you are ready, give the order, and the African legions will bring disaster to Theodosius. We have gathered all the soldiers, even border troops, auxiliary soldiers, all the locals. We will provide 20,000 men to Theodosius, and this apparent superiority will be his downfall."

Maximus didn't show it, but he had to be impressed. And he wasn't worried that the exposure of African borders would be exploited by any neighbor. Everybody knew that Maximus himself was in Africa and would cruelly punish anyone who took advantage of the occasion. There was always time to beat the heads of barbarians.

"The signals are ready?"

The question had been addressed to von Klasewitz. He smiled. "We have everything prepared. They won't be overlooked."

For a long time, they had discussed which kind of signals should be used. Was it the sound of the trumpets and horns normally used to direct the troops? Doubt had been expressed as to whether this would be sufficient given the battle noise of such a large number of legionaries, reinforced even by the cannons. Von Klasewitz had finally come up with the right idea, and the development had been done relatively quick. Nobody would overlook or ignore this signal, of that everyone was sure.

"I trust Gaudentius and his men," Maximus explained in a tone of conviction. "And not only he himself, but also all who serve him faithfully shall be richly rewarded for their patriotism."

The officer stiffened and smiled quite pleased.

The next few hours went by quickly. Von Klasewitz was busy supervising the landing of his artillery and at the same time preparing it to march. The new wagons proved sturdy and easy to maneuver, and his artillerymen were well-trained, so everything ran smoothly. As Magister Militium, he also had to take care of the proper preparation of the other units. By the time most of the soldiers had moved into the hastily constructed camp outside the city, it was already midnight. Maximus had ordered that the men would have a full day before the march started south, and von Klasewitz feared that it wouldn't be easy to comply – too much to do with the unloading of the ships.

When he himself fell exhaustedly on his bed in the early morning – not in the camp, of course, but in a villa in Hippo Regius himself, which had been made available to the Emperor and the highest dignitaries by the city's leaders –, he found no sleep despite his weariness. He had never held such responsibility before, and although many capable men took a great deal of work from him, both his own mistrust and the desire for perfection drove him to take care of things that another commander would've left to his subordinates.

It was hard for him to do that. Somewhere in his heart, he also knew the cause. If he had worked with people for a long time, it was easier for him to delegate. This had been the case with the construction of the three gigantic transports or with the construction of the artillery legion. In time, he had found one or the other, who didn't give him sleepless nights at the thought of performing tasks independently. However, his appointment as commander was too short a time to properly familiarize himself with his staff.

And even if he would've, the German was nobody who trusted other people much. He was very convinced that he possessed all of the necessary wisdom, and some, and he admitted that openly, at least to himself. Once he knew the only truth, he was willing to adjust, ready to adapt to the circumstances. Von Klasewitz held a lot of principles but was quite ready for flexibility. So ultimately, his arrogance towards the barbarians of the past – and in principle he meant all Romans – was still in his way. He was aware of that as well, but he didn't succeed in jumping over the last shadow. They couldn't know what he did.

He knew he had to change that. He had learned a lot in the last few months. He was a different man from the one who had fiercely instigated the mutiny on the *Saarbrücken*. He now appreciated the benefits of careful planning and the need for good and dedicated people. Once he was Emperor, it was impossible to take care of everything and everyone. He had to delegate. He had to trust people – to a certain extent.

And he knew what could happen if one trusted the wrong people.

But how did he separate the wheat from the chaff?

Was his knowledge of human nature sufficient? Could he see through the facades that many high-ranking officers and politicians had woven around themselves with sophisticated acting? Could he find counselors who recognized these things – and could he then trust these counselors to tell him everything truthfully and without ulterior motive?

Von Klasewitz sighed, straightened, reached for the wine cup next to him and drank. This restlessness of his thoughts led to nothing. He had to find peace. The heavy red wine he served himself might help.

114

He drank the cup, then lay down again, eyes wide, staring at the ceiling.

Sleep! Sleep! He wanted to force himself to find peace. But the inner tension had him firmly under control. He rolled back and forth for a few minutes, then poured another glass of wine, drank hastily without paying any more attention to the quality of the drink.

At some point, he succeeded in dozing off, but the dreams that followed showed him clearly that only his body had found rest, not his mind.

22

"That is not enough. Dig deeper!" Von Geeren pointed to the corporal beside him. "Like him. Otherwise, this isn't a decent cover. The enemy has cannons!"

It was tedious to have to emphasize that again and again. The infantryman in front of him just nodded and leaned down to drill the shovel back into the ground. Since the early morning hours, they were busy digging out the positions. They had to perform several functions simultaneously: providing a good position to hit the battlefield with targeted shots, adequate protection against the tyrannical traitor's cannons, and a mount against attacking ground forces that they would most certainly encounter.

Lucius Verilius didn't leave his side. The Centurion continued to be responsible for the safety of the infantry, as he had been in the Battle of Bagacum. His legionaries were to ward off sneaky attacks and at least buy the Germans time to reorient themselves. Verilius' men had suffered heavy losses at Bagacum, but his troops had been rebuilt immediately. The Centurion knew the hard task ahead of him, and he did everything he could to increase his men's chances. He gave advice where he saw fit and was not afraid to ride in the parade of von Geeren if he thought he was wrong. The installation of a mound here, the positioning of a sniper there – Verilius had now developed a deep understanding of the possibilities of rifles and didn't keep his opinion for himself. Von Geeren allowed him to do so. And he found that initial reservations of his men against the Centurion's harsh suggestions were beginning to fade. That was good, because the time-wanderers wouldn't be able to maintain their particular structure of command forever. At some point, they would be completely absorbed in the Roman forces, mingling with them, and there would be Roman officers giving orders. The more the Germans got used to such a constellation, the easier it would be for them to adapt to this future integration. Of course, there were reservations – or rather prejudices. Von Geeren himself fell for one or the other. But it was men like Verilius with their pragmatic professionalism that made them more and more irrelevant.

"Tribune von Geeren, this wall is shit!" The Centurion pointed to a part of the fort that the infantrymen were working on. Of course, it was remarks like these that, on the other hand, that led to the German to take a deep breath and fight a bit for composure. A little bit only.

"What are your suggestions for improvement?"

This was followed by a lengthy lecture, which proved, among other things, that the Roman legionaries had much more experience in producing ramparts, walls and ditches out of nowhere than the German soldiers. Von Geeren endured the flood of good advice with stoic serenity. His men had already stopped working upon hearing the word "shit," and looked expectantly at the Captain.

Once Verilius had finished, Geeren took a deep breath, forced a smile, and nodded. "That's how we do it, Centurion!"

He ignored the groans of his men. It may have been that he had given them extra work and injured pride. But if that did increase their chances of survival in the coming battle, he was ready to accept those injuries.

Von Geeren nodded to the men and moved to another part of the position they were currently preparing. Here, a position with three MG was set up. First, they had considered distributing the MGs widely, but then decided against it. The effort to protect the nests was too great and would stretch their forces too much, which increased the risk of losing the shooter. By concentrating the guns, they could increase the firepower as well as provide better for the safety of the men. The range of the machine guns was so great that they could spread the entire battlefield. Their biggest problem was, as with all other firearms, the remaining ammunition.

Von Geeren had made a complete arms inspection a few days ago. All rifles, pistols and machine guns were in excellent condition. The soldiers had the weapons well maintained, knowing that there were no spare parts and they were fully responsible for the functionality of their tools. Von Geeren had hardly anything to complain about. But the disillusionment had been great when it came to measuring the ammunition. For the approximately 100 still active infantrymen were only 40 cartridges available, the MGs were still able to fall back on about 2,000 rounds, which at their rate of fire, however, was not particularly comfortable. The handguns of the officers were also only partially operational. Consequently, von Geeren had warned everyone to shoot only when the target was clear and worthwhile to attack. Every shot had to find its victim. The MGs especially had to concentrate on short bursts of fire, used tactically.

All infantrymen also had been equipped with swords. Legionaries of Verilius had taught them to use the weapon in every free minute. Von Geeren had also participated in the exercises and realized that he was untalented for this type of combat. He had learned how to fight, but that was quite different from the work with the blade they had to learn here. The Roman short sword was essentially a thrust weapon, and the long sword was swung savagely, less used for a real fencing duel. His officer's saber had remained on the *Saarbrücken*. It was a fully functional weapon, but at the same time a piece of high symbolic power and nothing he wanted to break or damage in combat.

Soon, the day would come when their firearms became useless. If Dahms could organize his small industrial revolution, it would be a temporary state. Either he would be able to make new ammunition or replace the rifles of the infantrymen with muskets. He would definitely be able to conjure something in that direction, with time and peace and a safe place where all the resources were available to him.

Von Geeren shook his head slightly.

Here, he stood to command in a fight that would lead to creating conditions so that he could continue to win battles in the future. It wasn't surprising that at the moment he was thinking of a young woman, daughter of Prefect Modestus, who resided in Constantinople and who had never left his mind since her liberation. He had decided to return to the capital of the East, and he wanted to survive this

118

fight to put this intention into action. Well, at least that was one motivation he could make friends with. He looked for rest, and he was not the only one. Once the victory was achieved and Maximus was dealt with, some of the infantrymen would make their escape, and he and Rheinberg were well aware of that. The desertion of Ensign Volkert, who now served as Tribune Thomasius and didn't yet know that he had long since been forgiven – Rheinberg and Dahms had only recently told about their discovery to von Geeren –, was only the beginning.

Also a form of integration into the Roman Empire, von Geeren thought, and he caught himself shaking his head again.

So, just this one more battle.

And who knew, maybe he would afterwards belong to those who settled down. Nobody would blame him. Constantinople was an exciting city. Von Geeren was a practical man and had learned other skills besides warfare. He would find a living. For a change, not travel slaughtering through the countryside or participating in too many endless planning sessions – that was a very pleasant alternative.

"Captain, you had asked for me?"

"Ah, Sassmann."

Von Geeren waved the man over. Sassmann was always in a pleasant mood, had excelled himself in the liberation of Modestus' family and kept himself in good memory with his superior. With Sassmann, it was quite evident – Everyone knew that the man wanted to leave the army. He was a good soldier, but maybe just too good. To Rheinberg, von Geeren had suggested that one might give Sassmann another position in the service of the Empire and then have someone who could teach the legionaries how to handle firearms once they produced them.

The Captain had promised to think about it. The conversation with the sniper, with which he would've been able to find out what his preference was, hadn't yet taken place. There would not be much time left after the battle to do that; von Geeren felt it.

"I thought of a special role for you in the coming battle. Not easy, but tailored to your abilities," Geeren said quietly, pulling the man aside, slightly out of earshot of the other soldiers.

Sassmann's face remained unmoved. He knew what he could do and what kind of assignment he could expect. "I'm ready," he said.

"You will not dig ditches, Sassmann," von Geeren continued. "Actually, you're not going to be used in that position." He grabbed the man by the arm and walked with him away from the others, his head tilted to one side, and explained in detail what kind of plans he had for the sniper.

It was a long conversation.

23

"After all, it's not a *new* order we want to create," Maximus explained, giving Ambrosius a friendly nod. The Bishop of Milan had traveled as far as Hippo Regius, but now he wanted to leave and return to Italy. A final dinner together with the Emperor had been arranged in his honor, in a small circle. Petronius, who would remain with the Emperor along with three other priests, participated as well as some officers and advisers. The Magister Militium on the other hand had apologized for coordinating tomorrow's departure of the troops to Mactaris. Maximus almost envied the man for this task. It was tedious at times to listen to the Bishop's lectures, especially when they became more radical and demanding with each new conversation.

"No new order?" Ambrosius shook his head, smiling gently. "But, sire, that's exactly what we want to achieve. The unity of Church and Empire is exactly that – a new order! It is the order that prepares the return of Christ on earth, which will prepare humanity for him and welcome him. It is the eternal kingdom that governs the world in the name of the Lord, and points out to those who are not of the true faith the error of their ways and cleanse where necessary."

"I have no problem getting rid of the old cults and putting the Arians in their place," Maximus replied, frowning at the Bishop. "But I won't start, just because of my faith as a Christian Trinitarian Emperor, an attack against the Persians or to do more against the Huns than to defend myself as effectively as possible."

Ambrosius nodded. "That's hard to imagine right now. We lack the military means of power. But for that we have our new Magister, and as soon as Rheinberg is dead, the technology of the time-wanderers, which we can use under appropriate spiritual supervision, to solve this problem. Then Persians and Huns won't be an obstacle any longer. And until then there are still enough other areas to tackle. You have quite rightly mentioned the Arians and the ancient cults but also point to the Jews. They also have to be severely punished. Here, too, I see a good chance for forced conversions."

Maximus closed his eyes. "Why should we worry about Palestine now? I'm glad that those wild people, for once, are docile!"

"Docile? They are the murderers of our Lord! With a crooked faith that thinks to be better and more original than ours! They consider themselves the chosen people! Absurd! Only those of us who have accepted Jesus as their Savior are chosen. But the Jews killed him in cold blood!"

"Well," one of the officers said who had been listening to the argument in silence, "if I remember the records properly, nobody was murdered. The governor carried out a sentence because Jesus violated Roman law, which was then in force ..."

"Silly!" Ambrosius said. "It was the Jews who drove Pilatus to do it with their resentment and their envy!"

Maximus raised both hands. "I think this discussion will not take us any further!"

"But yes!" the Bishop demanded, looking very agitated now. "We nourish the Jews in our midst, on our breasts, they enjoy Roman civilization and security, and yet they are nothing but murderers! God wants to punish them, and we – we alone – are his tools!"

Maximus made a reassuring gesture. "I can't wage war against any ethnic group within the Empire. The Empire must have peace. Our situation is precarious enough so that I can't provoke another civil war! We should turn to more important questions."

"But that's important!"

"Noble Bishop ..."

"We have to make every effort to reconcile the purity of faith with the purity of imperial power! Both must go hand in hand, must *be* the same hand that carries the common sword, that of the word of Christ and the Lord's holy wrath! Only this unity will ensure that the right faith prevails and we will find salvation! This is no small matter! It's all about one thing – the salvation of all of us."

Ambrosius' voice dropped, took on a pleading undertone. "It's also about the salvation of the Jews – as well as that of the Arians and other heretics. We have a great Christian duty, a heavy responsibility to bring the truth to even those who are ignorant. And some ... well, some have to be more emphatically convinced to be blessed than others. It's only good for them."

Maximus took a deep breath. Those who knew him well knew he was struggling to maintain self-control. In contrast to Theodosius, the former governor of Britain wasn't considered to be particularly hot-tempered. But it was difficult to maintain a calm attitude if one was emperor and didn't quite receive the deserved respect.

"Bishop!" he shouted.

Maybe this rash form of address rushed a bit too loud over his lips. At any rate, Ambrosius narrowed his eyes and involuntarily straightened. Had he noticed that he was about to cross a finely drawn border?

"Your advice is dear and important to me," Maximus continued in a lower tone. "The benefit of the Church is very important to me. I reject the Arian deviants just as vehemently as you do. That's why I have already given you a free hand in this regard. The purity of faith is central to the Empire and, of course, to all of our salvation. But there are necessities and priorities in politics that are not always in harmony with the wishes of the Church. I must dedicate myself to these aspects as well."

He raised a hand as Ambrosius tried to insert something. The Bishop wisely caught himself and kept his mouth shut.

"To make matters worse," Maximus said, "the Church by no means agrees on everything. By this I refer not only to the fact that, especially in the East, the majority of bishops are attached to the Arian errors."

"There will soon be a cleanup to solve the problem," Ambrosius interjected. "It has already started in the West, and I am very satisfied with the first results. We are making good progress."

Maximus nodded. In response to the petition for clemency from many churches asking for leniency in regard to deserving priests, he had hitherto closed his heart, for he didn't want to meddle in these things, at least not right now, where other priorities were pressing. Maximus didn't grieve too much for dead Arians. He wasn't detached too far from the ambitions of Ambrosius in these matters. He only preferred other ... nuances.

"Even the Trinitarians are not in agreement on everything. The Bishop of Rome is not half as committed as you, Ambrosius. I have the impression that he could well imagine a less radical implementation of our common ideas."

Ambrosius didn't show any expression that might indicate a derogatory opinion about the Bishop of Rome.

"My brother has my greatest respect," he said. "His counsel is important to me."

"Not to mention other dignitaries," Maximus continued. "I have even heard of bishops who can find some truth in the tolerant ideas of Rheinberg, Trinitarians in their hearts, but ... pragmatically oriented."

Ambrosius clenched his teeth. The persons mentioned by Maximus disturbed him more than he wanted to admit. He was able to depose and punish the Arians with the help of the state authorities. But Trinitarians, whose only flaw was a lesser determination – that was a whole other problem. "That's an issue we can take care of it," he said. "I'm not too worried. These are no serious obstacles."

"Good to know. So we should wait a while, am I right? When it is clear what the situation develops into after the victory over Theodosius, we can devote ourselves to these things. We must not lose sight of other problems. The plague is one of them. It's spread worries us all."

Ambrosius spat and made a contemptuous tone. "The plague! So much is clear: Only those are affected who have attracted the wrath of God! The East has not yet fully succumbed to the orthodox view, so the plague is God's pointer, telling us that he's no longer willing to tolerate this kind of heresy."

"The plague has reached the West by now!"

"There are still many in the West who lack insight and righteousness. There, too, the punitive hand of God is felt. Maybe it's a lesson for them."

Maximus looked around. Officers looked at each other or turned their eyes to the ground. Of course, there was something true about the words of the Bishop, no Christian wanted to dispute this. But the officers had a very practical problem: If the plague killed their soldiers, there were simply no men left to go to war with. Without soldiers, it would not only be difficult to fight the external enemies but also the inner opponents, and those, to whom the special attention of the Ambrosius had been applied, would remain unmolested for the time being. Marauding priests couldn't nail everyone on the cross. A proper pogrom required professional planning and was best supported by those whose job was killing.

"The army of the East has been decimated by the plague!" Ambrosius trumpeted. "The Lord plays in our hands! Don't you see that?"

Maximus sighed. Ambrosius might know more about spiritual matters than he did, but as far as long-term military planning was concerned, he was an amateur.

"I also see that once we have defeated Theodosius, there will be no army in the East that can defend the Empire against our enemies."

Perhaps the tone of his answer had been a bit too sharp – or too patronizing. But Maximus allowed himself this tiny slip. His nerves were strained, and it was depressing enough that not his enemy was the reason for his stress but someone whose support he should expect.

Ambrosius stared at Maximus, as if he couldn't believe what he was hearing. Could the Emperor really be so ignorant?

Maximus got up before the Bishop could say another word. He would lose his patience, and above all, all self-control, if he continued this conversation. There were also, by God, more urgent things to discuss and decide. Apostates and heretics could wait.

There was always more than enough of them.

He nodded toward the Bishop and strove for a friendly tone and a smile as warm as possible. "I wish you a safe journey home, Ambrosius. Convey my best wishes to your brothers. I hope we'll meet again next time at my victory celebration."

Ambrosius bowed. "Thank you. I will pray for your victory." The Bishop seemed to realize that he wouldn't be able to finish his favorite topic tonight.

Maximus smiled wider. "Please continue the meal. I still have a lot of work to do. The victory will not fall in our lap without effort."

All rose as the Emperor left the room. When he was gone, there was an awed silence. Nobody wanted to look the Bishop in the eye or speak to him.

The dinner didn't last long.

24

It wasn't quite as easy to get out of Hippo Regius, as he had imagined. For one, Godegisel was in this city and on African soil for the first time; he simply didn't know his way around. Further, there were armed patrols everywhere, and many people were stopped and questioned along the way. When the legions were brought ashore, the civilians brought along were not allowed to leave the ships. But even when most of the soldiers had been moved into the military camp built in front of the city, the curfew hadn't been lifted right away. Godegisel was among the last to be landed. For a moment he had considered simply fleeing the ship – opportunities would have been enough –, but he had decided against it. It would've been very suspicious, and he just wanted to be a docile young man, interested in further employment, who had a hard time in life and didn't cause any trouble. He played this role so well that he got a recommendation for one of the big transports who hired sailors in order to travel the entire Mediterranean. Godegisel suddenly had a promising career at sea, but he quickly decided to pursue his original plan.

With the money in his pocket, his modest bundle on his back and a great deal of time on his shoulders, he was finally released ashore. Immediately, the young Goth hurried to the forum, because he hoped to get hold of a way to travel on as quickly as possible. He knew by now that Theodosius and his kin had taken positions in Mactaris, so the purpose of his journey was clear. And because it was so clear, this part of Roman Africa was for a long time shunned by traveling merchants, caravans, and all others who were not in the Emperor's pay and who wielded a sword for him. In other words, after a frustrating day of searching, Godegisel had to realize that he wouldn't find a harmless camouflage ride – no ox cart, no horse cart, no one, nothing. Everyone was waiting for the outcome of the battle, for the victor's orders, for the withdrawal of the troops. Only then would trade would resume.

That was far too late for Godegisel.

The night he spent in a sailor's tavern at the harbor, which offered reasonably pleasant accommodation. The food was decent, but the bed bugs numerous, and the roommates in the large bedroom were noisy, stank and behaved anything but reassuring. When Godegisel awoke in the morning, he heard during breakfast that the legions of Maximus were about to leave. Since the Goth had to arrive at Theodosius and Rheinberg before them, he didn't have too many options left. He hurried to the market early, bought a new set of solid sandals, a bag of all kinds of supplies, and was already on his way to Mactaris, always vaguely hoping to find a way to increase his travel speed on the way. He was good on foot, but the Roman legions knew how to march, and there was a danger that especially mounted advance detachments would catch up with him. Was he suspicious? He would rather not take that risk.

A long, exhausting walk was very good for him. The freedom of movement aboard the ship had been limited. And if he hadn't had such an urgent mission, he would've been interested in Africa that seemed to be nice enough here in the north, with its green hills, agriculture, and pleasant climate.

But he concentrated on making as much distance as possible. He marched through the day, except for a brief lunch break. As the sun went down, he prepared a shelter off the road, protected by a tree. He was now, especially without a horse, no worthwhile object for mugger, on the other hand, he wanted to take no unnecessary risk. The few coins remaining to him were certainly still of use.

Breakfast was meager, some hard bread, just as hard cheese, a sip of water. Without further hesitation, he set off again immediately, marched hard, pushed ahead, although his body began to protest after the first few miles. When he reached a market town, he was able to replenish his water supply. A farmer sold him dried and fresh fruit, his wife gave him freshly baked flatbread, all for a small sum. With no traders left until the great battle had ended, the whole country was in a strange state of stupor, and Godegisel was an almost welcome change.

He didn't spend much time stowing his supplies and marched on. At lunchtime, he stopped at the wayside to strengthen himself. He was disturbed in his meal when an ox cart loaded with hay rumbled out onto the street from a field. A wizened little man sat on the box, his skin burned deep brown, a cap pulled down his face so that one could barely see his eyes. When it became clear that the cart was turning in the direction that Godegisel wanted, he got up and waved. The cart came to a halt, the ox looked at the Goths with grateful eyes. Apparently the animal enjoyed the unforeseen break.

"How far in that direction are you going?" Godegisel asked the coachman.

The man shrugged and made a general gesture. It was clear that he was hard-pressed to give a useful estimate. "Hay for my master," he said, scratching his head under the cap. "Hay for the stable."

Godegisel nodded and smiled. "Can I travel with you?"

The coachman looked at him suspiciously. Godegisel sighed and pulled out a coin, letting it jump through the air. The coachman showed a remarkable and unforeseen agility, as he grabbed the metal with uncanny precision and let it disappear in his tattered coat in no time. Then he grunted and pointed to the seat by his side.

Godegisel swung onto the coachman's seat.

"This direction is not so good," the driver mumbled as the ox sighed and the cart lurched forward again. "There'll be a big battle soon."

"I've heard of that."

"All nonsense."

"Yes?"

The man looked up. "They fight up there, but nothing changes for us."

"What change do you think of?"

The old man shrugged. "I don't know. Would be satisfied if my son hadn't been drafted. But he was. It might be that he is over there now. Haven't heard from him for a while." He sank into silence again, moving his lips back and forth, as if more words wanted to push his way through his mouth, which he held back with force.

Godegisel remembered Clodius, whose son had long been sold as a slave and about whose fate he had learned nothing more. The young man knew many such stories. The long flight of his people from the Huns and the suffering after their arrival had given rise to many more such fates.

He wondered if there would be a time when events like this would become unthinkable.

He said nothing else to the coachman. He had experienced enough on his long journey through the Empire to understand how the big men's decisions influenced the common ones' lives and what kind of destiny lay behind him. Did Rheinberg think about the common people? He remembered that the Magister Militium had pushed ahead with the liberation of the slaves and had abolished the duty for a son to take up his father's profession. In an abstract way, he probably thought of the ordinary man, yes. But even so, not least because of his actions, the old man's son might soon die on the nearby battlefield.

"We leave them alone," the old man muttered. "Why can't they just leave us alone as well?"

Godegisel still didn't say anything. He felt the rumble of the cart under his butt, staring down at the dusty road in front of them, knowing the marching legions of Maximus behind him. His insights burned in his soul, he wanted to get rid of them.

"Do you want to go to battle, boy?"

Godegisel shook his head. "No I don't."

That wasn't even a lie.

"Hide yourself, I tell you," the coachman advised. "Hide yourself. That's all we can do."

Godegisel said nothing, and the coachman sank into silence.

Hiding, the Goth knew, was the last thing he intended to do.

25

"The soldiers of Maximus are on their way!"

Rheinberg looked up, glanced at Richomer, who had entered the tent, a piece of parchment in his hand, with which he waved.

"The scouts just confirmed it. Our African allies have reported it. The legions are marching."

Rheinberg stretched. The sudden feeling of approaching danger mingled with relief. The wait would soon come to an end. With this battle, everything would be decided. He shook off the fear. They had prepared themselves as well as they possibly could, had made plans, made alliances, resorted to treachery. They didn't have much more left to do now.

"I want scouts to keep a close eye on the advance but keep their distance. We don't want to stop the enemy because we are ready. Everyone wants it to be over."

Richomer nodded. "I have already given the appropriate orders."

The scouts wouldn't get in trouble. Unlike Maximus' men, they possessed the few precious binoculars of the time-wanderers. No one had to go near the armed caravan rolling toward them. Already on the way there, Rheinberg had identified good observation posts, hills, buildings, far away, just within sight of the binoculars, where scouts could hide without being immediately in danger.

"Let's inform the officers down to the centurion," Rheinberg said. "They're supposed to shut up, but they'll be able to smile meaningfully when asked. I want tension to build up. This sharpens the senses, and the soldiers can gather the energy they will soon need."

Richomer grinned. "I'll call a meeting."

"Does Theodosius know?"

"He was informed. He said the details were your problem. Tonight he wants a brief meeting, but otherwise he just walks through the camp and talks to the soldiers to give everyone some courage and confidence. "

Rheinberg was pleased. The Emperor did what he did best in his position, now that everything was planned and decided. Theodosius was a passionate man, and he radiated these feelings. He could talk to the simple legionaries who had accompanied him a long way. He would evoke the memory of Gratian, the vision of a new Rome – a place where faithful and brave legionaries who had proven themselves had untold opportunities to make a difference. He wouldn't threaten and discipline; he wasn't a sergeant. His job was to inspire. Would Maximus do the same? He was told that it was his great strength to take care of the affairs of his simplest men. Maybe that was also the motivation for the Spaniard to try harder for an emotional bond with his troops. It was a weapon that cost little but could make a big impact when the going gets tough and the battle unfolded unpleasantly.

Unpleasantly …

When Richomer left the tent, Rheinberg had to think again about what would happen to him if they lost this clash. He knew some of his men were planning an escape for such a case, but he didn't feel that he liked the idea. The *Saarbrücken* would certainly flee and try to seek refuge in the East. Perhaps she could take Theodosius with her, and then he could hold himself for a while as the Emperor of the East – again an interesting historical parallel to the Theodosius of his past, who had also had to share the Empire with Maximus for a while.

Only in that timeline there hadn't been the plague and the Spaniard had won in the end. But this time the omens would be reversed, and Rheinberg wasn't sure whether alone with the *Saarbrücken* he would succeed in turning the rudder once more.

He could no longer stay in his tent.

He had to go out to meet with the troops too. He had to feel their readiness, their confidence and their hope. Maybe it would help to get infected.

He wandered through the army camp. It was gigantic, because now also the African troops had arrived. Almost 40,000 soldiers were gathered here, one of the largest armies in the history of the Roman Empire. Should he feel proud to command such a machine? Or should the responsibility rather inspire fear?

Rheinberg didn't want to decide for one or the other. He found that focused humility was the right attitude for this moment.

Some of the legionaries spoke to him. The commander was not known as aloof. Many only greeted him. Two offered him a helping of porridge, and once Rheinberg accepted the offer, praising the cook ironically, earning laughter.

He didn't want to inspect anyone, but overzealous NCOs called their men to attention as he approached, and then it was his job to calm the general agitation. He assumed that the weapons and armor were in good condition everywhere. And if not, well, that wouldn't change too much.

He didn't want to spread fear.

Not all of the men noticed him with excitement or special respect. Not all soldiers liked him. He was still a foreign man who didn't understand much of what made up the soul of these troops. Some felt threatened by the new weapons, some by the changing times. Rheinberg couldn't persuade anyone to like him. For those who had reservations, there was still the iron discipline of the Roman legions.

Rheinberg hoped that would be enough.

Especially with the tents of the African troops he met many questioning looks. It was a slightly cooler, restrained politeness he felt, nothing that surprised him a lot. They practiced, they marched, they rested, let the signals sound. But in the end, it was two armies that were to be put together in a short time. The African generals had asked to keep the coherence of their units because otherwise they feared confusion in battle. Rheinberg had quickly seen that, too, and accepted. The African troops were placed on the two wings. The army of Theodosius would be the center. That's how it had been decided a few weeks ago.

It was all a little like patchwork. So much could go wrong. It was these imponderables that robbed Rheinberg of sleep. This feeling of not having everything under control – as if that was ever possible. But in these times when safety and quiet were strange concepts and the threats piled up, the illusion of control was even more important. It allowed him to maintain his sanity. If the illusion was destroyed, what was left but trusting God?

And that, in turn, was something that Rheinberg unfortunately found very difficult. If God loved sending him and his men through time, pulling them out of their familiar world and confronting them with challenges of that sort, what kind of trust would he have to face such a God?

Rheinberg spent a good two hours wandering around the camp, always willing to be stopped, didn't hurry, didn't seem to be rushed. And what he was most aware of wasn't enthusiasm or trust or fear … but consistently professional serenity. He exchanged many words. He was asked many questions. Fear of what was to come lay only subtly above anything, no matter how professional and relaxed the veterans were. There was so much at stake, not the least their lives.

Control, Rheinberg thought. He felt the illusion melt like sand in his hands.

Trust in God. Confidence. It really couldn't get any worse.

They'd succeed if they kept everyone together and, as a military unit, mastered this last great challenge.

When Rheinberg returned to his tent, this was precisely this insight he sought. After all, he was not a politician, not a revolutionary, not a visionary, not a creator of a new empire, but only one thing – a soldier.

Maybe that was what ultimately gave him the necessary rest.

26

If only he would've been allowed to do his duty in Capsa.

But no.

But no.

But no.

Lucius Strabo stared at the dusty road and turned to his two comrades. The Centurion had said this morning that they would no longer neglect the patrols despite the fact that the Prefect had withdrawn almost all mobile troops north toward Hippo Regius to fight a civil war there.

Strabo was grateful for not belonging to that contingent. His need to be smashed by one of the spellcasters of the time-wanderers was limited. Here on the southern border of the Roman Empire on the African continent, the situation was calm and manageable. The adjoining kingdoms behaved modestly and didn't seem to have any intention of exploiting the current exposure of the border. It was all very peaceful.

Maybe that was why they had neglected the patrols a bit. Nevertheless, Strabo had no sympathy for the Centurion's zeal. In fact, there were very few border guards in the area, just enough to give the appearance of public order. Everyone was afraid of the outcome of the great battle, so everyone remained covered and quiet. No matter who won, the frontier troops would return, and anyone who had used the time of their absence to do evil would be punished, regardless what the new Emperor's name was.

Strabo therefore found it unnecessary to punish him and his two comrades by marching south along the road to the border post near the beginning of the desert, where nothing was happening and nothing would.

What a torture.

Of course, Strabo thought, the order could also have been causally related to the fact that he and his two comrades had spent yesterday evening their free time in a bathhouse to use the services of some whores, to then determine that their cash for the payment was not quite enough. When the owner of the bathhouse used muscular help, the legionaries retained the upper hand, but the ensuing complaint to the commandant's office did more than muscles and clubs could. The debt was withheld from their pay, there was a sermon, there was special service – cleaning latrines, what else? –, and this patrol smelled strongly of additional punishment. His two comrades, too, seemed to have come to a similar conclusion, for many of the curses they uttered along the way contained artful and imaginative variations of the name of their Centurion.

Justice was sometimes overrated, Strabo thought.

Besides, the whores had been old and not very enthusiastic. If someone still had to pay off debts, then the bathhouse owner to his customers for not properly rendered services.

With that in mind, the man consoled himself, as he trudged along the road. He would spend the night at the small border station, which was known to have no food supplies and very hard beds. The porridge from the ingredients he brought would have to be sufficient, and from that Strabo always got bloated, which in turn would lead to an interesting night in close companionship with his fellow sufferers.

This was one of those days when Strabo counted the remaining years of his service. It was a depressing activity, having spent the first ten years three months ago and then had decided to benefit from the recent military reform – retiring after 10 years with bonus and land title – or continuing to ten more years in the next higher rank. Strabo had joined the army mainly because it was well-paid, he received medical care and a certain social prestige, especially when he was promoted. And so Strabo had signed, been promoted, and now had another nine years and nine months' service, a decision he was beginning to seriously question just then.

Next to him his old friend Lacius, who differed from him by the fact that his ten years were over in two months, and he would start as a shoemaker in his father-in-law's business in Hippo Regius, matched with the prospect of inheriting the shop from the old man in the not too distant future. This process was now simpler than before, because the economic reforms had led to the breakup of the guilds and free career choice slowly began to assert itself as a principle. Lacius had used the favor of the hour in his own way, and that he would bring his retirement bonus as a dowry into the workshop, the old man had liked particularly well. Lacius wouldn't make Strabo's mistake. But Strabo also had no wife who could have directed him on the right path.

After all, he would now know a reliable source of neat footwear in the future, and that was a good thing.

"We'll arrive at the border soon," Lacius muttered, taking a sip of watery wine. "How long are we supposed we stay there?"

"Until the Centurion sends new men, we'll patrol the road," Strabo said.

"Who would know that we're actually doing that? There's no one the asshole can send to check on us."

"He'll suspect we're just going to sit in the shade and get on his horse himself to kick our asses," Decius, third in league, suggested. He rubbed his crotch. "Damn, the whore yesterday was so exhausted, I barely got a shot. I should get compensated."

"You'll probably have to lay hands on yourself," Strabo commented. "It will be some time before you see another woman stupid or desperate enough to get involved with you."

"The Centurion needs people for the watch," Lacius said with hope in his voice. "He will not let us waste out here forever."

"We have to cool down, he told the Optio," Decius muttered.

Strabo nodded. Given the summer temperatures, that would be difficult for them.

In the distance, he recognized the squat stone building of the small border station. The men stationed there would be happy to escape this godforsaken place. In the surroundings one could find – except from the road – only a few skewed houses from which farmers sold snacks for travelers. The nearest village was almost as far away as the nearest major city, Capsa, from where they had traveled. There

137

was a village on the other side of the border, in the area of the Garamantes, but they were not allowed to cross the line. And there wasn't much going on over there anyway.

"We're almost there," Decius muttered. "I hope the well has not silted up again."

Decius had been stationed here once before. His statement led to sinister fantasies in Strabo's mind, in which a shovel and a lot of sweat played an important role.

He had no choice but to surrender to fate anyway. There would be better times. The building was then clearly visible. In front of it, two legionaries stood watching listlessly as a trader trotted down the street with three loaded donkeys. The pack animals carried vegetables. Here, too, the reforms had made it easier for the legionaries to do their work – food was no longer levied. It was good to always have enough to eat, the time-wanderers had decided.

A point Strabo had no objection to.

He stopped, took a sip of his own and sighed. Casually, he looked up to see if any other lonely traders came from the south of the road, promising at least some variety.

Then his eyes narrowed, and he raised a hand to shade it. His eyes wandered past border posts and donkeys.

What was …

He cleared his throat.

Decius and Lacius stopped, following his gaze.

Strabo narrowed his eyes.

"Say," he said slowly, with a slight tremor in his voice, "what is this?"

27

Ox cart or not, Godegisel was overtaken in the end. When the old coachman had shooed him off the cart and headed for the *latifundia* of his master, the Goth had already identified the riders in the distance – and not only him. The old male had advised him to stay away from the street for now, for marching legions paid little heed to lone wanderers. This was all the more true of the equestrian unit, which approached the marching man at a steady pace. Of course, the animals were not rushed unnecessarily, they were rarely sped up to a trot. Not only because the riders didn't want to increase the distance to the foot soldiers too much, but also because excessive speed would have unnecessarily fatigued the animals. But a slow horse was still faster than a Goth, and the time came, already in the early evening, when he had to hide himself in a lonely tree, standing on the side of the road, and let the seemingly endless rider column pass by. He continued his way for a while on the adjacent fields and meadows, but this was an increasingly dangerous undertaking, especially in the dusk.

He finally prepared his modest bed about fifty yards from the military road. It was fortunately warm and dry, so his night wouldn't be too hard.

The sun had just set, and Godegisel had sunk into a first gloomy slumber when light woke him again. He opened his eyes and started up.

Torches were waved in front of his face.

"Hey, wake up!" a raspy voice snapped. "Who are you?"

Godegisel scrambled to his feet. Three legionaries stood in front of him, holding out torches. They hadn't drawn their weapons, probably because they realized that the sleeper was unarmed. Godegisel looked at the military road. A torchlight procession marched along there. The legions used the safe road to get through part of the night and would probably only make a relatively short nocturnal break. It was not quite a forced march when no soldier would sleep at all, but it had become very clear to the Goth that if he couldn't organize a horse, the troops would arrive well in advance of him. And if he couldn't convince the three men here of his harmlessness, then he soon wouldn't have to worry about this fact anymore.

He raised his hands, showing empty palms. "I didn't do anything! I only wanted to sleep!"

"Show what you have."

Godegisel bent down and handed the soldier his bundle, which he shook carelessly on the ground. He bent down to the rest of the hard cheese the Goth had left, bit in, grunted, and began to chew.

"Where are you going?"

"I'm looking for work on a *latifundia* or as worker in a city," Godegisel explained. "I have no real goal. I'll stay where I'm paid."

"Hm. There's not much on you," the legionary grumbled. "What kind of work are you capable of?"

Godegisel understood that the physical signs of his plague might prove helpful now. He pulled on his collar to show the scars.

"I survived the plague," he explained. "I can work, even if I look weak. I can clean your armor!"

Laughter answered him. Godegisel felt the mood relax.

"You take a risk, my boy," another man said. "One might think you're a spy."

"A good spy who sleeps by the wayside while the legions march past him, and who doesn't even hear them to wake up in time," Godegisel replied with a grin.

Another laugh answered him.

"Still, Decurion, we should take him to the commander and have him interrogated," the third legionary now said, who had not spoken for now.

Godegisel stiffened inside. Interrogations meant torture. And under those, everyone broke. That was also true for him, he had absolutely no illusion.

140

But the decurion didn't seem to think that necessary. He waved it off. "No, that's a waste of time." He turned to Godegisel. "You can go back to sleep here, but we're not the only patrol tonight. I would advise you to take a good distance from the marching column. There are fields over there where you can find shelter, or else you'll be woken up a few times tonight – and possibly by men who are not as understanding as we are."

Godegisel humbly bowed his head. "Yes, sir. I understand. I'm leaving immediately."

"Pack your things!"

Godegisel bent down and did as he was told. The chewing decurion, in his sympathetic way, had finished eating the cheese, but the young Goth was smart enough not to object to this kind of toll.

No interrogation, no torture. Everything else was incidental right now.

He packed up. He had some nuts and dry flat bread left for breakfast, but he was used to this kind of deprivation. Once again he thanked the decurion almost submissively, who acknowledged it with a grin of approval, then turned and stumbled away from the street into the darkness. The starlight helped him find a dirt road, and he didn't look back until he was reasonably sure the legionaries couldn't see him anymore. Then he paused, looking at the torch-shaped chain, which was still clearly visible. Maximus didn't hide his advance. That wasn't necessary. If it was true what Godegisel had picked up at sea, then Maximus couldn't lose.

The young Goth felt despair rising. How could he manage to warn Rheinberg in time? He had to wait until the legions had passed. He couldn't take the risk of being picked up a second time. He would just unnecessarily challenge his luck.

Another ten minutes later, Godegisel had reached what he considered a safe distance from the troops. He found a large stone on the roadside, which was well suited as a seat. He felt exhausted and overwhelmed. His body felt more tired than he was allowed to be. He didn't know if it was just imagination, but he felt his pest marks as if they were burning or itching. He controlled himself, didn't want to make it worse by scratching or rubbing wildly.

He rested his head in his hands. The darkness of the night was also spreading in his thoughts. But why? Was it so bad if Maximus won the battle? He was certainly no worse emperor than others, yes, he seemed to be competent in many ways. He would pursue a more radical religious course, but that was nothing that affected Godegisel any further. He was Arian, like most Goths, but it was unlikely that anything as radical as pogroms would come about. Underpopulated Rome needed the Goths. Maximus knew that too. And he himself, Godegisel? He could do anything, become everything. Sailor. Wagoneer. He could produce charcoal.

Yes, charcoal.

Godegisel rubbed his eyes.

He got up.

He opened his bundle, pulled out his modest supplies. With methodical movements, he put nuts and bread in his mouth, chewed and swallowed. He ate until there was nothing left, and it didn't take long. Then he reached for the water hose, drank it half empty. He then tied it on his back.

He looked down at the rest of the baggage, shaking his head gently.

He would drop all of it.

He took a deep breath.

He was such a fool! But he just couldn't get out of his skin.

Godegisel, the Goth, began to run.

28

"Is he serious?"

For a moment there was total silence in the Emperor's tent. The congregation was silent, because they had all been taken by surprise. When a messenger arrived at the camp and wanted to hand over a message from Maximus, hectic activity had broken out. Theodosius had summoned all the important men and then read the letter aloud. No one seemed to want to be the first to speak, even the Emperor's unbelieving question remained unanswered.

Theodosius looked at the parchment. Rheinberg said nothing. He was pale. He didn't want that. His rejection had nothing to do with the suggestion of Maximus. The usurper wanted to talk, suggested a pre-battle meeting. Talking instead of fighting – or talking before fighting. Both things were quite right for Rheinberg.

But it was not just the two emperors who were supposed to meet. No, Maximus suggested that the two commanders should also be present. That, too, was basically to be expected. But it would mean that Rheinberg would meet with von Klasewitz.

And Rheinberg didn't want that.

Would he be able to control himself? Would he be able to offer the mutineer, the traitor, and the deserter the minimum of courtesy necessary to keep the meeting from becoming absurd? The thought of the nobleman still and again triggered a storm of emotions in Rheinberg. Everything boiled up in him. Contempt. Hate. It couldn't be called anything else.

Rheinberg didn't want to vouch for his behavior at such a meeting.

That was possibly shameful for someone in his position. But it was the way it was.

"I think it doesn't hurt. And I think it's an important, indeed necessary conversation," Richomer said. He leaned forward, his eyes fixed on Theodosius. "Don't get me wrong. I'm ready for battle. I think we have a good chance of winning. But if there is a very small chance to come to an agreement ..."

Protest rose. Officers took the floor. Rheinberg frowned, resisting the urge to let Richomer run the knife for completely selfish motives. He took a deep breath.

"Richomer is right!" Theodosius said loudly. Immediately silence returned. All eyes turned to Theodosius, who then nodded measuredly.

"Richomer is right," he repeated. "The chance is very small. But he wants to talk to us, in a limited circle, without a large audience. This is more than just a propaganda trick. Whether it is just a necessary formality for him to save face, I don't know. He has Gratian on his conscience and is about to kill another emperor. Perhaps he seeks legitimacy for his actions by giving me the chance to reject a peace offer that is formulated in such a way that I cannot possibly accept it. But that doesn't matter, because I have to commit to the meeting for exactly the same reason. If I reject the meeting, his moral position would be better. But I have the same concerns as he does, strange as it may sound now."

The Spaniard looked at Rheinberg. "Of course, it's very hard for you."

Rheinberg hid his slight surprise at this demonstration of empathy. He bowed his head and ran his hand over his hair. "Your Majesty, I find another question a lot more interesting – what happens when he makes a serious offer, one that is not so crazy that we cannot accept it," he replied, eager not to discuss his personal misgivings.

"What kind of offer could that be?" von Geeren asked, who was also a member of the War Council.

"The same thing he offers to Theodosius in our past," Rheinberg explained.

Theodosius looked at him. "What was that?"

"Civil war also happened in our past. Even there Maximus has killed Gratian by betrayal. Then, for a while, the conflict stagnated; Theodosius established himself in the East, while Maximus consolidated his rule in the West. During this time, Maximus tried to agree with Theodosius that they would, as before, share the imperial rule, and thus end the civil war. Maximus reckoned that the effort to rebuild the eastern army and protect the eastern borders was too much to justify further confrontation. Maximus underestimated that the East was by far the wealthier part of the Empire. Theodosius, angered by the betrayal of Gratian, didn't accept the offer, rebuilt the Eastern Army, and eventually forced Maximus to his knees."

"The situation is different today," Richomer mused. "The East is threatened by the plague, we no longer have a working army there. And we must seek the decision in Africa, where we more or less fled to."

"Yes, but the situation is not so different for Maximus," the Emperor said. "He doesn't necessarily have an interest in a never-ending civil war. He too knows that the plague will not stop before reaching the West. A completely paralyzed Empire is not a very attractive alternative for him either. If we were to accept such a proposal, it would serve him well. He has made his decisions in Rheinberg's past on the basis of a certain attitude, and this personality he also has in our time, that's for sure. I think Rheinberg is right: Maximus will suggest that we stop the war and share the Empire."

"If so, will we accept that proposal?" von Geeren asked. Again, all eyes turned to Theodosius, who stared into the flames of the cast-iron hearth that was set up in the tent. The Spaniard didn't press for an answer. He thought carefully. Rheinberg was sure that Theodosius didn't consider this question for the first time. The man thought ahead, in spite of his spontaneity, was someone who acted with perspective. His emotional outbursts were better controlled than with the historical Theodosius, of whom Rheinberg knew. Did this also mean that he was equally determined to reject an offer made by Maximus?

Rheinberg looked into the Emperor's focused face, and it seemed to him that an answer was emerging – or was it only his own weariness that made him hope for something similar. Yes, of course, it would be a thorn in his side, if von Klasewitz would be permanently established as the Magister Militium of the West, a constant reminder of betrayal and mutiny. But wasn't ready to pay that price? In Constantinople, he would be able to rebuild with his people what had been destroyed in the West. If they survived the plague, many new possibilities would arise – and he was sure that the West would depend on the economic and technical superiority of the East immediately, no matter how hard von Klasewitz tried. He lacked the *Saarbrücken* and, thus, the very basis for a faster technical development. He was alone.

"What if Maximus demands a price for peace – a prize like the *Saarbrücken* or a share in her?" another voice asked, which had hitherto held itself in the background.

Rheinberg looked up, suppressing a smile. The Emperor's council also had a particularly capable and intelligent Tribune named Thomasius. Volkert. The deserter, whose career had been so different from that of von Klasewitz – and whose motivation for desertion was so much easier to understand.

"We won't be able to avoid sharing technology," Rheinberg said.

"Maximus vilifies our 'magic,'" Volkert replied.

"Ambrosius vilifies it, and that's only because Rheinberg preaches tolerance," Theodosius said. "If Rheinberg would've used his fire catapults immediately against Arians and other heretics, Ambrosius would've called him an angel sent by God."

Volkert nodded. "But do we want Ambrosius to gain access to this power through Maximus?"

"He already has guns," Rheinberg pointed out. "Much worse cannot come in the foreseeable future. A more liberal and prosperous Eastern half of the Empire offers refuge. We could even benefit from it."

"This will lead to another civil war," Volkert insisted. "If Maximus realizes that lots of smart and industrious people are leaving the West because their religion is not tolerated there, then he'll eventually have to risk war if he doesn't want his half of the Empire to bleed out."

Theodosius nodded.

"All this is worth considering. Maybe the common enemy will help us too. If the threat from outside is large enough, someone like

Ambrosius must also realize that there are more important issues. I even believe that Maximus will come to this insight very quickly."

"So what will the Emperor decide when the offer is made?" Richomer asked frankly.

Theodosius smiled at him. "I'll think more about it. But if the framework is right, then I'm inclined to agree. If in doubt, it gives us some time to force the decision later – and time is helpful for us, once we have the plague under control. Or Maximus manages to get the radical religious leaders somewhat contained, at least enough to keep them a bit quiet."

Not all were pleased, but many were relieved, as Rheinberg observed. He stretched, feeling the tiredness in his bones. It had been a long day.

"Who should come with you for the meeting?" he asked.

"Maximus asked for a small setup. Me, then my Magister Militium and Richomer. Two servants and the usual bodyguard. Meeting point is an old farmstead not far from the battlefield. Well visible from all sides. We can easily have troops ready, as well as Maximus."

"When will his troops arrive?"

"Advance units are expected tomorrow afternoon."

"And Maximus himself?"

"Marches with the main line. Two more days, not longer. He also asked for the meeting at that time."

Rheinberg nodded.

"Then it is decided."

The meeting was over. Rheinberg walked into the open. He was tired, but an inner turmoil told him that he wouldn't sleep yet. The decisions taken tonight would probably hunt him like a demon, and he feared that he wouldn't get rid of him anytime soon.

A demon who looked a damned lot like von Klasewitz.

29

"I just can't believe it. That's treason!"

Petronius stared at Thidrek, the young priest who had just brought him the questionable news. Ambrosius' confidant relied on the young man whom the Bishop had given him to accompany Maximus to Africa, an upright Christian, totally dedicated to the cause of the Church. And ready to do things for that cause for which he had already received extensive absolution in advance.

"I heard it in Maximus's tent, sir," Thidrek said submissively. He often stayed there, reading from the scriptures, officiating for the staff, ready to render any service. A useful traveling companion, as the Emperor also found, and a silent and inconspicuous one. Exactly what Ambrosius expected of him so that he could position himself to do what was to be done one day – and given the current developments, this day would not be long in coming.

Petronius was upset, and he wasn't just pretending. The fact that Maximus began to become pragmatic in office had already been recognized and criticized by the Bishop early on. But to make such a defeatist, monstrous decision!

Actually, both priests were very tired. The night's sleep was short, then they would all march on, because tomorrow should be establishment the camp, from which they would seek the decisive battle.

Decisive battle!

Petronius laughed.

If it ever came to that!

"He just said that, brother? Are you quite sure?"

If Thidrek was offended by the unbelief of his elder, he didn't show it. He nodded determinedly.

"That's how the words fell, Petronius. He wants to offer Theodosius a peaceful solution. The Empire shall be divided – his dominion in the West, that of Theodosius in the East."

"Incomprehensible! The Spaniard will be, in his half, the liberal ruler, making the kind of decisions that fill us all with such great disgust! The Arians will be spared, and not only those – all other sects and the representatives of the traditional religions also will enjoy liberty! And there are so many more Arians in the East than in the West! Our purges no longer make any sense. That would de facto mean the division of the Church!"

Petronius spoke in rage – in a subdued voice, but with quivering lips and wild gestures.

"That's finalizing it! Ambrosius was right with his doubts! Maximus threatens to deviate from the right path, he lacks assertiveness and honor! Make peace with Theodosius! What an absurd performance so close to victory!"

"It seems that Maximus isn't so convinced of this victory."

"Nonsense. The Lord is on our side! We cannot lose!"

"He means that if Theodosius can escape, the civil war will drag on much longer."

"Then the Spaniard must die!"

"And then there's the problem with the plague and again ..."

"Be quiet now, Thidrek! Shut up! Enough! I don't want to hear anymore of this idiocy!"

The young man dutifully closed his mouth. Petronius wasn't really angry with him. He had only reported what he had heard, and that was exactly his job. The priest didn't have an easy task anyway. He would die soon. Whoever murdered the Emperor, the bodyguards would execute immediately, there was no doubt about that. Petronius prayed for the young man. He was sure that the Lord would take him into his kingdom in heaven. Every heavenly reward for his just deed was certain.

Petronius forced a smile.

"Thidrek, you did well and thank you for reporting to me immediately. Our shepherd, the great Ambrosius, appreciates your commitment beyond gratitude."

Thidrek smiled happily, and there was again this zealous glow in his eyes, that unconditional obedience, for which he had been chosen by the Bishop.

An important quality, Petronius thought. The fact that Thidrek also wasn't necessarily one of the brightest helped in this context. The Lord provided His servants with the right combination of spiritual gifts to fulfill His will. The priest found that in the less gifted the Holy Spirit sometimes burned intensely. This certainly made sense, especially in order to have pious followers who, without much thought and not plagued by doubts, executed the will of the Lord – and thus the will of the Church.

Petronius himself was certainly destined for higher office in the Church, a bishop's chair, a responsible task.

So everyone found his place.

Yes, Petronius was extremely pleased with the world in which he lived.

What undermined his satisfaction were men like Maximus, who forgot in their so-called pragmatism that the world was heading toward the Last Judgment, and it was necessary to prepare the ground for the return of the Savior. And part of this certainly not easy task was to eradicate all heretics from the face of the earth. A Herculean challenge, but anyone who was firm in faith would face it with determination, as did Petronius.

His eyes fell on Thidrek, who was clinging to his lips and smiling happily as he became aware of the attention of his spiritual leader.

Petronius returned the smile.

"Thidrek, it seems your hour will come soon."

"I'm ready!"

There was no pretense, one heard that clearly. Here someone spoke who was completely committed to his cause.

"You have prepared yourself?"

"Every night I pray and submit to the exercises you have taught me. I cleanse my body and mind, immerse myself in the scriptures, burn the words of the Lord into my soul, that they may be my constant guidance and strengthening."

"Uh, yes, very good. And the knife? Is it ready?"

Thidrek nodded eagerly. "Sharpened is the blade, sharp as the wrath of the Lord."

Petronius didn't begrudge the young priest his pathos. If it helped to get into the right mood to kill Maximus, only to be slaughtered after that, then he wanted to be lenient. The result finally counted and nothing else.

"That's satisfactory, Thidrek. A deed like this requires both aspects – the sharpened mind and the sharpened blade. As you are a tool of God, the knife is yours. Just as God loves you and promises his blessings, so you must love and care for the blade. Just as God takes you by the hand and leads you against his enemies, you lead the weapon in his name. There is never a greater unity of human and divine will. You are blessed, Thidrek, truly blessed."

The young man smiled pleased and bowed.

"Go and indulge yourself in prayer," Petronius told him.

Thidrek nodded, said goodbye and stepped outside. Petronius was sure that the young man would not sleep much today, but that wasn't too bad. The thought of his own destiny, clearly drawn before him, now filled him with vitalizing freshness.

He watched Thidrek, then turned his attention to another thought.

Bishop Petronius of Ravenna.

That was what Ambrosius had promised him over and over again. Sure, the congregation had a say in it, but if the shepherd of Milan recommended him, it was certainly nothing more than a formality.

Petronius stretched. Ravenna was not without prosperity. He would occupy the villa of Senator Viscasius. Viscasius was one of the senators who had sided with Theodosius. Once the Spaniard was defeated, it would be easy to dispossess Viscasius and see to it that this particular piece of his heritage came into the hands of the Church. And it was a short step from the hands of the Church to reach the hands of Petronius.

Yes, if he looked at it from this angle, it was, in the end, about the same thing.

He listened.

Thidrek had begun to recite psalms. He would now be busy and safe in his contemplation.

Petronius smiled.

There was still some leftover from his wine. Maybe he found some just sleep when he helped himself out with a glass of the red.

30

The planned meeting came about.

Nobody had seriously objected, and the Emperor had decided. Rheinberg's discomfort had not subsided, but he knew the inevitability of coming events and realized that his place was now in the second row. That felt somewhat comforting.

It came about without any problems, without delays and because both sides wanted it. The venue was well-chosen to minimize mutual distrust. When the delegations arrived, they gathered in a large room prepared by the staff of both leaders. It was a brightly lit place, its wide windows inviting and distributing the sunlight. In the center stood a huge table, on each side of which chairs had been placed, each one a particularly well-upholstered armchair worthy of high-ranking dignitaries. It had been meticulously taken care that the layout and equipment looked absolutely identical for both sides to avoid being offensive or disparaging through any unwanted symbolism. On a side, snacks and drinks had been served, only trifles, but due to the variety offered, enough to cater for a legion. Some wine was available, cooled in special amphorae. The cutlery was of exquisite quality, the crystal glasses each one worth a fortune. In addition, the property had been cleaned, the toilets had been restored, and, as well, a second room for negotiations was being prepared for if the delegations would split for some reason or the two emperors would have a personal conversation – which Theodosius secretly expected, or at least hoped for. In the end, it depended on both of them. And it helped to focus thoughts together and to avoid any interference.

The greeting was conducted in cool courtesy. It wasn't to be expected otherwise. One would hardly express love after having been at war for some time.

"Let's sit down!" Theodosius invited. He had quite noticed that Rheinberg and von Klasewitz had not shaken hands. Rheinberg's face was unmoved, he tried not to show his feelings, and so far did his job quite well. Von Klasewitz didn't necessarily mirror this; his whole attitude seemed arrogant, even triumphant, as if to show his former captain how far he had come. The deserter was a personified provocation for Rheinberg, and Theodosius could only hope that Maximus had him under control.

The erstwhile British governor was friendly and anything but provocative. He avoided quips and derogatory remarks, and did everything he could to pretend to be serious with Theodosius. This relaxed everyone visibly. Even if the time-wanderers didn't like each other, it became clear that the two Emperors could talk without getting at each other's throats.

Two servants – one from each side – served silent wine. Everyone drank thoughtfully.

It was Maximus who finally spoke. "Theodosius, thank you for following my suggestion."

"Thank you for making it."

The usurper nodded. "I think it's important that we explore ways to prevent the big battle we are about to embark upon."

"Why should we stop? The Empire belongs to the victor."

"Because I'm not sure about that logic, I'd like to talk."

"What's wrong with my logic?"

Maximus smiled. Both of them knew what was wrong with that. But it was necessary to lay the ground to get to the heart of the matter and to assure one another that indeed both assumed the same. The biggest obstacle to successful negotiations was tacit assumptions about reality – as soon as it became clear that it would've been better to avoid this silence and to clear up misunderstandings, it was often too late and everything failed.

"The plague has arrived in the West," Maximus said.

Theodosius nodded. "That was expected."

"The Huns are a serious danger. The time-wanderers were correct in this."

"It's good that you see that. Where did they err?"

154

Maximus hesitated. "I don't think all of the reforms that Rhein-berg has initiated make sense." He gave the man a brief look, but Rheinberg sat quietly, his face unblinking, unresponsive. "Of course, this is about important spiritual questions. On the other hand, Rheinberg has also questioned a system of power that has existed for a long time. I fear that his reforms could harm the position and reputation of the Empire in the long term."

Rheinberg leaned forward. "Why this?"

"This new atmosphere of liberality that you've created makes me uncomfortable," Maximus went on. His tone wasn't accusatory but analytical, almost passionless. "Not too long ago I was listening to a son of a senatorial family speculate that it would soon be time to give the Senate new and real power. The ancient republican sentiments, which are especially to be found in the tradition-conscious families with a long pedigree, are boiling up again – or have been newly awakened, I don't know."

"Republican elements are perfectly compatible with the Empire," Rheinberg replied softly.

Von Klasewitz snorted. "Silly," he said in a sharp voice. "Party bickering and the authority over the budget have destroyed so many things for the German Empire, I cannot list all of them. I can only point to the curse of social democracy, the criticism in regard to nobility, the cries for rights to be given even women. German society had decomposed by these elements, its natural resilience and its virtues radically questioned. The strength of the Roman Empire has always been in preserving monarchical principles!"

"Rome has fallen."

"A military problem that can now be solved."

Rheinberg opened his mouth to reply, then obviously thought bet-ter of it. At another time, he would evidently have liked to have this discussion, but here this squabble could only be counterproductive. He would convince no one and von Klasewitz ... Rheinberg cast a glance at Theodosius, who listened with interest. One could not be so sure.

Hopefully, Freiherr von Klasewitz had not put an idea in the mindset of the Spaniard.

"War between us is not the solution to this problem," Maximus said. "We need the army to defend the imperial borders. We agree that the Empire is economically in a very difficult situation. When we kill each other, our enemies benefit from it. We're acting stupid if we keep this up."

Theodosius nodded. "What's your suggestion?"

"We share the Empire. The West to me, the East to you. We cooperate in defense against external enemies, we ensure internal trade and shipping on the Mediterranean. All other domestic issues will be solved by the respective Emperors to their taste. No mutual interference."

Theodosius looked at Maximus. Exactly the proposal they had expected, Rheinberg thought. And Maximus seemed serious. There was no sign that he was doing a charade here. It was visible from the outside: Rheinberg felt an unnaturally strong sense of relief. Should this war really end here? Could all of them now focus their energies on solving the really important issues? Rheinberg definitely had no problem finding his new home in Constantinople, if that was the price he had to pay. Dahms' facilities could also be rebuilt there. He stared at von Klasewitz. He would learn to live with that, too. Somehow.

"I expected that suggestion," the Spaniard said truthfully.

Maximus smiled. "Of course you did."

"I've discussed this idea with my advisers for a long time."

"What conclusion did you come to?"

"Not everyone was happy about this idea."

"That goes for my side too. But we are the leaders. We decide."

"Do we always?"

Maximus' smile widened, and he bowed his head to the Spaniard. "We can try, can't we?"

Theodosius nodded. "So we'll do that. We'll have to discuss the details, but I'd like to let you know that I agree with the proposal."

Maximus hit the table with the palm of his hand. He was beaming. "This is ..."

"Treason!"

Heads moved up.

One of the servants held up his meat knife. Rheinberg blinked. The man was ... he knew that odd person somewhere.

"Treason!" the man said again, then threw himself on Maximus. Rheinberg left his seat like everyone else, but it was Maximus himself who brushed away the advancing blade with a swift reaction. The blade cut his arm open, not deep, but it started to bleed violently. Shouting everywhere. One of Maximus' bodyguards stormed in, recognized the situation, raised his sword, and dropped it into the thin body of the old servant, who fell to the ground with a gurgling sound.

He was still clutching the blade as he died.

Theodosius's guardsmen stumbled in, caught sight of one of Maximus's men killing the servant, and Rheinberg shouted, "Stop! Stop it!"

But the soldiers, in their savage effort to ward off an actual or perceived threat to their respective lords, charged at each other. Theodosius took a few steps back.

Rheinberg put himself protectively in front of him. One of Maximus's men was struck down before his eyes.

"Get out of here!" Rheinberg shouted to Theodosius. The Emperor just nodded, staring at the scenery in complete astonishment, as if he couldn't believe what had just happened.

"Rheinberg ... we have to ... we have to ..."

"We have to get out of here!" Rheinberg completed the sentence. There were calls from outside. Weapons clinked. The entourage of the two emperors had met and begun to fight. All the painstakingly controlled pressure had erupted in a bloody, unpredictable spectacle.

Rheinberg pulled Theodosius through the door, raised his own sword defensively, and saw another servant, this time one of Maximus, crouching on the floor before him, his eyes at least as confused and painful as that of Theodosius.

"Right this way!"

Theodosius had recovered, didn't have to be pulled anymore. Men of his bodyguard approached, the blades bloody, and took them both in their midst. It took less than five minutes before they sat on their horses and galloped back to the camp. They barely looked around.

They didn't believe that they were being followed.

As they restrained the horses, Rheinberg looked questioningly at Theodosius. "Who in God's name was this servant?" he asked the pale-looking Spaniard. The Emperor had obviously not processed the events yet. The mayor's question tore him out of his thoughts, he regained his composure quickly, visibly grateful for being able to analyze what had just happened.

"That ... that was Elevius, Gratian's former servant."

Rheinberg hit his forehead with his hand. "Who was dumb enough to let him serve for this meeting?" he asked.

Before Theodosius could reply, they reached the Emperor's tent and dismounted. Anyway, it was just a rhetorical question because it wouldn't undo what happened.

They stood in front of the tent. Excitement prevailed in the camp. Men returned. Rumors spread. In minutes, every legionary would know what had happened. In minutes, everyone would realize that any hope for peace had been shattered.

And when the Emperor finally opened his mouth to say a word, someone stepped out of the tent, a thin, run-down figure whom Rheinberg didn't really recognize, until he opened his eyes and pulled the man into the light of a torch.

There was no doubt, even if he had to get used to the change in sight a moment. Much had happened to this man, and little of it pleasant.

"Godegisel!" he exclaimed. "What an evening!"

Nobody had expected the appearance of the Goth. And a look into the face of the unexpected visitor gave an idea that this reunion didn't bring any happy news.

The man smiled weakly. "I have bad news, my lords."

Rheinberg laughed, and it sounded not amused, but desperate. He took off his helmet, scratched his head. "Godegisel, we've just had a catastrophe."

The Goth wanted to say something, but then Theodosius approached him. "We have bad news, too, young man. You look awful."

Godegisel nodded and let himself be led inside. They gathered at the fire and gratefully accepted goblets of wine. Rheinberg chose the heavy red wine that he normally renounced and poured the contents of the chalice into his mouth with hardly tamed wildness.

It took a while for them to calm down and discuss the issues ahead. Their excitement was contagious, and time and again their conversation returned to the events they had just encountered. No one understood it, and only gradually did they realize that a unique, terrific historic opportunity had been lost here and that they were now faced with a battle that they almost had avoided. The pain associated with this realization went deep and troubled them, and the wine didn't soothe the nerves either. It took almost a half-hour of perplexed discussion to remember the Goth again, who patiently and quietly waited to be given the floor.

Rheinberg took a deep sip of wine and wished he hadn't banned spirits from the camp. A bit of the hard stuff would suit him right now. As if that thought affected his body, he immediately choked on the wine.

"Give it to us!" he coughed, holding out the goblet. He looked at Godegisel.

"You should drink, too, Goth. You are not yourself anymore."

The Goth shook his head. He had refused any of these offers, but had taken food and water on his own. It had been a miracle that he had been recognized and not kicked from the camp as a tramp.

That would have been bad.

"I have experienced terrible things," he said, "and terrible things will happen."

"Much worse it cannot be," Rheinberg said.

Godegisel measured him with a long look. "Don't say that."

31

There was no clearer and more definite reaction than this. If anyone had entertained any hope that the events of the previous day wouldn't prove to be the end of the already very short negotiations between the two Emperors, then now it'd become finally evident that these hopes were in vain. The troops of Maximus went into position, the enemy offered battle. And Theodosius had no choice but to accept the offer.

Not all had escaped alive. Some soldiers and almost all servants had been butchered. Maximus himself seemed to have recovered well. But the door to further negotiations had no doubt been closed.

Rheinberg watched as the generals gave their orders. For him, there was currently not much to do. The battle plan had been discussed so often, everyone knew exactly what to do. The troops, which had been transferred from Italy, stood in the middle, a mighty block, which should move at first as little as an anvil, on which the opponent was steadily beaten. Positioned on the wings were the auxiliary troops as well as the units of the African prefects, more agile, ready to exploit any weakness of the opponent. Von Geeren's infantry would position itself on the right wing and try to target the enemies from there. It was about hitting at least some of Maximus' men in important tactical positions. To bring movement into the formation was of great importance. Cavalry stood ready to launch an assault on von Klasewitz's artillery positions – swiftly and stormily, as had been ordered. Every available horse had been mobilized for it. The cavalry was currently far away, in order not to be in the immediate field of vision of their opponents. Rheinberg hoped that their definition of the "right time" to which the attack should be commenced turned out to be correct.

After all, there was good news too.

Rheinberg couldn't stop smiling slightly, as he thought of the reaction Godegisel had caused the night before. He had told them of the treachery of the African troops with a straight face, and Theodosius had only grinned. Rheinberg had told the baffled – and given the hardships he had undertaken to deliver the news, perhaps even a little offended – Godegisel that their own plan had worked out. Maximus should believe that he had the African troops under control, the Goth was prepared to expect that they wouldn't change sides at the crucial moment but continue to fight for Theodosius. With that, the tactical plan of Maximus would dissipate and he might – ideally – come to the conclusion that continuing the battle was not worthwhile.

In turn, Rheinberg didn't believe in that. This was too much to be expected. If the usurper saw even a small chance, especially with the traitor's cannons, to win the battle, he would be persistent, no matter how much the setback disturbed him.

It would be a long, bloody battle. And an unnecessary one.

Godegisel had heard his explanation with ever-widening eyes and shook his head several times in disbelief. He then spoke of his experiences with his own people, the failed ambassadorial mission, and his eventful journey back to the court. His story had been accompanied by general tension and great praise. In the end, the Goth had shown that he was glad on the one hand that his information was not as catastrophic as he had feared ... but on the other hand hinted once in a while that he was not sure if this wonderful plan could really be implemented the way it was planned. What if there was betrayal in betrayal?

Rheinberg hadn't pursued this train of thought. But it had given him a restless and very short night. Godegisel's story had moved him deeper than he wanted to admit. Theodosius seemed to be carefree and optimistic again – or perhaps simply on principle, because the Emperor was expected to radiate optimism and trust God in every situation.

Godegisel had then withdrawn. He was weakened, and nobody resented him for not wanting to participate in the fighting. Everyone found that he had done more than his own and had gone through a lot of trouble. Now the task was in the hands of others.

"Half an hour, everyone's in position," Richomer said. The previously rather vague concepts of time of the Romans, which were based primarily on sundials, had given way to exact information. All the generals had received one of the few pocket watches they had collected from the crew of the *Saarbrücken* and were kept protected like eyeballs. Dahms had stated that he should sooner or later be able to construct large wall clocks or grandfather clocks, that the miniatures of a clockwork that anyone could carry with them, however, would be unattainable until further notice. The tools were lacking to construct the tools necessary to make such a small device possible.

Rheinberg watched Gaudentius, the leading prefect of the African provinces, mount his horse and wave to him. The Prefect apparently felt the need to be with his men once the battle began and to issue orders directly at the scene. Rheinberg couldn't blame him. There was a lot at stake, and you never knew if one of the subcommanders was in your opponent's pocket. It was good to keep an eye on everything personally. Gaudentius knew the battle plan and knew which commands meant what. He would do well.

Rheinberg turned around. Godegisel had come to his side, wearing a full Roman officer's uniform. He had slept long and had breakfast extensively, and he had asked to be a witness to the battle. Rheinberg had allowed him to do so. It was amazing how calmly he acted next to the one who had killed Jonas Becker. Godegisel himself had changed, too, and that didn't even mean the extent to which the disease had marked him. The young nobleman was now a different person than a year ago, when he stood on the battlefield close to Adrianople against Valens. One could actually say that about everyone. When this was over, he would ask the man how he thought about his future. He couldn't quite imagine that the Goth would simply return to one of the villages in the East of the Empire to live an existence as a rural nobleman. From what he had reported on the failed negotiations with Engus, his relationship with the Gothic leadership was more likely to be somewhat cold.

162

Before the Goth could say anything, someone else came to Rheinberg, someone whose visit he had silently expected. The tribune Thomasius – Ensign Thomas Volkert – approached him, gave Godegisel a quick look and made his salute.

"Tribune," Rheinberg said, and bit back a smile. "Questions about your orders?"

"No. The orders are clear."

"Then you should be with your legion."

"Yes, General."

Rheinberg looked inquiringly at Volkert. "Something is on your mind."

The man looked down. "It's ... private."

Rheinberg raised his eyebrows and waved to Godegisel. The Goth bowed and disappeared. Now the two men were alone, at least as alone as one could be given the circumstances.

Volkert sighed and started to speak, but Rheinberg raised a hand and told him to keep silent.

"I can imagine what this is about!" Rheinberg said.

"Really ... I ... oh."

With a second delay, Volkert noticed that Rheinberg had not spoken to him in Greek or Latin, but in German. He stared at the Captain – and he was his Captain, more than anything else – and lacked the strength to speak. "Since when?" he finally managed.

"Since our meeting here in Africa," Rheinberg explained. "You are forgiven, Tribune. I have made a mistake. I have to apologize to you for that."

Volkert was still staring. One couldn't see the burden that had fallen from his shoulders with these words, yet his body seemed to tighten, to stand upright, and his eyes shone, knowing that these worries had now been removed from him.

"I ..."

"No, seriously, Volkert," Rheinberg interrupted. "What you have done is phenomenal. You are an excellent officer, and you have made difficult decisions. I brought you into this malaise – but look what you made of it! What a career! You deserve respect and recognition."

Volkert bowed his head, probably feeling his face heat up. At that moment, he wasn't the brave and successful Tribune but the timid Ensign.

"Whether you want to remain Thomasius or become Thomas Volkert again – you have to decide that," Rheinberg continued. "But all doors are open to you. After the victory over Maximus, you can be sure that the highest offices will be available to you. You will start the family you have wished for and play an important role. By the way – congratulations. You are going to become a father."

"Uh ... yeah, well, thanks ..."

Rheinberg grinned, approached the embarrassed man and placed a hand on his shoulder. "Survive the battle. Help us to achieve victory. Forget what was. We are on one side, as it always has been and how it should be. Are you ready?"

Volkert's eyes tightened, he nodded.

"Then go to your men. Survive, Volkert. We want to be victorious. But we don't need more sacrifices."

Volkert saluted. He couldn't say anything else than the ultimate reply every subordinate officer had at his disposal. "Yes, sir."

32

Von Klasewitz passed the batteries, inspecting everything exactly as he was expected to. He had barely slept after that fateful night of the failed encounter between the two Emperors, when things had worked out so well without him having to intervene any further. He was very glad that this so-called peace hadn't materialized, and when he looked at the blunt pipes of the guns, as they threateningly extended their dark openings toward the battlefield, he felt great joy and confidence, a feeling that animated him more than strong coffee.

He felt almost euphoric.

His good mood was transmitted to the men, with whom he had in recent months – with considerable self-control – built an emotional bond. He spread more than the quiet confidence of the competent leader, he exuded joyous anticipation, yes, almost enthusiasm. He joked, praised and slapped shoulders.

And his gunners had indeed done an excellent job. The endless drills, day and night, had paid off. The cannons were in excellent condition, perfectly cleaned, perfectly aligned, stocked with all supplies. Here was the only serious problem that von Klasewitz was willing to acknowledge – lacking in gunpowder. The production just couldn't keep up with the growing demand, especially not in such a short time. He hoped the battle would not last forever. If the plan of Maximus was fruitful and the African legions changed sides in due course, it was not to be expected anyway. At the latest then, the united armies should be able to finish the men of Theodosius even without cannons. It would anyhow be difficult to identify clear targets. When the trick was done, a confusing battlefield was the consequence. Maximus had been reminding him insistently what he thought of the idea of his own soldiers being accidentally hit by the murderous shot of their own guns. Von Klasewitz could only agree with the Emperor on this point. He definitely didn't want to have to explain occurrences like this.

He needed every living and loyal legionary once he was Emperor.

That was the real reason for his euphoria. The approaching battle, the approaching triumph – good. But what came afterwards was even more important. Petronius had taken him aside, revealed his plans in detail. As soon as the victory was over, Theodosius was imminent, when it was clear that there was no salvation for the Spaniard, no result other than surrender or death, Maximus would be attacked. Von Klasewitz, whose guns were silent on this phase anyway, had to get near the Emperor's location in time to make a determined move to keep the army going, and shortly after the triumphant victory, he himself would take the purple. Petronius had left nothing to chance. A lot of money had changed hands. It was necessary to make the transition as smooth as possible, also in regard to the reaction of important high-ranking officers and civil servants, especially those on the ground.

Smooth.

Von Klasewitz shook his head. That he would ever catch thinking so – he, the man of action, who had always considered male assertiveness and bravery as the true nobility of mind and deed as so important! How had he always looked down on the politicians of his time, their intrigues, their clandestine backroom meetings, the balancing, the mumbling, the compromises, the half-heartedness, the bickering, and the platitudes – even the Emperor was often helpless in navigating the meaningless and dishonorable activities of this caste, only to watch in honest indignation. Von Klasewitz had felt this shame almost physically.

But now, himself on the threshold of absolute power, he had to realize that without that kind of behavior he wouldn't be able to make it, especially if he wanted to yield that power in real life. People, including henchmen, had to be involved, they had to be assured of their own share of power, given a say in decisions, given consideration for their preferences. And though all of them were somehow servants of the Empire, that didn't mean they were always in agreement with the Emperor, and depending on their personality this criticism was expressed in one way or another.

That would be difficult for von Klasewitz. Gratian had listened to the dissenting views of his counselors, Maximus even encouraged dissent among his highest advisers, and Theodosius also appeared not to be averse to a lively and varied discussion. When he became Emperor, he couldn't just pretend it was a practice of the past, especially not if he wanted to get the fickle and the disapproving on his side.

He would have to listen and smile pleasantly when someone politely but surely wished to direct him to the right path.

The nobleman paused for a moment and shook his head.

Well, maybe one didn't need to smile too friendly.

But he wouldn't be able to avoid listening. He wasn't allowed to send critics immediately to the lions – this noble tradition had already fallen out of fashion in Christian Rome anyway – or otherwise muzzling polite dissent. He wasn't even allowed to demote those disapproving of his actions right away or to send them to a lonely post, at least not as long as their statements were uttered within a certain frame of respect, deference, and politeness.

Of course, these weren't very pleasing prospects.

On the other hand, he should be able to enjoy other aspects of his new reign that would benefit him greatly. Everyone needed his hobby, with whom he could live out his interests. Otherwise, if he worked adequately and maintained the balance of forces that secured boundaries and was a good Christian, it should be possible to pursue other inclinations without causing too much disapproval.

Von Klasewitz unconsciously licked his lips. That would be very, very stimulating.

A legionary came to attention as von Klasewitz approached him. The German had taught his men the way German soldiers showed respect and discipline; this had previously been unknown in the Roman army – above all because clicking heels as a way of expressing respect in sandals or rather soft boots didn't produce this most satisfying sound. But von Klasewitz had missed it, he wanted to admit that, and his gunners took it as a special sign of their privileged position, as a privilege, to show their readiness this way.

With that, the German concluded, everyone got something out of it.

"Cannon 7 loaded and ready!" the gunner yelled at him.

"Thank you," the German replied, keeping his eye on the arrangement in front of him. In fact, the report was true. He didn't see any blemish. Von Klasewitz leaned forward, eyeing the black cannon barrel. The greatest danger was in fine hairline cracks, which were often difficult to see with the naked eye and which could lead to catastrophic consequences if the cannon was fired several times. One more reason not to let the artillery fire last too long. After all, it could happen that he himself was nearby when a cannon was torn and the bystanders were cut down by metal splinters.

And of course that had to be avoided in any case.

Von Klasewitz slapped the proud grinning man on the shoulder and mumbled something appreciative.

This one was replaceable.

Johann Freiherr von Klasewitz wasn't.

33

Volkert took a deep breath. The weather was still cold. Standing in front of his unit, he watched the line of men as they persevered in formation, all eyes on the mass of legionaries who had lined up on the other side of the battlefield. The distance was considerable, as the armies were large and both sides had no interest in the two bodies merging prematurely. Von Klasewitz wanted to use his guns as accurately as possible, and they wanted to do the same with their shooters. No one asked the poor victims on this "field of honor" who would either eat bullets or cannon shot.

But they kept their discipline. If Roman troops had nothing else, discipline had been taught to them. Eternal, indelible discipline. Many of the men looked at him. He was "the Tribune," even for those who didn't know his name. The one who killed the Magister Militium, who revealed the betrayal of Sedacius. He who left with a transport ship and arrived with a flotilla. The Tribune. Volkert accepted it. It helped him to establish authority. And there would be plenty of opportunity and necessity for that today.

Volkert saw some of the men puttering around like a girl before the decisive entrance to a reception. In was much the same, except that the men were less concerned with their appearance and more about whether the equipment was reasonably safe and comfortable.

Volkert himself had renounced all unnecessary ballast. He wouldn't be right on the front line, for the first time in his career as a Roman soldier. His rank was now so high that he was expected to take a command position behind his men and keep track. That didn't mean that the fight would not reach him. Officers who marched directly with the ground forces were always involved in the clashes, if only because of passion and thirst for blood – or perhaps despair. But he wouldn't participate in the first rush, the first clash. That was still quite dangerous. Von Klasewitz's guns would try to avoid the front line at some point at the beginning of the battle, as it was very likely to hit their own men. Instead, they would concentrate on the rear units, in no way mistaken in assuming that they would be able to do the relatively biggest damage there – exactly where Volkert would stand.

He actually stood. He renounced his horse – it was too good a target, and he didn't want to be buried under or with the animal. He wore nothing but sword and shield, no spear, and he had nothing but a water bottle with him. The helmet was firmly on his head, already somewhat dented, although repaired. Equipment was scarce in the army of Theodosius, and they used everything until it was no longer reparable. That was also true for officers.

Volkert tried to radiate confidence, though he felt otherwise. But he kept his doubts under control. He could neither run away nor had a particularly great influence on the course of events. The battle would begin, and at the end there would be victors and defeated. What Volkert was more interested in was the fact that there would be at the same time survivors and dead, and he had the firm intention not to belong to the latter. There was a lot to live for – Julia, his daughter, his newly found freedom and identity, an end to his hiding, a new life. It would be a bitter irony of fate, if at the moment when everything seemed to turn out for the better, a shot fired by his former first officer would wipe out his life.

Volkert had developed quite a sense of irony. He had found an opportunity to talk to Godegisel, the young Goth, barely older than himself. The man's highly adventurous story had been fascinating. Godegisel also had some hopes, as Volkert himself did. And an even deeper mistrust. In contrast to the protestations of Rheinberg, he believed that the apparent betrayal of the African troops could turn out to be a factual one.

Volkert looked to the right wing, saw the formation of the provincial troops preparing for the attack.

He felt Godegisel's doubt echo inside. In addition to a sense of irony, he also developed one for betrayal and ambush, as did the

Goth. He decided to keep a careful eye on the movements of his neighbors and comrades.

He looked up. The horns sounded. Her whining, slightly weird tone yelled across the battlefield. And then he heard a similar sound from opposite, the enemy. It was the formal initiation of mutual slaughter.

Commands were roared. Volkert remembered the howling, how the rehearsed commands almost automatically left his throat. He remembered the first time he had commanded Roman soldiers in a surprise raid of the Sarmatians when he was on his way to Noricum with his cohort. Hardly a year had passed since then, but it seemed like an eternity. He had given himself command at that time in an effort to turn a desperate situation, the first step of a career, which had led him to the current position, and at a rapid speed. The first dead friend, the Greek Simodes, who had remained on the battlefield. Not the last man who had died when Volkert gave orders. He would never be able to put it that way.

He heard a distinctive voice. Secundus had an even stronger lung than he himself, a piercing and startling voice that the otherwise lethargic legionary was capable of.

The men began to march, all at once.

The ground was a better meadow, muffling the sound, but when thousands of feet trampled, there was no grass left to suppress that noise. Volkert saw himself progressing. He had drawn his sword, as every legionary had done, though there was nothing for the blades to do yet. The closed phalanx of the comrades conveyed a false sense of security, at least at the present stage. Only those who marched in the front saw the adversary's wall approach at them with the same mechanical tirelessness. Volkert knew how it was over there. In the first row either the very timid stood, who were driven by their comrades or the military police, or the very brave and serene, who pursued the craft of slaughter with emotionless routine.

Then white clouds of smoke rose in the air, and Volkert thought to hear a soft singing. It was unmistakable.

The traitor's cannons had begun to fire.

Volkert estimated the distance to the opposing battle line, within seconds, came immediately to the conclusion that he was still far enough away, and shouted, *"Abdite!"*

The drill worked. Like a man, the legionaries threw themselves flat on the ground and pulled the shield over their backs. Not a second too late: The mighty clouds of shot fired by the cannons spilled over the lying men. Many were lucky and were unhurt. Some shot was held by the shield or the helmet if the speed of penetration was not too high. But then came the screams as the metal balls tore skin open, exposing veins, tearing limbs. Volkert dared to look up, feeling that he himself had been spared, staring directly at a man in front of him who was looking with incredulous horror at the hand-sized wound on his leg, from which the bright red blood of the arterial blood shot violently. Volkert had barely risen halfway, as the legionary already lost consciousness.

"Elevate!"

They couldn't stay here. They had to go ahead. And they were no longer allowed to prostrate themselves when there was a danger that the opposing lines would storm and trample over them.

They stood up, swift, precise and marched forward. Roman discipline took them over the fallen and wounded comrades. Grass and earth mixed with blood. The orders of the officers were muffled by the lamentations of the victims.

Secundus screamed, *"Elevate, Culi! Elevate!"*

Was it really helpful to call your own men assholes? For Secundus, it seemed to work. His voice ripped up the soldiers, driving them forward. Then again clouds of smoke, a rumble of thunder and Volkert roared out his "Abdite!" one last time, for the enemy was approaching. He threw himself to the ground, heard the disgusting noise as the cannon shot tore flesh and opened wounds. Again, miraculously, he was unhurt.

"Elevate!" Secundus roared. *"Culi ignavi! Elevate!"*

Volkert got up. Now the men were even lazy asses. Secundus really knew his way around in proper leadership.

He heard a lot of screaming and the clinking of metal on metal from the front. The first lines had collided. Then he heard the shots of the German infantrymen, not the wild bangs he had expected but a very low cadence, deliberate firing, clearly to save ammunition and let each shot find his target. Then again the crash of artillery and this time no command to cover, because more and more of the legionaries were busy in the melee.

Some of the legionaries in the back rows threw themselves to the ground anyway. Volkert noticed that the shot hit, took lives. The cries of the wounded shook his soul. Around him, men fell, clasped their hands on gaping wounds, dropping their weapons.

"Why am I unhurt?" Volkert wondered, looking down at himself. Inviolate.

He stumbled, just caught himself. A man was lying in front of him, bloody blisters spilling out of his mouth. Shotgun pellets hit him head-on at the chest, crushing the bones. Volkert saw ribs sticking out of his skin, blood spurting out. The wounded man was still alive, wheezed something, moved his lips. He looked pleadingly at Volkert, almost compelling. The German knelt down, held his outstretched hand, tried to say something reassuring – but what did one say to a man who was nearly dead and writhing in pain?

"What's your name?" he finally managed.

The dying man coughed. "Olavus ... Olavus Scintilla."

Scintilla. The spark. This one would go out soon.

"Say ... tell my father I fell in the battle. Honorably."

"I will tell him. Where can I find him?"

"He lives ... near Augusta Vindelicorum ..." Olavus coughed again, spitting blood. His eyes became cloudy. "Promise me. My dad always said that I'd never achieve anything."

"I'll tell him," Volkert assured him. He saw a faint smile slip across the dying man's bloodied lips, then his eyes broke, and he collapsed, his cramped body suddenly relaxed.

Volkert closed the dead man's eyelids. For a tiny moment, the battle didn't seem to take place around him.

34

"Careful! Careful!"

Von Geeren's words of warning made the young infantry soldier look up guiltily. He fired five shots into the crowd of legionaries in quick succession, apparently believing that he would always find a victim. Of course, that wasn't wrong, but von Geeren had repeatedly told the men to aim carefully and be absolutely sure of their targets. Randomness was a waste of ammunition, even if the five shots had been, indeed, five kills.

A brief rattle distracted him. The machine guns fired no single shots, but short volleys, especially on those enemy legionaries who were too close to their own position. The big storm on the infantrymen's positions had not begun yet. The cannons of the enemy concentrated on the area where they could do the most damage. The shotgun packs loaded by von Klasewitz had a devastating effect on the tight formations of the legionaries. Von Geeren knew that there was no time to rehearse new tactics, but the traditional Roman modes of organized slaughter made less and less sense. This wasn't the way they should throw away their men. A loose formation with a lot of cover was necessary, flexible, and mobile, in which each soldier could find cover for himself on the basis of his individual decision, with assault attacks only from under the cover. If the primitive hand grenades had spread and firearms were in common use, the battle would be different, more fluid, more flexible.

Von Geeren knew that he wouldn't have understood these thoughts at home in Germany. He had always had the impression that the military leadership had gladly accepted the ever better weapons, but the tactical implications of a resulting war of aggression largely bypassed them. Von Geeren didn't know what this war would be like before he had departed the German Reich, but he feared that the battles would be very bloody and above all completely wrongly fought.

He observed all of this now, not of immediate use in comparison to pressing issues, but nonetheless. If he survived here, he would develop a new military doctrine for the Roman forces with Rheinberg and those Roman officers who had proved to be more flexible in their thinking. The sea was Rheinberg's job, but for the land forces, who were far more important to the continued existence of the Empire, this challenge rested on his shoulders.

The infantryman in front of him fired, carefully, deliberately. Von Geeren saw an enemy legionary throw up his arms and fall to the ground, unable to move. A clean hit, an efficient use of ammunition.

"Okay then!"

Von Geeren crept on, from position to position, admonishing, praising, correcting. His infantrymen were disciplined, almost methodical, and yet the captain was watching with great concern as the ammunition melted away. He hoped again and again that this battle wouldn't last much longer. If this went on, they would, despite all the caution, plant their bayonets at the end of the fight and barricade themselves in the trenches, nothing else. Then Centurion Verilius would fight with his men. They could handle the sword better.

As if the commander of his bodyguard had listened to the mention of his name in the German's mind, he suddenly appeared beside him. His face was serious. He had bad news, one could tell immediately.

"They are coming, Tribune von Geeren!"

The Captain didn't have to think long about what Verilius meant. It was inevitable that the enemy would do everything possible to attack and eliminate the infantrymen's positions. The shooters out of action would move the balance of power quite massively in favor of Maximus. And that was also true in the other direction, where a cavalry unit was already riding in a wide arc on the way to attack the cannons of the traitor. There too, another Verilius would stand in front of von Klasewitz and soon – or even now – utter the ominous words.

They are coming.

But the reciprocity didn't make it easier for von Geeren.

"How is the situation?"

"They diverted a whole legion for us," the man said, his expression gloomy. "In ten minutes, my men need some protection."

Von Geeren nodded. That meant he had to pull off essential firepower from the actual battle. But what was the "real" battle? Everything was connected. A purely defensive position, however, was inflexible and reduced tactical options. Von Geeren hated being forced into such a stance.

"I'll give the appropriate orders."

"I'll call when it gets really hot."

The positions of the infantrymen had been carefully chosen and prepared. They were sitting on a hill, in a strong entrenchment, on all sides with a free range and a short line of defense. Maximus, too, had recognized that, and therefore assigned significant forces to eliminate this threat. Von Geeren remembered the Battle of Gaul. There, legionaries had come so close that they had been able to throw their primitive hand grenades. It could actually have been easier for Maximus if he had ordered the cannons to be aimed at the Germans.

Von Geeren was certain that von Klasewitz had told him exactly that. The traitor had to guess that his adversary expected no less and had built appropriate defensive positions that would protect well against the gunshot. It would be pointless to bombard a well secured place for an endless time with artillery, which was able to do so much more devastating effect on the free, unprotected battlefield.

The Captain was not sure if he should classify that as a blessing or a curse. But it seemed to make von Klasewitz predictable. What other conclusions could be drawn from this?

One more thing he would worry about later, when it was all over, and if he was still alive – and von Klasewitz had escaped from their grasp to cause further unrest. A decent jail, better still, a clean execution was a result he wished much more intensely and would finally make his reflections about his adversary superfluous.

He heard a curse, ducking into the position from which the wordy filth had emanated. One of his marksmen handled his weapon, obviously jammed. Von Geeren said nothing and just watched as the man began to solve the problem. His comrades continued to fire methodically.

Von Geeren crawled forward, looked at the battlefield. The lines had met. The cannons punched holes in the sea of bodies. His men frayed it from the side. Nevertheless, the legionaries on both sides showed a remarkable discipline. Gone were the days when the soldiers ran away like headless chickens when they came in contact with rifle fire. They may not fully understand everything that killed them, and many may still believe it to be the work of demons or sinister sorcerers whom they couldn't oppose. But the training was worth it.

Von Geeren shook his head.

A nice reward. The legionaries had learned to continue fighting under cannon and rifle fire and keeping their lines. They had learned to become classic cannon fodder, except for those who came close enough to pay back the gunman.

The improved discipline had one effect above all else: Dying was in full swing.

35

Maximus stared down at the battlefield. The canons of his Magister Militium fulfilled their purpose better than expected. Their massive onslaught didn't only drive like the sword of God through the crowded mass of his opponents, it also did a lot for the motivation of his own legionaries – because so far the German had managed not to hit his own soldiers. Maximus' followers watched as the opponent's men were mowed down, and to many it seemed like observing the hand of God. The attack was motivated and powerful, supported by the prospect of a decisive victory.

Maximus also had to realize that his enemies' firearms didn't even have half as much of a psychological impact. The occasional bang of the rifles was almost lost in the noise. Yes, men fell under the targeted shots of the time-wanderers, and, yes, there was an urgent need to eliminate this threat.

Appropriate steps had already been taken.

But it seemed as if the enemy would run out of breath. And even the rapid guns, which von Klasewitz called "machine guns" with a certain respect in his voice, didn't have the massive effect as a thunderous salvo from the mouths of the Imperial artillery, which drowned out everything visually as well as acoustically. It was right to channel all resources into building these pieces, rather than getting lost in other projects. This battle sealed the fate of the time-wanderers, and Maximus respected von Klasewitz for his good advice. And he knew that he would win this battle mainly because he had the traitor on his side.

Certain consequences would be inevitable.

Maximus kept his eyes fixed on what was happening in the battle. His generals had the situation under control. Things developed as planned. There was no immediate need for him to give orders.

His thoughts wandered again to von Klasewitz. By no means had he missed how Petronius had wandered around the man. He just had more important things to do than to worry about him. But he himself felt that the representatives of the Church were not quite as enthusiastic about him as they had been at the beginning. He couldn't even blame them. But what should he do? Although things had largely developed as he had planned, it was clear that the arrival of the time-wanderers had upset everything. The events of the great migrations from the East also made developments unclear. Both events had to be taken into consideration. How could this goal be achieved by putting everything on one side and completely neglecting the counterweight?

The imbalance was magnifying and would harm the Empire, Maximus was sure of that. But men like Ambrosius and Petronius didn't share this perception. And von Klasewitz was someone who would obviously do anything to achieve the highest office, no matter what the consequences.

There was only one supreme office left to him.

Maximus pressed his lips on each other.

He would really have to deal with this as soon as this was done. "Sir?"

Maximus turned. Marcus Vetius was one of his generals who were responsible for leading the battle. An old veteran of his time in Britain, he had never shown much enthusiasm for the "disreputable" weapons of the time-wanderers, and although he recognized the effectiveness of the guns, their use seemed to cause him physical nausea. But he was of unquestioning loyalty and did what was expected of him, even under the constant bellowing of the despised weaponry.

"Is it time, Vetius?"

The general nodded. "There are different points in time when it makes sense, sir. But there is no use in giving our allies the agreed signal if the cannons have killed too many of them. The Magister Militium … is good at targeting and especially good in hitting the enemy in the middle of his formation. But this opportunity will dissolve more and more, and the wings are more involved into the normal fight man against man. Our allies will die for the wrong lord if we delay too long."

Maximus nodded. "We don't want that."

"I'll show you, Sir."

Vetius stepped beside his Emperor and began to explain the situation. In short order, he convinced Maximus.

"Notify von Klasewitz. As soon as I give the signal, the cannons have to fall silent. We want to make sure that as few as possible are hit by our own artillery. The allies are traitors to Theodosius, now they themselves shouldn't get the impression that they have been betrayed."

"I will send the messenger immediately."

Maximus' gaze wandered over to the signal trumpeters. The men stood not far from the small cluster of generals commanding the battle from the background. At the German's suggestion, they had added a number of additional horns to the ensemble, which sounded particularly piercing, with an absolutely unmistakable sound, blown by men with an impressive chest. As soon as they were released, another novelty would be visible.

Von Klasewitz had been inventive. And he had terrified his followers, even the Emperor himself, with his new method of sending a clear message over the battlefield. "Rockets," he called the simple things of reinforced parchment filled with gunpowder that were rammed into the ground on long sticks waiting to be used. As soon as the legionaries heard the hornists' signal, they would set fire to short matches and send a battery of fifty of those projectiles hissing into the sky, hard to miss. A marvelous demonstration of power that would confuse the enemy and give their secret allies a clear command. When the rockets flew, it was time to plunge Theodosius and his followers into the abyss.

That was the agreement. The prefects of Africa would order their troops to turn their weapons against the enemy. Thus, the soldiers of the Spaniard would be enclosed from three sides and would not be able to resist this superiority for long.

Maximus hoped for a quick surrender. He didn't want to shed Roman blood unnecessarily. In fact, after some time in which to cool their anger and forget their frustration, he thought of including the then-captured legionaries in his own army, as had been his practice before. Rome remained Rome. Only from some of the senior officers could he expect that they were difficult to be persuaded to obey him. But here, too, Maximus didn't want to cause a bloodbath. Many would simply be removed from their posts and sent to a private life. Some would be pacified with an attractive civilian position. All in all, Maximus intended to be very reasonable and act appropriately. Even Theodosius, should he not choose to commit suicide and be taken prisoner, would be allowed to live, in exile, but without further impairments. Those who had to be symbolically killed were Rheinberg, his man von Geeren, and Magister Dahms, although the loss of his special knowledge was certainly regrettable. Still, it was unavoidable. Ambrosius insisted … and von Klasewitz as well.

Maximus sighed.

That's the way things were.

It took a few minutes, then Vetius came back to him. He indicated a bow.

"The German sends his respect," he said with an undertone that seemed a little lacking in it. "He's ready to stop the fire once the order is received."

Maximus nodded. Once more, he took a hard look at the billowing battle in front of him. He squinted. Among the inventions for which he had serious need were the glasses that could make him see over long distances. Given the fact that he had always had a mild visual impairment, this achievement was very important. The German had hinted to him that properly cut glasses, well-adjusted, could correct his deficit. Maximus had intended to devote as much resources to this opportunity, for military as well as personal reasons.

Maximus scrambled to his feet and raised a hand. A legionary who had been waiting for that gesture raised his own and looked in the direction of the Emperor. Only when he performed the movement a second time for confirmation, was the signal given. The Emperor didn't hesitate any longer.

Moments later, the buglers put the powerful instruments to their lips, took a deep breath and pressed their lips to the mouths of the instruments. Moments later, the mournful song resounded, penetrating to the core, producing by over a dozen powerful instruments, echoing across the battlefield.

It was as if everyone was pausing to listen to the sound.

Just a moment.

Then it hissed loudly, and the rockets raced into the clear air, a whole bundle of long, sometimes even colorful smoke trails behind them, where von Klasewitz had experimented with admixtures to black powder.

A loud "ah and oh" could be heard. It came from both sides, for although their own officers were instructed, none of them had ever actually seen such a thing.

An almost reverent moment.

Then the trap snapped shut.

36

"What's happening?"

Rheinberg took a few steps forward, as if he could improve the clearness of the binoculars, with which he had armed his eyes. The horn signal had caught their attention, and Rheinberg was not the only senior officer straining his eyes to see what was going on.

"The cannons are silent!" Richomer cried. Rheinberg listened. He now realized that he suddenly missed something from the sound of the battle. Indeed. The cannons had stopped firing.

And then ...

Rheinberg stared into the sky. A whole phalanx of white and colored plumes of smoke rose into the air and made a loud, piercing hiss. Rockets! Von Klasewitz had given the missile to the Romans, no more than firecrackers, but certainly a very impressive display.

A signal for whom?

A signal for what?

"There! Damn it! Rheinberg! Treason! It's really betrayal!"

Rheinberg made a mournful sound when he saw it too. The banners of the African troops turned, the men on the wings made a 90 degrees movement sideways, toward the center on whose side they had previously fought.

"Godegisel was right!" Rheinberg finally said. "The prefects did not deceive Maximus but us!"

Rheinberg watched the scene like paralyzed. He suddenly couldn't say another word. The right wing penetrated with force into the no longer allied center, surprised the legionaries, drove a wedge into their formation. The left wing had bigger problems. Some officer had paid attention and given his own orders at the first sign of change.

Everything threatened to break up.

And Godegisel had been right.

They had all been terrible fools.

Rheinberg stared at her downfall, incapable of any meaningful reaction.

"What ... we have to withdraw the center, now!" Theodosius exclaimed, who now had an overview of the situation. That had been Rheinberg's first reaction, but he raised his hand, lost the paralysis that had afflicted him, and tried to keep his mind calm.

"Not so fast!" he explained. "Von Geeren is in a good position to attack the right wing. He should give everything he has. There is no time for exaggerated caution. The center seems to be steady on the left, someone was paying attention."

Rheinberg turned to the men. Theodosius looked excited, almost panicked, while Richomer made a calculating impression.

"General," Rheinberg told him, "you yourself take our new right flank. Take the reserve and the Imperial Guard. I want you to move forward as soon as von Geeren clears up there and has unbalanced the African forces. We have to clean up before we can press against Maximus. The silence of the cannons helps us."

Richomer's back straightened. He clenched his clenched fist against the breastplate.

"I obey!"

As soon as he said that, he turned and ran to his waiting horse. Rheinberg looked at Theodosius.

"Your Majesty, we must retire elsewhere. I suggest that we hide with von Geeren, he provides the best stationary protection on the battlefield. The Guard must intervene in the fight."

The Spaniard nodded. "So be it, my friend. I hope you know what you are doing."

"If we remove your person from the battlefield, our formation collapses," Rheinberg said.

Theodosius nodded. He knew what had happened when Gratian had been killed in the first battle against Maximus. The Emperor was a symbolic and actual figure central to the fighting morale of men. Theodosius was soldier enough to know that well.

"We're on our way immediately, Magister."

Rheinberg turned around and shouted orders. Horses were brought while Richomer, at the head of the Guard, ran down the hill. Then came the frantic rattle of rifles, especially the MGs, who were now faithfully executing Rheinberg's orders. Long volleys of bullets drove into the now so close enemy and plowed through the densely packed formation, which was torn open by the violent gunfire. Only a few more minutes, and the once strong right wing would panic and fall apart. Von Geeren, that was Rheinberg's confidence, would have the situation in view and stop the fire in time, so as not to endanger his own men in the center.

A legionary appeared beside him, the horse in the reins. Rheinberg nodded to the man and swung himself onto the back of the animal. He looked down again at the battlefield. Von Geeren's fire achieved its effect. The ranks of the African troops were clearing. Their formation collapsed, entire centuries melted away like ice in the sun. Were those not the first troops to break loose and sought their salvation in desertion? Rheinberg paused a little longer. Richomer's unit got ready, and then the signal. The general had chosen the right time. The Germans stopped their fire almost immediately as Richomer thundered down the hill with his men, heading straight for the dissolving phalanx of the traitors. That had to have a murderous psychological effect on the men! Rheinberg found himself grinning triumphantly. Richomer drove his soldiers toward the African forces like a storm front, and when they collided, the traitors were driven back with a primal power driven by anger and bitterness.

Rheinberg's gaze shifted to the left. The center held. There you would have to attack next. The situation was still precarious, but things had certainly not developed as the former British governor had imagined.

Rheinberg smiled. Von Geeren had really exceeded his expectations. How he managed to "smell" Richomer's attack, so to speak, and give the order in time to stop the fire ...

Just at that moment, he heard the rifles speak again. He turned on his horse and peered in the direction of the infantrymen. The binoculars limited his field of vision a little, but what he saw made his newly-felt joy disappear again.

The reason why von Geeren had ceased his fire was not his excellent sense of time or the clear analysis of the situation. It was the simple fact that he had to reform his entire troop.

The position of the time-wanderers was about to be overrun. Rheinberg saw and heard rifle fire, but he also saw and heard clashing blades, and that much, much too close.

He tore his horse around.

Theodosius was on his way to this maelstrom. Hopefully, he had thought better of it in time and started his retreat. The Emperor had only a small bodyguard of perhaps a hundred legionaries with him.

An uneasy feeling raised inside him.

Perhaps the Emperor had thought that these men and his presence would be able to fend off the attack on the riflemen, that they would be enough for the Spaniard to do the job.

Rheinberg let the binoculars wander, adjusted the magnification, found himself in search of the banners of Theodosius, as they moved towards the position of von Geeren. He didn't find them at first, almost got scared until he finally succeeded. His fears were confirmed. Theodosius had made much better progress than he expected, and made no attempt to move away from the scene.

That was not very clever ... that was just too ...

Rheinberg stared down at the battlefield. A strong conflict raged in him. What should he do? He had an army to command. But what use was that command when the Emperor was dead and the infantry was wiped out? He had to set priorities, as always. And at that moment, he found it more difficult than ever.

He pulled himself up and waved. He also had a bodyguard, another one hundred men.

It was time, thought Jan Rheinberg grimly, as he pulled his pistol and checked the magazine. Time to get his fingers dirty.

37

"Holy shit!" Volkert bellowed, thrusting his sword forward. The blade pierced the legionary's chest, who had neglected his cover at the wrong moment. He staggered back, and with a sucking sound, Volkert's sword was yanked free from his ribs. In an automatic movement, the German pushed forward a second time, pierced the enemy's throat and watched grimly as the dying man fell to the ground.

Another soldier stepped into the resulting gap.

"Traitor!" Volkert roared. "Kill them!"

His anger spread to the men beside him, who used his cries as an incentive to fight the former allies even harder. Everyone shouted encouragement to each other, confirming themselves in their anger and contempt.

Volkert's sword pushed forward again, slipping off at a quickly uplifted shield. He quickly took a step back, lifting the deflected weapon to his own defense. The counterattack of his opponent went into the void. Obviously surprised by his opponent's quick and light-footed reaction, the attacker leaned his upper body a little too far forward, extending his sword arm too far in an effort to catch Volkert.

The German gave a satisfied grunt. The African troops were not elite units, but little more than glorified border troops without a real enemy on the continent. There were many of them, and they were clearly determined to implement their betrayal as effectively as possible, but Volkert's men had already fought too many battles to be intimidated by troops of this quality.

Volkert's blade descended and severed his opponent's arm just below the elbow.

The man screamed, staring in horror at the pulsing blood shooting from the stump, and stumbled. Volkert had an easy time. His blade thrusted forward, a second graceful cut, and when Volkert pulled it back, the man in front of him was already dead. The corpse fell, Volkert took a big step, stood in front of the next foe. Everything was tightly packed here, restricting freedom of movement. There was no turning back and forth, merely over the dead bodies of the enemies. Volkert was happy with that. All caution, all doubts had disappeared. In a frenzy of bloodlust, he had roused his men when the extent of the betrayal had become clear. And he had reacted quickly, with other officers smart enough to follow his example.

Volkert raised the blade, stepped forward. The metal shone red with the fresh blood of his judgment, ready to dispatch the culprits he had already condemned to death. Here and now, he was the judge of the Empire, and the determination and precision with which he made his way through the mass of enemies animated his comrades.

"Traitors!" Volkert cried, when a hostile decurion stared at him in fear, barely lifting his arms before he fell to the ground, bloodstained. "Traitors must die! Forwaaard!"

A polyphonic answer returned his command, a great rumble of thunder from the throats of hundreds of legionaries, who threw themselves forward again and again, thrusting, hacking, slashing, beating and bringing death many times over those who had once imagined themselves as their brothers in arms.

"Rooome!" Volkert roared, as he took another step forward.

"Rooome!" the men echoed around him, and the word spread, drowning out the calls of pain, the horns and trumpets, the loud orders of the opposing officers.

"The Tribune! Follow the Tribune!" he heard a strong voice from the crowd, and again this idea continued to spread, from throat to throat, and soon the cacophony of voices mingled.

"The Tribune! The Tribune! Rooome!"

Volkert felt carried forward by these voices, no longer knowing whether he was still leading or being led by his men, but this distinction became increasingly irrelevant anyway. Like a determined wave of deepest contempt, the compact unit of several hundred legionaries streamed against the treacherous wing of the African forces and demanded a blood toll that the traitors could never have expected to pay.

Time lost its meaning. Pain receded into the background. Hit and thrust. To look at the enemy, to assess, to react, to act. Every opponent was different. Everyone was a traitor. Traitors died that day, and they all were supposed to roast in hell.

Volkert's anger was more than contempt for the enemy. It was also contempt for himself. The deeper he rose into the wild intoxication of killing, the more often he saw the image of the dumb Sedacius plunging into his own sword with a determined movement, over and over again. Treason! Volkert knew exactly what price to pay for betrayal! And he judged all those who had dared to do so, as he challenged God to judge him for his own. That drove him. That pushed him forward, and he was just as ruthless to himself as to everyone else.

A howl went through the crowd, as the bodyguard of Theodosius went into battle. He felt the resistance of his own opponents weaken, as if they were no longer as sure of their cause as before.

A wild laugh escaped Volkert. If they all doubted, he didn't. Once more, he took a deep breath and yelled with all his might, "Rooome!"

A chorus answered him. All of them listened.

But the delay was short-lived, the rising sense of triumph premature.

Trumpets and horns from the enemy's side. Maximus's army started an assault, flinging forward, and Volkert watched with horror, as it gnawed at the lines of his own unit fighting on two fronts, and his forces were now rapidly dwindling.

A shout, a scream that made Volkert turn his head. He stared at the image, not a hundred yards from him, saw General Richomer being dragged off his horse, how he was beating around and how others were rushing to his aid, then a spear shot out from below and broke forcefully through the chest plate of the general. Blood spurted out of his mouth as he was dragged limply and cut to pieces by triumphant legionaries.

Volkert turned away his eyes. The bloodlust had gone, the madness of the fight that had driven him forward. He felt his men make room for him as he turned away from the front. He had to give orders again. How many officers of what rank did command down here? Where were they? Where was Theodosius and where was Rheinberg?

He turned around himself, desperate for answers, for an overview, for some orientation in this chaos of betrayal, pain and death.

What happened here?

38

"They are too many!" one of the legionaries informed Rheinberg.
"They are just too many!"

Rheinberg raised the pistol, sighted one of Maximus' men, and
pulled the trigger. The success was inevitable on such short distance,
the soldier staggered, fell to the ground.

Another one stepped into his place, throwing something. Rheinberg felt pushed down when someone pulled his arm violently so
that he lost his balance and fell. Dirt and loose earth pattered down
on him as the crude hand grenade exploded. He felt something pene-
trate his thigh and send painful waves through his body. Rheinberg
raised his head, wiping earth from his eyes. The grenade thrower
was pierced by a spear and dropped dead to the ground, felled by
one of the legionaries of Verilius. Rheinberg looked down, felt his
thigh, and raised his bloody hand to his face. With difficulty, he
straightened up. The wound was full of blood, but the shrapnel
had missed the central veins, tearing out only a palm-sized piece of
muscle. Rheinberg reached for his bandages and pressed one on the
wound, then wrapped it tightly. It would do – it had to.

While he was taking care of himself, two legionaries stood guard,
but no one approached them. The rattle of the rifles, the cries of the
dying and the wounded, Rheinberg tried to ignore it for a moment.
When he was done, he got up again, trying not to burden the
wounded leg. Painful waves flushed through his body, black clouds
danced before his eyes. He stumbled. Someone supported him.

"Lord, there are too many of them!" the legionary whose name
Rheinberg didn't know uttered.

He was right. The troops Maximus had sent against von Geeren's
position were too numerous. Theodosius and his guardsmen were
directly involved in the fighting, as were Rheinberg and his men.

"Captain!"

The voice made him turn around. A German corporal waved to him, his face dirty, an assault rifle with an attached bayonet in his hands.

"There!" Rheinberg ordered. Supported by the legionaries, he hobbled in the direction of the man. Moments later, they were sitting in a ditch. Next to them were three infantrymen who ignored the newcomers, instead shooting at the enemy legionaries. On the ground lay a figure with a chalk-white face, breathing hard, sweat on his forehead.

Von Geeren.

Rheinberg knelt down, ignoring the pain in his leg, and looked at the Captain's eyes.

"Ah ... Jan," he muttered with sudden recognition, indicating a faint smile. "We have no luck today!"

His voice was barely audible in the noise, but Rheinberg was close enough to the man's face to make it out.

"Got me badly. Hand grenade. Don't look at it."

Rheinberg's gaze instantly wandered down the injured man, pausing briefly on the chaos of blood and flesh that was von Geeren's abdomen. "The paramedic ..." he said, but Geeren raised a hand.

"Takes care of people who can be saved. You know what? I feel nothing down there. Nothing. The spine has cracked. Bad crack. Can't move anything. It's not a life for which I want to survive, Jan. It's not how I want to be."

Rheinberg swallowed, felt tears come to his eyes. He grasped the limp hand of the dying man and searched for words ... comfort, encouragement, something. Von Geeren seemed to notice that, for again that faint smile slid crossed his lips.

"All right, Jan. Time is up. Hope it's not in vain."

"I ..."

"That's okay. It's better this way. Take care of yourself. Keep yourself down. No reason to end this way. Fuck the Romans. They're crazy, really."

Then his eyes suddenly unfocused into the void. He was dead. Rheinberg stared at him, speechless, feeling his body tremble. He closed his eyes for a moment before stroking the captain's eyelids. Then he sat down, felt the pain in his leg and took a deep breath. The corporal looked at him questioningly.

"Who is the highest-ranking infantryman?" Rheinberg asked flatly.

"Lieutenant Paulsen. Should I get him?"

"No. Just tell him that he is now the commander of the unit."

The man nodded.

Rheinberg raised his pistol. "I have about twenty shots left for this one, Corporal. I won't take them with me. Twenty more shots."

The man grinned at him and nodded.

Rheinberg looked down at the motionless body of von Geeren. He would mourn, at the right time, and there would be a decent burial. He would let the funeral procession take place in Constantinople, so that a daughter of Modestus would have the opportunity to say goodbye to something that might have been.

Rheinberg tested his weapon and waved his two guards. "What's your name, men?"

The one man, tall, broad-shouldered, with no front teeth and bushy eyebrows, almost requiring a barber, bowed. "Titus, sir."

The other legionary, smaller, stocky, but with powerful arm muscles, almost as massive as thighs, smiled at the commander. "Marcus, sir."

"Marcus will help me walk," Rheinberg ordered. He was able to grab the smaller man well, and he had the stature to support an extra weight. Willingly Marcus stepped next to him and helped Rheinberg into the right position. Titus stood in front of them, sword ready, and looked at the commander. "Where to, sir?"

"We run to the Emperor."

The legionary probably wanted to say something about "running" – at least he pursed his lips briefly as if trying to get a word out –, but then he changed his mind. Rheinberg shook his head gently. The comment wouldn't have been necessary.

"Forward!"

They climbed out of the ditch with difficulty, and Rheinberg saw with a glance that the fight was still in full swing. The Emperor's banner stood just a few hundred meters away. The position of the infantry wasn't yet overrun. The dull hammering of a machine-gun sounded, probably a central reason for the slower progress of the enemy. Then again the crash of a hand grenade, not far, followed by screams, curses and orders.

Rheinberg turned his eyes to the Emperor's banner. Theodosius and his men supported the troops of Verilius. The Emperor was no stranger to war. He had fought under the protection of his eponymous father in Britain, against the Alemanni and several times against the Sarmatians. Only the unlawful execution of his father for alleged high treason had interrupted a brilliant military career. But he had learned the craft for many years. Rheinberg could at least be reassured of that. The Emperor was a field commander far better than himself.

However, he had ensured that both his wife, who had never met Rheinberg, as well as his little son Arcadius remained in the Spanish province in relative safety. That might have been a great comfort to him now.

Rheinberg pointed to the banner. "There!"

He raised his weapon, but there was no target. Was it just an assumption, or had the focus of the fighting actually shifted to the men led by Theodosius?

Rheinberg suspected that he had to hurry.

39

"Victory is ours!"

Maximus beamed, and he looked with great joy at the battlefield. What a wonderful, glorious day! Alas, the betrayal of the African troops had not led to the immediate collapse of the enemy forces. Richomer, whose corpse lay on the battlefield, had been able to help one of the heavily beleaguered wings with Theodosius's reserve, and on the other hand, some officer had been able to gather and motivate his own men. But now, with the storm of the main force, it became more and more clear that the army of Theodosius was doomed. On top of that, the German cohort was struggling to survive – with the Spaniard in the thick of it. In the near future, all of their problems would be solved at once.

Maximus felt a slight regret. He would have preferred a peace agreement. But fate had decided otherwise. Who was Maximus for wanting to contradict the counsel of God, who so obviously wanted to give him victory?

Marcus Vetius was with him, as was his Magister Militium, the time-wanderer. More officers had gathered, all of them standing at this spot from which they had a fair view of the events on the battlefield.

"We must press them further," Vetius said, pointing with an outstretched arm at the formations that had been wedged together, ultimately distinguishable only by the banner and sign bearers. "The men of Theodosius hold and retreat only slowly. The formation is still stable. There must be officers on the ground to keep the legionaries together."

After the death of Richomer, they had tried to get an overview of the still active generals of Theodosius. Arbogast, it was said, was still in command, but many other high-ranking officers had fallen to the treachery of the African forces, and Rheinberg himself was busy guarding the lives of his time-wanderer marksmen and, as it seemed, his Emperor.

"I'm dispatching my guard to reinforce the attack on the Germans," Maximus decided. "Not only do I want this danger to be eradicated, but I want Theodosius to die foolishly in their so-called protection."

Vetius nodded, but made a worried face. "We are exposing your own protection, sir!"

"I'm not in danger," Maximus replied with a dismissive gesture. He gave von Klasewitz a questioning look.

"The troops who fought my cannons were withdrawn to reinforce the battle," he explained. "The artillery is no longer threatened. I therefore suggest that the Emperor will accompany me to the artillery positions where many men can provide security. It gives the Guard the freedom to kill Theodosius and his people, as you ordered."

"That sounds like a very satisfactory solution," Maximus smiled. Vetius took a long, critical look at von Klasewitz but kept any dissent to himself. His rivalry with the German was well-known – and Maximus promoted it to some extent –, but if he rebelled too loudly at this time, it would be regarded as a petty disagreement, especially in view of the fact that objectively nothing spoke against the German's proposal. It was reasonable.

Much too reasonable perhaps for the taste of Vetius.

Maximus smiled. When all this was over, he would appoint the General to oversee the conditions in Africa. In fact, this would require a lot of "oversight," because sooner or later Maximus would have to replace those prefects who had so easily changed their loyalties – and that as silently as possible. Loyalty was a scarce commodity in the Roman Empire, and those who proved that they didn't have it in abundance were always insecure companions.

"We should think of other precautions," Vetius said. "When Theodosius dies and the time-wanderers escape, they still have their ship, which they can use to cause a lot of trouble. And there remains a pretender to the throne."

"Ah." Maximus frowned. "The little Arcadius. Will that be necessary?"

Vetius shrugged. "He is unimportant as a person, but as a symbol ..."

Maximus thought for a moment. He wasn't as passionate an advocate of child murder as many of his predecessors. On the other hand, there were the necessities of the state and the possibility that the prediction of Vetius contained a kernel of truth.

And there was a nice opportunity to give the Magister Militium a task that could discredit him a bit, at least to some of them. It was just a matter of putting the matter in an order that would enable him later ...

Yes. That was a good solution.

He looked at von Klasewitz.

"Vetius is right. We have to make the most of our victory and not leave any loose ends lying around. Magister. I entrust this important task to you. Once the battle is over, take as many men as you think necessary and travel to Spain to the lands of Theodosius' family. Deal with Arcadius and his mother, as you think necessary. I leave you the details; you will surely make the right decision. But it's a problem that needs to be solved."

Maximus saw how the German hesitated, then nodded and took a firm posture. "I'll do what I have to do, Augustus!" he said clearly, and there was no sign to Maximus that he wasn't serious about it. Maybe the German didn't even understand the possible implications of this assignment. As far as Maximus had been instructed, it was rather uncommon in the future of the time-wanderers to have unpleasant offspring removed for dynastic-political reasons. Certainly a far more civilized time if these things were no longer necessary, the Emperor thought. But it was just another era, and as much as everyone wished that one day it would be the same here, it was just the way it was. Von Klasewitz would have to deal with the necessities of the present he lived in, whether he liked it or not.

Maximus sighed.

He was glad to have this annoying topic off the table.

"Vetius, send the Guard. I want Theodosius to die. Make sure he finds his end on this battlefield!"

The General punched the breastplate with his fist and turned, eager to carry out the Emperor's command.

Maximus turned back to von Klasewitz. "And you, General, accompany me to your cannons. I want to praise your men for their work and watch the outcome of the battle from there."

He turned and looked at his entourage – several more officers, servants, and some clerics, some of whom looked rather timid, as they watched the Emperor's Guard leave its rearward position and move toward the embattled position of the time-wanderers. Maximus suppressed a smile. The civilians were not to blame. Such a battle was not for everyone, and the presence of the Guard had certainly been reassuring. But the artillery troops were supposed to scatter the fears of the timid.

"Up, all of you!" he exclaimed loudly, smiling broadly. "We enjoy the grand finale and our victory!" He pointed to von Klasewitz. "Follow this man, and don't be afraid!"

Everyone laughed. The mood became lighter. The idea of victory made them cheerful. All would be rewarded richly. *Latifundiae.* Positions. Slaves. Gold. They had put their bet on the fate of Maximus and had been rewarded – surely by God himself – for it. There wasn't much to do. Now it was time to enjoy the fruits of victory and to set themselves up in a new phase of life in which the key factors would be wealth, power, prestige and more wealth – and the promise of even greater blessings in the Last Judgment, because the losers were now all those who opposed the true word of God.

Someone clapped the German on the shoulder. "Well, time-wanderer, take us to your men. We want to enjoy the victory and hear the rejoicing of the legions. Our triumph – and yours!"

Happy laughter followed the pithy words.

Von Klasewitz turned his head away. Nobody should see that his face showed more expectation than triumph.

40

"They're sending their damned guard!" Theodosius cried. He stood in front of a dead legionary, struck down by one of the bullets from Rheinberg's pistol. That one of the adversaries had come with determination and brute force to threaten the Emperor in person, said something about their situation. And it would become much worse now.

Rheinberg nodded grimly. He still had seven cartridges in his gun. He assumed that every shot had been a fatal hit, and it was so depressing that this alone had barely stopped their approaching demise. Seven more shots. "Lord, we must endeavor to remove you from the battlefield," he finally said, earning exactly what he had feared – a savage, angry look from the Spaniard.

"No chance, my General!" was the expected answer. "I'm not running away anymore. The decision is here and now. Our lot is in the hands of God!"

The fact that many of the officers accompanying them – no generals, who had been badly worn out by this battle, and the death of the Richomer had left a particularly painful gap – nodded in approval, showed Rheinberg that in close proximity to the Emperor he wouldn't find any allies. He wished Renna had not stayed in Hadrumentum to plan for their defeat and escape in case of emergency. He could have used him well by now.

Rheinberg made a fool of himself. Renna wouldn't be able to do anything more than to die gloriously here. But Rheinberg felt ... left alone.

And the stubbornness of the Emperor didn't help him at all.

"We have to retire," Rheinberg insisted. "The *Saarbrücken* can take us in Hadrumentum and ..."

"No, time-wanderer. I'm not running away," Theodosius interrupted firmly. "This is going to be fought out here and now."

"The betrayal of the prefects has put us in a hopeless situation."

The Spaniard didn't listen. He turned and headed for the next skirmish with his bodyguards. He turned his back on his master, a more than merely symbolic act. Rheinberg stared after him, felt the conflicting emotions, wanted to follow the Emperor and protect him, and yet he sensed that he would do nothing but kill himself.

"Titus, Marcus, see where the detectors and signalers are. The Emperor wants to fight, I have to give orders."

"They are off, sir, near the old command post."

"We'll go back there."

The two legionaries didn't conceal their relief at his decision. With his arm around Marcus' shoulder, Rheinberg let himself be helped, and slowly they got away from the fighting. The pain in his thigh was significant, the bandage soaked in blood. His old knife wound had started to hurt as well, a clear sign that he was about to reach his limits.

"The enemy's guard is approaching!" Titus observed, and Rheinberg looked around. It was a torrent breaking over the positions of the infantrymen, and Rheinberg felt the guilt that he was not down there with his men and dying with them.

Dying, they did. The fire continued, and the bayonets and swords flashed. They didn't go easily and without resistance, and many more Romans died than Germans. But the legionaries knew what was at stake and threw themselves on the infantrymen, coming closer and closer, hurling their grenades and spears, leaping into positions where they could use their melee skills to their full potential.

The gunfire became less. That certainly had something to do with the almost vanished ammunition stock, but above all with the fact that those who could shoot died.

Rheinberg felt bitter bile rise in him. He had led all of them to death. Many more, thousands, had previously shared their fate. And there, on the battlefield where the legions were still fighting, more died. In the end, their death was due to his hubris, and for a moment, the idea of finding the end for him was not so frightening anymore.

"Sir. Sir." The voice of Titus tore him from his gloomy thoughts. "The Emperor's banner has fallen."

Rheinberg turned his head clumsily aside, didn't want to look but couldn't avert his gaze. The situation was confused, but the Emperor's sign had fallen. He raised his binoculars to his eyes, saw Maximus' men triumphantly throw up their arms, then there was a legionary holding something up, and when Rheinberg focused his optics, he recognized the severed head of Flavius Theodosius, Emperor of Rome, who didn't want to run away.

"Lord, the army will break when it finds out," Titus whispered in a sinister voice. "The army will break."

"Take me to the signals," Rheinberg replied hoarsely. "We'll see what to do. If we have to order retreat, then we do it. I don't want a slaughter. We have ships in Hadrumentum. We can save the survivors."

"But where to, sir?" Marcus asked quietly. "East, where the plague rampages?"

"To Spain maybe," Titus suggested. "Spain is calm and loyal to Theodosius. His son Arcadius lives there. He is the new emperor."

Rheinberg looked up, mustered the legionary in surprise, then nodded slowly. "No stupid consideration, Titus. I should appoint you general."

The legionary raised his hands defensively. "It's enough for me to simply survive the army, Magister."

Rheinberg could argue little against his priorities.

He felt carried away by the legionaries as they marched him over the hill to the old command post. Rheinberg focused on two things: the pain in his leg and handling the current events. This was already the second emperor to have died since his arrival, and in contrast to Gratian, whose early death, if inclined to cynicism, was already "destined" by fate, Theodosius now fell clearly before his time. Instead of dying a natural death, he was killed in a battle, many years before he could do or refrain from acts which earned him the epithet "the Great" in Rheinberg's time line. Rheinberg didn't know if the Spaniard had reproached him in his last moments. Both had so basked in the skillful manipulation of Maximus by the apparent betrayal of the African prefects that they hadn't wanted to realize that Maximus had thought further ahead. Godegisel had warned them. How did the Goth feel now? Rheinberg hoped that he was safe somewhere and was no longer involved in the fighting. That would have been too much to expect after all. If he was smart, he would have made his way home, whatever he now called home.

It took a while until they reached the position. Rheinberg broke away from the legionaries, beckoned to the signalmen who immediately got into position, reached for binoculars, and spent a minute watching the situation. He was not an expert in ancient land battles, lacking experience and in some ways intuition. But most of his officers were dead. He had to make a decision. His inability didn't relieve him of his duties.

And that duty was a bitter one now, he realized.

Miraculously, the troops of Theodosius withstood. But it was only a matter of minutes before the formations would break apart.

Rheinberg came to the conclusion that all that remained for them now was the most orderly retreat possible. In fact, however, he assumed that it would rather lead to a wild escape. Who was there to give the men guidance? Rheinberg felt that at this moment, in this situation, he lacked, title and office or not, simply the necessary legitimacy.

He had seldom felt as much of a foreign body in this epoch as in these moments.

Rheinberg sighed.

Self-pity hadn't helped anyone yet.

He brought the binoculars to his eyes. The left wing held with remarkable steadfastness. Whoever was in command there knew how to motivate and command the legionaries.

Maybe not everything was lost yet.

41

Someone handed Maximus a goblet of wine, he took it and drank. The mood in the Emperor's tent improved with every passing minute. The victory was imminent, and they all knew it. Theodosius had fallen. The battle was over. With a little luck, this civil war was also completed. Maximus was the sole emperor of all of Rome, and that was more than he had dreamed of before his insurrection began.

His troops were led by senior officers who could handle the rest of the battle without any problems. Maximus had retired to his tent with his retinue, the Magister Militium, and good old Vetius. It was time to eat and discuss how to proceed, but it was also time to celebrate.

"What's to happen to those legionaries who surrender and do not flee?" was the first question that Maximus was asked.

The Emperor had already provided well-considered answers to all these things, which he now had to clothe in proper orders. "Everyone should be shown mercy and pardon. I don't want torture or mistreatment. They will be disarmed and guarded for a short time, then they will all be offered an opportunity to return into the service of Rome."

Everyone nodded. Nothing else had been discussed before and everyone saw the need.

"What's to happen to time-wanderers?" was the next question.

"Nothing should happen to them either. The normal soldiers and officers should be granted mercy. Only Rheinberg will be killed."

This had also been expected. The order was now valid, and the men of Maximus would strive to carry it out faithfully.

Von Klasewitz asked for attention.

Maximus waved to him.

"All weapons and other equipment of the time-wanderers should be diligently collected and treated with care. They are to be transferred to me," the German said, and this order was also recorded.

"In addition," Maximus went on, "a message should be sent to Hadrumentum for the ship of the time-wanderers. It should contain an offer of peace and cooperation, under the new captain, von Klasewitz." He looked at the German. "We should imply that the new captain has many duties as commander-in-chief and therefore will not be able to stay permanently on the *Saravica.*"

Von Klasewitz grimaced but was too smart to protest.

"The messenger should take one of the time-wanderers, an officer best, to witness the outcome of the battle and its consequences," Vetius suggested, and this, too, met with general approval.

"What orders do we give our legionaries?" Vetius then asked.

"First of all, there are three days of rest so we can take care of the injured and gather strength," Maximus explained. "Wine and beer are to be richly served, and we want to organize a banquet. The African prefects have promised slaughter animals and exotic fruits, all of which we want to offer the men. Then we return to Hippo Regius, where we want to take another break for a few days, so that the men can prove their strength in the brothels. Then we will move to Italy, if we have found an agreement with the *Saravica.*" He looked up to von Klasewitz. "If we don't conclude one, I doubt the time-wanderers will simply sink our fleet. It seems to me, no matter what the Magister thinks about his old command, that there are men there who are familiar with a notion of honor and chivalry. Or am I wrong?"

His gaze fell on the young priest Thidrek, who stood beside Petronius and was busy pouring a cup of wine for General Vetius, softly, quietly, submissively, unobtrusively as ever. Petronius caught his eye and nodded gently.

Von Klasewitz felt his heart begin to beat.

So it was decided! Then his hour had come. Now he just had to play the cards that God had placed in his hands.

He took a deep breath and didn't show his sudden excitement. He had to be as surprised and horrified as anyone else. He collected himself. *Just don't make a mistake,* he thought forcefully, fighting for the necessary self-restraint and concentration.

Petronius spoke up. "Noble sir, there are more decisions to make, if I may remember."

Maximus' face darkened a shade. "Of what nature are these decisions?" he asked a bit curtly.

"All those in the army of Theodosius who want to decide to join the now unified forces of the empire have to abjure the various heretical misconceptions and to commit to the Trinitarian orthodoxy of the Empire. We have reliable information that among the soldiers of Theodosius are not only Arians – that would be bad enough – but also many followers of Mithras and a number of Asian and Germanic cults, all of which have been tolerated. It is this false tolerance we have argued against, my Emperor."

"You don't have to remind me what I'm arguing about," Maximus muttered, narrowing his eyes at Petronius.

"I just wanted to mention it again. This is a great opportunity to send a message of orthodoxy and truthfulness. It must not only be a precondition that all accepted legionaries publicly confess, no, consequences must also be drawn for those men who refuse the deed."

Maximus' face got something lurking. There was the innocent horror in the face of General Vetius, who already imagined what that meant, but had not yet produced a word.

Reverent silence descended upon the congregation. Everyone followed the argument. No one doubted that this was one of importance.

"What kind of consequences are we talking about, Brother Petronius?" Maximus asked.

"Well," he replied in a tone of voice as if he were uttering something absolutely natural. "Of course those who refuse must be severely punished. I'm quite in favor of their execution. If we don't show determination, there is a danger that they will join stubborn loyalists of Theodosius and continue to cause trouble. We must eradicate the spread of heresy, once and for all, especially here in the legions, the most sacred part of the imperial body. A healthy Christian legion is at the heart of a healthy Christian Empire, and all illness and infection must be removed from the body with the purifying power of fire and sword. When the body is healthy and resilient, freed from every wound, it can withstand the challenges of the future with equal strength and determination."

Vetius turned his head and looked at Maximus imploringly. The Emperor also knew why. It was surely not the case that all soldiers in his own army were upright Trinitarian Christians. Should he let those who didn't follow this particular faith with the same enthusiasm as Petronius become victims – after they had just given their blood for him in a great battle and won?

Maximus nodded imperceptibly to Vetius.

The General understood the hint and relaxed.

But the veteran apparently didn't represent the majority, as Maximus noted with a glance in the round. Many high-ranking officers expressed their approval of Petronius' words, nodded, made supporting remarks. And the Magister Militium? Apparently von Klasewitz was trying to keep a polite distance, but there was certainly a reason why Petronius looked at him once or twice from the corner of his eye. Did he just want to confirm if the commander-in-chief responded favorably to his words? Or ...

Maximus felt a strange discomfort seize his body. Of course, he only imagined the worst. Now, in the hour of his greatest triumph, nobody could seriously ...

"Lord, as a representative of the Church, I await your answer!" Petronius' voice woke him from his dark premonitions.

Magnus Maximus, Emperor of Rome, would say the truth. "If we do that, we'll tear up the legions!" he said firmly. "We have to convince people about the right faith. Send your priests to the legions to preach and convert the men. In this way, we reach them much better, and it is more reliable to rely on conviction than on coercion. We won't slaughter those we fought with and whom we offered the Emperor's Gold to risk their lives for me. That would cause great unrest, and our enemies would take advantage of this unrest with great joy. No, Petronius, won't do that!"

Maximus looked at Petronius, who was obviously outraged.

"My Emperor! How can you make such a mistake?" Petronius said.

"If you let the seeds of heresy sprout in the legions, you endanger the unity of Church and Empire. Restlessness is our least problem when God turns His grace away from us and we thus become easy prey for all those whom the Corruptor sends against us. Only with an absolute purity of faith at all levels of the state will we be able to win God's help in the fight against the enemies and to be victorious. No short-term sacrifice, no temporary difficulty, can be too great for that. It is your duty as a Christian and an Emperor, now that the Lord has put victory into our hands, to stand up for this with all your strength and toughness. Otherwise we are doomed! Otherwise this battle was in vain! Otherwise, the victory is stale and useless!"

Maximus looked around, reading in the faces. Many – far too many of his officers and advisors – seemed to like the priest's words.

He took a deep breath. There were words on his lips that would hopefully smooth the waves and soothe them all. He needed them all here, as allies and loyalists, if he wanted to complete the great work of unifying the Empire. Later, he supposed, he would talk to Ambrosius – about the role that Petronius played, about what was at stake for the Church, and what was the Emperor's business, where the limits were which both sides had to respect.

Yes, respect.

In the end it all came down to one thing: Petronius – and through him Ambrosius – lacked the necessary respect.

Perhaps one saw his indignation at this realization on his face, because suddenly the men in front of him moved back a step, as if they were afraid or would recognize something in him, which reminded them to be cautious.

Respect was good. If it didn't exist, fear was an adequate substitute, Maximus thought.

But no words left his mouth more. It was too late for that.

The sudden pain in his back made him flinch.

Weakness seized his body, a deep, very deep tiredness.

Shouting. Fear. Satisfaction. Steps. Something went completely wrong.

Maximus looked down at himself. His blurring gaze recognized the point of a blade sticking out of his chest from behind.

A good attack, he thought, strangely detached as his legs gave way under him.

Carefully executed, his last thoughts were. The blackness surrounding him took away all the pain.

He didn't notice how Vetius cut off the head of the priest Thidrek, who had held the blade. He was no longer aware of how the General then rushed at Petronius, guided by a sure instinct that this had to be the author of this cowardly murder. Gratefully, Maximus could no longer witness the swift death of Vetius under the blades of those officers who had plotted in favor of the cause of the Church.

Thus, on behalf of Ambrosius, Petronius cleared the way for establishment of the Christian Empire they both dreamed about.

Magnus Maximus had not suited them well, in the end.

42

The purple mantle stank. Von Klasewitz tried not to turn his nose up, but perhaps this highly symbolic piece of clothing had already seen better times – or simply didn't adjust well to the stress of the long campaign.

He craned his chin forward, trying to look as majestic as possible. He recalled the photographs of Emperor Wilhelm II, carefully trimmed to publicize the dignity of the German Empire, trying to push the crippled arm far out of sight, and above all to convey the impression of energy and masculine determination through his distinctive countenance.

It turned out quite well that the photographic art wasn't invented yet. The sculptors would, in due course and with detailed instructions, create a fitting picture of the new Emperor in order to spread his statues throughout the Empire. There was still time and opportunity for one or the other correction. Von Klasewitz liked the idea. He on a horse, sword raised. He in thinking pose, considering important issues. He, gazing far into the future, planning, forward-looking, visionary. He, with mildness and care in his attitude, the protective father of the Empire. He, with a glazed look, holding the cross on his chest, immersed in spiritual contemplation, a faithful servant of the Church, filled with the Word of God. Von Klasewitz decided to write down these and other ideas in a quiet hour. He found that the current postures of the imperial statues seemed a bit too one-sided and monotonous. He would make it his personal project to develop the propaganda effect of this art to its full effect. Variety, the representation of all important aspects, all facets and nuances, was as much a part of it as the observance of certain basic rules. Von Klasewitz was especially looking forward to this task and the first results. To be allowed to look at himself in marble, larger than life-size, certainly a little idealized here and there, he regarded as big pleasure.

But now it was not about eternity, and at the moment in which he had to prove dignity and seriousness, and a sharp-smelling purple mantle shouldn't stand in his way. Everyone looked at him expectantly. The officers on Petronius' side had supported his proclamation to become Emperor, as expected. The only troops in the immediate vicinity – the artillery legion in particular – had also made it clear by loud cheers that this development enjoyed their support. And given that the rest of the army was still slaughtering the rather stubborn followers of the deceased Theodosius, the partisans of the dead Vetius had held back nobly, in order not to share his fate. They would pretend to accept the sudden development, at least for a while. And if they afterwards refrained from intrigue and subversion, they would find that von Klasewitz, Emperor and Augustus, would stretch his hand in peace toward them.

If not, he'd have to take measures.

And so he became Emperor of Rome. Of all of Rome. Theodosius was dead. His army dissolved before the eyes of the new Emperor. Von Klasewitz, who would rule as Johannes I, had no intention of repeating Maximus' error and show too much leniency. Yes, there were military and political necessities, but some things needed to be done in a less subtle way than Maximus had intended. The new Emperor was firmly convinced that it was necessary to state an example. Known Arians or followers of ancient cults would be publicly executed, if they refused to repent and adhere to the Trinitarian creed. Petronius had provided a greater number of priests who were able to perform proper baptism ceremonies in a short time, so that there would be no lack of opportunity. Anyone who stuck to his outdated or false belief would bask in the joy of becoming a martyr for his faith. If this was the wish of the unlearnable, von Klasewitz was quite ready to fulfill it. Petronius would have no reason to complain, nor would his master, Bishop Ambrosius. Von Klasewitz intended to strengthen and expand Christianity, especially in Africa. He knew from the future what was to come, that Islam would quickly enjoy great success on the continent. It was already necessary to take precautions in order to show the limits to the Sultans of the future. Von Klasewitz didn't believe that he could prevent the emergence of this religion, but its spread should be controllable. When he had discussed these things with Petronius, he found in him a strong supporter. Measures to strengthen Christianity were also to be taken in the Asian East of the Empire, so that in the future crusades would prove unnecessary and Constantinople would remain forever Constantinople. Klasewitz wanted to do what he could to ensure this. And to put a stop to the decay of the Empire, a strong official church in conjunction with a strong state was the only effective combination. Here, the new Emperor was absolutely in line with the Trinitarians, and if there was blood to be spilled along the way, he didn't care. And if it was the blood of little children – such as a certain boy called Arcadius, who didn't yet know of his imminent demise back in Spain –, then this too was to be accepted. Von Klasewitz would certainly be given absolution by appropriate authority in good time.

He was now, so to speak, close to the source of any blessing.

Everything was fine.

Everything developed well.

Johannes I felt at peace with himself, a satisfaction he hadn't felt for a long time. It remained to kill Rheinberg. Best of all, death to all the other senior officers who were with him. None of them would ever serve him faithfully. Removing them was a greater gain as the concomitant loss of expertise was a step backwards. He would then, out of the crewmen and NCOs, all in all easily malleable, promote men of low status to new officers, personally indebted to him. Yes, a little purge. That wasn't a bad idea. And some of the older NCOs ... this man Köhler, should he ever return from his crazed expedition, had to be considered as well. The man had carried his experience like a banner and sometimes even dared to question the German's orders. Yes, Köhler would have to die too. But some African savages might already have eliminated him.

So be it.

Von Klasewitz rose, adjusted the stinking purple. Enough of the musings. Now it was time for action. He would step out of his tent and give his orders as Emperor. Clean up with the remnants of the troops of Theodosius. To witness the beginning of a new era. Who would have thought about something like this, when ... in the future ... they left Wilhelmshaven? His biggest goal at the time had been to become an admiral, a senior officer, as befitted someone of his lineage. And now he had exceeded those expectations by far. The nobility in him had prevailed. No officer, no mere nobleman, not one among many, but one of highest nobility, the climax, the epitome of par excellence, equal to the person to whom he once swore the oath of service as a young ensign.

What a wonderful and infinitely satisfying feeling.

He would enjoy it all of his long, long reign.

It was finally clear that his assessment of being simply someone better than most other people in the world was absolutely justified. No arrogance. No presumption.

It was just the truth.

Von Klasewitz stretched. A servant was already about to open the entrance to the tent, but the Emperor raised a hand, admonishing the man to wait.

Johannes I took a deep breath.

Then he stepped outside.

43

That was it.

With burning eyes, Rheinberg stared at the battlefield below. The remaining officers had gathered around him, many of whom he only knew the names. A small group of infantrymen had also saved themselves on this hill. All were silent, filled with bitter helplessness, resignation. Rheinberg didn't have to look anyone in the face for a long time to capture the general mood. There was hardly anyone to give their cause a chance, not one who still expected them to turn the tide of events.

Nothing. No chance. Rheinberg felt a deep disillusionment in itself. So many victims. Twenty men of the company of infantrymen may have survived the massacre, many weapons were lost with the dead. And the legions – they behaved amazingly brave. Rheinberg had heard that many officers and NCOs had gathered around "the Tribune," which he had identified as Thomas Volkert. The young man seemed to have earned a legendary reputation, and the men seemed to trust him to do wonders. He commanded locally, along with several other leaders, but ultimately nothing more than an attempt to retire in an orderly manner.

The men of Maximus didn't want to allow that. They wanted an absolute victory, either by complete surrender or annihilation. They were obviously angered by the continuing resistance they had to fight.

Rheinberg didn't command any army anymore. He felt that things were slipping from his hands. He felt lost. What else was left to do? Save lives. Prevent another massacre.

He had to surrender. Only then could he prevent the senseless killing from continuing.

"Gentlemen," he said, his voice a bit brittle, in search of the old firmness, an expression of his emotional state. "Gentlemen, we must surrender."

No horrified looks, no incredulous amazement. There was no one among the officers here who didn't see this as the only possible consequence of the situation. Nobody harbored illusions about his personal destiny. With luck, the simple legionaries and NCOs would suffer no further harm if they surrendered peacefully. For the higher ranks was either the career at its end or possibly even their life.

"You have to run, my lord," one of the men advised, knowing that Rheinberg's days in captivity would inevitably lead to his inglorious death. "Escape to Hadrumentum."

"Yes," a soft voice inside him said. She sounded female, reminded him of Aurelia. "Fly while you can. Escape to the *Saarbrücken*!"

Rheinberg quarreled with himself. Cowardice. He had many mistakes to blame himself for, numerous weaknesses that had ultimately led to this disaster. But cowardice? That wasn't a tactical retreat, that was … panicking. Could he do that?

Did he want to do that?

Rheinberg took a breath, struggling for an answer.

"First surrender," he said hoarsely. "Call that Tribune to get ready to lay down his weapons. He has to give up, so that the men will not uselessly follow him to death."

Faces showed mourning when Rheinberg said that. Everyone felt the utmost respect for the young Thomasius, and everyone was saddened by the realization that by capitulating he would finish such a promising career and possibly his life.

"Sir!"

Rheinberg turned around. A rider slid off his horse in front of him, his face sweating with sweat.

"What is it?"

"My Lord, Maximus is dead!"

As if thunderclapped, Rheinberg stared at the man. He was among the band of scouts who, armed with binoculars and operating off the battlefield, watched the goings-on around the enemy Emperor in the hope of obtaining information that would prove important.

Like this one.

Important. But really crucial? Reason for hope?

Rheinberg controlled himself, fought down the wild feeling. Maximus was dead, but his army victorious. What happened?

The scout seemed to have foreseen the question, for without being asked, he continued.

"The observers don't know the details, sir. We only know that the body of Maximus was carried out of the tent. Then there was some turmoil and a lot of walking around. Finally, the purple cloak of the dead was carried back into the tent. We can safely assume that a successor who was appointed Emperor is already in place."

Rheinberg nodded. A terrible thought took possession of him. Von Klasewitz was the Magister Militium of Maximus, and he was a man of betrayal and intrigue. What if he was behind the surprising death of the usurper in order to put himself on the throne? To make this possible, however, he needed numerous allies, and there were certainly competitors. Rheinberg knew too little about the background and details, but the idea that the traitor would now call himself Emperor of Rome, was terrifying – not only because now, in the case of inevitable surrender, it'd certainly sealed his own fate.

Of course, that didn't change anything. So much was clear: Cowardice or no cowardice, he wouldn't expect other men to die for him if his cause has become hopeless.

"Anyway," Rheinberg emphasized slowly. "We surrender, no matter in front of which man I'm forced to throw my sword to the ground. We will ..."

"Lord, there's something else."

The scout was respectful, but his voice had that an urgent undertone that put the content of the message far beyond the personal well-being of its deliverer – so he dared to interrupt a general. Not that Rheinberg was so petty as to complain seriously – and the tone made him sit up and take notice.

"Speak, my friend," he said, smiling as warmly as possible.

"We're under attack ... I think."

Rheinberg noted the hesitation, but he just shook his head. "I've noticed that we're being attacked. We're on a battlefield too."

The messenger turned red.

Rheinberg was immediately sorry for his remark. It really wasn't a good idea to make fun of the unfortunate choice of words of a legionary. He sighed, took a deep breath and said, "Sorry, friend. Report exactly what has been observed."

The man didn't have time to be offended. Something burned on his soul. "An army," he gushed.

Rheinberg closed his eyes, collecting his patience. "Yes?" he said slowly.

"It's marching toward us. I mean, all of us. To this position. From the south."

Rheinberg's eyes widened.

"I beg your pardon?"

"The advance departments are clearly visible with the binoculars. It is an army. A big army. Many riders. You will be here in minutes, master."

"Banner? Signs?"

The man shrugged.

"I've never seen anything like it before, sir."

44

Sassmann let out a breath.

45

"Tribune, we are finished!"

Volkert turned to see the legionary who had appeared beside him. He had just bowed over the dead body of another tribune, felled by a blade, and with that the group of officers who held the remaining units of Theodosius under control had shrunk by another valuable member.

"What are you talking about?" he snapped.

"The Magister Militium prepares capitulation. When the signal comes, we should lay down our weapons. Be ready!"

Volkert didn't doubt the veracity of this statement. But he doubted if he would be able to implement that order without resistance. God, what had they been fighting for all along? But he immediately called himself a fool. The signs were obvious. The collapse of the formation was imminent. The only thing left was to prevent a slaughter. So he would do what he had to do.

Even if it hurt his soul.

"I understand," he told the man. "Tell the Magister Militium that we'll obey the signal."

Volkert turned away, didn't want to talk about it anymore. He took one last look at the dead officer at his feet, then raised his eyes, his gaze fixed on the faces of his hopeful-looking centurions and optios, the backbone of his army.

Ha, that was funny!

He had actually thought of "his army."

Volkert wiped away the thought. Nothing and nobody here belonged to him. Many of the men obeyed his orders, and he had made a contribution to ensuring that not everything had fallen apart hours ago. But his energy was exhausted, his resources became more and more limited, and he lost hope as well as the raging fury that had driven him both forward. Resignation spread. Even though Rheinberg didn't stand a chance and was willing to put his life in the hands of the Maximus – which in all likelihood meant his death –, everything was indeed lost.

Lamentation didn't help.

He now had to save the lives of his men, even if it was his last act. Certainly his last as a Tribune. Easy come easy go. The new Emperor would scarcely want to keep him in his service, and if he did, he wouldn't want him in that rank. And Volkert didn't want to serve this new Emperor, no Magister Militium like von Klasewitz. If he survived this, he would have to seek another employment.

The pain was under control for him. He didn't long for further battles and promotions. Why not become a peaceful wagoner? He had traveled enough to know what challenges could get in the way.

Volkert stretched, looking for Secundus. He would miss this friend, the old crook, the good-for-nothing, more than anyone else.

Trumpets became audible.

That wasn't the agreed signal.

"Tribune!" a centurion called to him, gesturing excitedly, pointing with his outstretched arm.

The cries became louder, no screams of pain, but of surprise, horror, unbelief.

They came from his men.

They came from the army of Maximus as well.

The fighting faltered. The clinking of the swords faded away. It was as if someone had taken all the energy out of the struggle, as if a cloth was sinking over the battle. Heads turned, eyes were opened, questions were asked.

Volkert turned, stared, didn't really recognize anything, reached for the binoculars and brought them to his eyes. At first, he remained at a loss, saw nothing that could justify this excitement.

But then.

He saw a black wall approaching. A broad, mobile wall consisting of riders. They carried colorful banners and flags in weird shapes. Such breastplates Volkert had never seen before, such helmets were alien to him. The colors and signals said nothing to him. The faces of the men, if he could catch a glimpse of them, looked determined. Everyone was dark-skinned and they came from the south.

Volkert flung himself around, ran up a hill, wheezed, paused, and again brought the eyepiece to his eyes. Riders, thousands of riders, and behind them the approaching band of foot soldiers. He had been in the Roman legion long enough to estimate the size of the host. How many were there? At least 20,000 men. A large army, powerful enough to make a difference, sweeping away the exhausted fighters.

But whose warriors would attack them? Did they only take the chance, now that Rome was weak? Or …

Who was *that*?

Volkert lowered the binoculars, realized his mouth was open. He didn't have … that was not …

He looked again, searching, focusing. His eyes caught the group of men, splendidly dressed, nobles, officers, and there were a few who stood out because they wore Roman uniforms or …

Those were Köhler and … there, Behrens … and Neumann, the doctor of the *Saarbrücken*!

Volkert cried out, lowering his binoculars.

Men who had followed him, Secundus beneath, stared at the hysterically laughing Tribune who had fallen to his knees, head back, as he threw his arms up to the sky and cried aloud in a language that none of them understood could.

"That can't be true!" Volkert shouted again and again. "That can't be true!"

He got to his feet.

"Secundus!"

"Tribune?"

"Give the orders. All signals of surrender coming from Rheinberg are to be ignored."

"What?"

"Can't you hear well?"

Secundus looked around, but then his confidence in his friend's abilities won, and other subordinates nodded. They ran, shouting orders that their enemies had to hear.

Volkert laughed. It was a liberating laugh, a sobbing, painful outburst of emotion. This battle was over, that was true.

But with God and all powers of fate, not as Maximus had imagined. Anything but that!

"We'll attack again!" he yelled, whirling around himself. "Listen to my orders! We attack again! Our allies have arrived!"

Was it the halo of the "Tribune" that gave it credibility? Was it the desperate hope of the men for a miracle, an intervention of God that would save them from the deepest distress? Was it the realization that the great, alien army could be just as much a blessing as a curse and they just assumed it was the former?

The order of the Tribune was carried on. The word "allies" spread. The men of Maximus heard it, too, seemed hesitant, disoriented and perplexed. As the legions of the opponent raised their swords again to continue the battle, they defended themselves weakly, seemed very defensive. Their confidence, their courage for victory had faded.

They were in the majority, but they retreated.

Volkert ran like a dervish across the battlefield. He ordered, drove the men forward. He encouraged. He shouted, *"Foederati! Foederati!"* And his words were carried on. Soon the voices of the legionaries mingled with sudden enthusiasm. Some shouted "Tribune! Tribune!" others bellowed "Rome!" and others again carried the word of the newly arrived allies across the battlefield. Movement came into the units.

Volkert looked at the rider's wall, as it paused on the edge of the battlefield, seemed to orient itself. He ran through the swirling crowd of fighters, ruthless, as fast as he could, toward the newcomers, began waving his arms, making loud noises. Well, didn't they notice him? His own men made way for him, for them he had to act like a madman who had succumbed to the stress of the battle and spinned totally out of control!

He felt his legs get heavy and dropped his sword and breastplate. He ran like never before in his life, and his legionaries made way for him, staring at him like a man possessed. Then Volkert broke free of the formation.

He saw Köhler's eyes fall on him, the Roman officer opening his arms, madly screaming, how he touched Neumann and seemed to say something.

"Köhler!" Volkert roared, waving with his arms again. "Köööhler!" He stopped, gestured to his side of the battlefield, gesticulated. "Here! Köööhler! Here we are!" His words spoken in German made the difference.

Orders were given. Many a battle cry echoed across the battlefield. Köhler and Behrens rode up to Volkert, who stood, breathing heavily, his hands on his thighs. He had exhausted himself completely.

"A horse!" He heard Köhler's voice. "A horse for the man!"

Volkert saw one of the dark-skinned warriors bringing him a horse, and in a trance he mounted the animal, staring at the battlefield.

"Forward, my boy," Köhler muttered to him, and recognition flashed in his eyes. "Now show me where the party is on."

Volkert picked himself up, commandingly raising one hand, then spurred the horse, felt a crowd of soldiers begin to move behind him as he rode ahead of them, unarmed, and heard himself again, shouting to hoarseness, "Rooome! Rooome!"

And the men of Theodosius received the call, witnessed how the Tribune – *the* Tribune – led an army of foreign riders into battle, how it the dumbfounded men of Maximus struck like a hammer and how the army of the usurper stumbled the onslaught of the new arrivals, was overrun as it broke, fled, vanished, as their own officers threw away their weapons, as signals were overheard, how banners fell, insignia were trampled to the ground, how formations broke and how the pain engulfed the army of Maximus, the pain of defeat, the pain of strange blades, the pain of shattering hooves.

The pain served by *the* Tribune.

46

It was a cold morning when Jan Rheinberg met with the returnees from Aksum. In addition to the three Germans, the Trierarch Africanus and Ouezebas, the leader of the united Aksumite-Garamantite troops were present. Outside, everything was cleaned up.

It could not be called anything else.

The legions of Maximus had collapsed and hadn't withstood the onslaught of the Aksumite army for long. The death of their Emperor had certainly not helped to strengthen their fighting spirit. When it became known that von Klasewitz, wearing the Emperor's purple, had been shot dead the moment he left his tent, Rheinberg understood the enemy's relative insensitivity. He actually understood them very well, as his own soldiers barely escaped the same fate.

The traitor's corpse had been discovered when Rheinberg's men had taken possession of the enemy's camp, which was now serving as a holding area for prisoners of war. The gunshot wound had been unmistakable, and when, after the battle, a visibly weary, but ultimately contented Private Sassmann spoke again, it had also been clear who was responsible for it. Sassmann had acted on special orders from von Geeren. An ultimately very wise decision, as Rheinberg found, and one that relieved him of a great burden.

Other burdens remained, of course.

Still, his heart was light as he sat down with his comrades and their new guests and friends. To see Neumann again was of particular pleasure to him, and for the first hour he did nothing but listen to the physician's account of his adventures in Aksum. That it had been the old Aksumite Emperor who, in the face of disturbing news from Rome, had come to the conclusion that relations with the Empire could be "placed on a new footing," something Rheinberg found remarkable. The old man hadn't taken part in the long and exhausting journey for understandable reasons, but found himself eloquently and convincingly represented by his designated heir apparent, who intended to use his special position as a believer in the gratitude of Rome without false timidity and modesty.

"We certainly have no further problems here," Rheinberg said when it came to the current situation. "The defeated troops are in custody and largely demoralized. We will integrate most of them into our own legions after a while, they are too valuable for us. The treacherous prefects have been apprehended and whimper for mercy, they are robbed of their troops and have put their bets on the wrong horse. They will lose all their positions, and many will probably lose their lives as well. The whole thing is high treason, and there we can indeed show no weakness. Ultimately, that will be a matter for the new Emperor."

Neumann looked questioningly at Rheinberg. "What's the situation, Jan? I heard you have no ambitions."

"I'm not von Klasewitz. I don't think I could last long as an emperor. I'm still too distant from everything, from the legions, the Senate, all the important forces that an Emperor must rely on. Half of Christendom hates me because I don't advocate any intolerant, state-driven Christianity. With these Romans, my reputation is completely burnt. And let's face it – as a field-commander I didn't excel in any particular way. As soon as it becomes clear what the new power structure looks like, I will leave office. I will command the *Saarbrücken* and do everything we can to continue the work that we started before the civil war at Ravenna. There are so many projects and ideas – we have to resume that work. I heard coffee roasting is now on our list."

"That's right, my friend," Neumann confirmed with a smile. "But to come back to my question: Arcadius is therefore the new emperor? Under guardianship of his mother and the Senate? Will that be the solution?"

Rheinberg shrugged. "Something in that direction is certainly under consideration."

"And the *Saarbrücken*?"

"We return to Italy with the army and re-establish our rule. The

East is reasonably safe in this respect, but we now have to change some of the Western staff at court and in the provinces. Here I hope, however, that I can act without causing too much bloodshed. I don't want to drag a trail of blood behind me in the next few months."

Neumann looked at Rheinberg but said nothing. The sharp wrinkles on the young man's face testified to the strain he had endured, both physically and emotionally. The loss of von Geeren and many of his comrades weighed heavily on his consciousness, and this without speaking about the deaths of many Roman friends and companions. Neumann was aware that he had arrived at the last minute. They had marched day and night to even make it. If Maximus' men had known how exhausted and on the edge the soldiers of the relief army had really been, they probably wouldn't have surrendered so easily.

But Neumann was glad that it had developed this way.

"Does Maximus still have troops in Italy or Gaul? Certainly his loyalists in Britain are firmly in the saddle," Köhler said.

Rheinberg smiled weakly. "Loyalists, yes, but only with limited power. Maximus could risk the battle against us because he pulled together all the troops he could get hold of. There are still the Border Guard castles in Gaul, which he has – reasonably – bared, but his most powerful units are here – and our prisoners. We shouldn't expect any serious resistance. Other things worry me much more – the role of Ambrosius in this intrigue, the spreading plague, the imminent danger of the great migration, which we have by no means already overcome. Whoever ultimately takes over the leadership of the Empire, the list of challenges he faces becomes longer with every minute I think about it."

"And in this situation you want to give up your position?" Neumann asked. He strove to avoid as much as possible an undertone of disapproval.

But Rheinberg knew the doctor long enough to suspect what the question was. "Yes, my decision is clear. With the demise of our infantry, we no longer have any significant resources for land battles. We will build on the previous work of the deceased von Klasewitz and develop the artillery, and Dahms will have the opportunity to pursue further projects. But the coming conflicts should be led by someone who has experience in battle on land while being able to tactically combine the innovations with the proven methods of our legions. This person is not me."

The last sentence sounded pretty categorical, and Neumann obviously knew when a topic had reached a deadlock in a discussion. So he just nodded and accepted the decision, which certainly had a lot to it. To find a new commander-in-chief, who had the qualities mentioned by Rheinberg and at the same time was ready to show loyalty to a child emperor, was certainly one of the great list of challenges he had spoken of. Making this choice would be one of Rheinberg's most important legacies.

Neumann wanted to express a comment on another topic when the tent door was turned. A Roman officer entered with a worried face, which immediately electrified everyone. The excitement of the battle wasn't gone for long enough not to expect that fate had more bad surprises for them.

"Lord, something is happening in the legions," the man reported, and seemed undecided how to proceed. Rheinberg rose with an alarmed expression.

"What happened?"

"There has been a large gathering of officers. They decided to talk to the troops."

"You're among them?"

The man was feeling unwell in his skin. He was an officer, a legate, so he knew exactly what had happened. Apparently he had been chosen to deliver the message to the meeting. The man was young and had a very harmless-looking, round boy's face. Perhaps this was the decisive selection criterion for this task.

"If you want to follow me ... nothing will happen to you, my lord. The point is that we want to inform you about certain ... decisions. The Aksumite guests are also invited. It's all very peaceful."

Rheinberg's concern dwindled slightly. The man sounded sincere enough. He waved to the others, and together they left the tent. As they stood outside, they discovered that the legions had started to assemble outside the camp. Rheinberg and Neumann exchanged a look, then followed the officer, marching out. Now he was overcome by a certain amount of anxiety. Rheinberg knew the history of Rome and the way legions had made policy over the centuries. The tough men in the uniforms of the Empire had the habit of using that hardness against their own leaders, too, if they no longer lived up to their expectations. The consequence, if you were lucky, was that you were allowed to return to a private room to plunge yourself into your own sword.

Rheinberg's abdominal muscles tensed. He struggled for self-control, but his historical education thwarted him. Sometimes it wasn't good to be well-educated.

They were led to the field.

Only now did Rheinberg realize that the legions were grouped in a rectangle around a small podium. It reminded him in a fatal way of a place on which public executions were celebrated. He looked into the faces of the men, sought and found no hatred, no anger – no, the mood seemed rather relaxed, he saw men smiling, some nodded to him, all seemed very festive, almost happy.

This atmosphere was transferred a bit to Rheinberg, who took a deep breath and looked at the podium. There stood the highest ranking surviving officers of his army, and in the middle of it was a wooden chair with someone sitting on it …

… a purple coat.

Rheinberg stopped dead in his tracks.

He almost hit his forehead with the palm of his hand, but he stifled that gesture. Relief gripped him – and anger at his own stupidity.

What a fool he had been!

The situation was obvious! Tired of wrestling, blessed with an army commander with a rather weak popular base, the legions had, of course, done what they had always considered their right for many centuries – sometimes more successful, sometimes less.

They had appointed an emperor, evidently from their midst.

Rheinberg nodded, continued on his way.

Maybe that wasn't such a bad idea. It eliminated the lack of guidance, pushed a little boy out of the lurch in Spain, made things clear, and was based on a proven, if doubtful, tradition. And with luck, they would let him live. He had never distinguished himself by any particular cruelty, and he could expect that one would deal with him just as graciously.

As always, in such cases, it simply depended on whom the legions had chosen.

Rheinberg and Neumann looked at each other, their eyes met those of Köhler and Behrens. Everyone had obviously understood what it was all about. In a few moments, they would get to know the new Emperor.

Rome had decided to act without asking the time-wanderers.

Even that, Rheinberg thought to himself, didn't feel wrong.

As they approached the platform, a figure rose, a little reluctantly, as Rheinberg observed.

Then he stopped again, surprised again and embarrassed by his lack of foresight.

The officer who had been accompanying them cleared his throat. Then he spoke loud and clear.

"Lord, the legions are presenting the new Emperor of Rome, Thomasius, whom we all call the Tribune."

Rheinberg stared at Thomas Volkert, who returned his gaze a little tiredly.

That was ...

"But no ..." Neumann whispered, aghast. "But that is ..."

"Yes, dammit," Köhler said, very softly but not quiet enough for Volkert not to hear it. A thin smile crossed the face of the former ensign and deserter. There was no anger in it, no arrogance, not even triumph or pride. Just tiredness and ... calmness.

Then he leaned forward a bit and said softly in German, "Captain, we mustn't worry about my unreasonable love interest anymore."

Rheinberg grinned involuntarily and shook his head.

"No, Volkert, you have improved yourself." He paused. "Or do I have to address you differently now?"

Volkert made a defensive gesture. "Most of them were quite surprised when I told them I was a former deserter of the time-wanderers. But then there was no going back anymore – not for them, and unfortunately not for me either."

He sighed. He looked over the assembled crowd. Rheinberg followed his gaze and felt the expectation that lay upon him like a veil. There was still something to do, one last, symbolic act that would give all this legitimacy and completion.

"I didn't care for this, Captain. I didn't really want it."

Rheinberg nodded and looked into the tired face of Volkert. He believed him every word.

"I know that feeling too well," he said.

Closure and legitimacy. Rheinberg was ready for it.

He waved to his comrades and everyone did the same, knew what was expected of them.

He took a step forward and dropped to his knees.

It was time to swear allegiance to the new Emperor.

Epilogue

Godegisel stood in the familiar clearing, saw the great mills that glowed softly, and looked at the two men crouching beside the big heaps, each with a stick in one hand, a mug in the other, from which they now and then took a sip. He didn't know if he was ignored or if the two charcoal workers hadn't actually noticed him, but that didn't really matter anyway. He looked at Alewar and Fridunanth, who had accompanied him on the trip to Gaul. Not even three months had passed since his appointment as a Roman knight, closely followed by his appointment as Senator for the Goths. He had moved into a house in Ravenna – again and still the capital of the united Empire – and another one assigned to him hastily in the eastern settlement area of his people. His personal retinue was small and made up of reliable men who had served his family during the great exodus. After all the experiences that Godegisel had to go through, he was reluctant to travel alone.

He stepped into the open, leading the horse by the reins.

One of the workers looked up, looked surprised, noticed the good clothes, the three horses, the swords and bows, the beautiful bridle. Something went *click!* in his mind, and he nudged his colleague, took off his cap, got up, and bowed.

"Lord, I greet you!" he said in a submissive voice. Godegisel just nodded.

He wasn't here to scare people.

"Don't worry. I don't bother you for long, my friend. I'm looking for someone."

The relief was immediately visible on the faces of the two men. The speaker shrugged.

"There is no one here, my Lord, far and wide. I can show you the way to the next village if you wish."

"Thanks, I'm coming from there. I'm looking for a young woman whose father was formerly in possession of this place. Her name is Pina."

The two men exchanged a look that Godegisel didn't know how to interpret.

"My Lord, the government has taken the mills away from Pina, since women are not allowed to do this kind of work."

The young Goth nodded. "These laws are being changed."

The two men looked uncertain. "We've heard of that, sir. Will they take everything back from us?"

"No, I don't think so."

Relief was visible, but Godegisel grew a little impatient.

"What happened to Pina?"

"She went to the village. She works in one of the taverns, I heard. She did ... she didn't receive a lot of money for this place."

Now the insecurity of the men turned into a hint of fear.

"My Lord, we only operate the mills. An official snubbed her and made sure the purchase price was very low. We can't help it," the spokesman hurried to say, clenching his hands slightly around his cup. The stick had been dropped, wisely.

Godegisel took a deep breath. "I don't blame anyone."

They all knew that working in a tavern was limited only in the best case to serving the guests with food and drink. It was rather expected that the bartenders – regardless of whether they were still "girls" or not – were also busy as prostitutes.

"In the tavern, then?"

"I don't know in which, but I heard it."

"I thank you."

Godegisel gave the man two small coins, which he immediately made disappear, and turned away. Minutes later, they were back on the horses and followed the forest path that led to the military road. Godegisel didn't feel well. Of course, he should have foreseen what had happened. Had he stayed, Pina might have been spared that humiliation.

He could only hope that it was not as bad as he feared and that he could make it up. He didn't expect Pina to greet him with open arms, but perhaps she would accept his offer – a small house, an income, not an obligation. Godegisel didn't want to owe anything to anyone, and just as he had returned his wages and clothes to the foreman in Ravenna, he was driven by the desire to pay his debts to Pina as well.

There was something else that drove him, but he hid this deep in himself. It was a hope that could hardly be nurtured after all this time, after his reckless disappearance. But he was a human, and humans hoped.

In the first of the two taverns, they had no luck, at least they didn't find Pina there. They were referred by the host to another establishment, and with a knowing grin that Godegisel didn't like.

When he entered the second tavern, it was already early evening. The taproom, which contained a good dozen tables, was neatly staffed. Cervisia and wine and small cups of the brandy of the time-wanderers was served. A sign over a back door indicated that there was a small bathhouse attached. Everything smelt of brothel, and that was by no means unusual. It was usually not possible to clearly distinguish one from the other.

The clientele consisted of ordinary people from the area, many agricultural workers, a few passing wagoners, ordinary civil servants. Godegisel suspected that slaves were also served here. The Emperor had announced that slavery would be abolished at the beginning of next year. This hadn't led to much disturbance here in the area, there were few large *latifundiae* and the region was sparsely populated. Each freedman should be assigned land, either here or in other regions of the Empire. There was a lot of available land, especially since the plague had raged in the East. The Emperor wanted as many fields as possible to be worked on, and he had realized that free peasants had a much greater interest in these efforts than unfree farm laborers, who usually didn't partake much in their earnings. Godegisel wholeheartedly supported this policy of Thomasius.

The looks he got were curious but not hostile. The young Goth stood out of the crowd here, better dressed, though he was by no means intrusive in his higher social position. That he and his companion Alewar were entitled to carry weapons, was striking enough. The other man of his entourage had stayed outside with the horses.

The landlord personally didn't hesitate to rush to the two new guests.

"What can I bring for the gentlemen? There's another nice place over there!"

"Are you the owner of this tavern?" Godegisel asked unfriendly.

The slightly fat man looked at him from under bushy eyebrows.

"Yes, sir, my name is Iavus. I'm at your service. A relaxing bath maybe?"

The wink was unmistakable. Godegisel forced a smile. "Later, maybe, good Iavus. I'm looking for a Pina who works for you here."

The host's expression got something lurking – and a trace of fear was also noticeable. "Pina? Are you not satisfied with her services?"

"I would like to speak to her."

"She's cleaning the kitchen."

"I am going to see her."

"Oh ... no ... I ... I call her."

"We'll sit down there."

Godegisel pointed to the table in a niche that still had two seats and where only a bearded journeyman was sitting in front of an empty cup, into which he stared, lost in thought – or drunk. He looked up as the Goths approached.

Godegisel put a coin on the table. "Drink on me, friend, but do it elsewhere."

The bearded man didn't ask twice, let the coin disappear and cleared the table.

Then, out of nowhere, Pina stood in front of Godegisel, who had barely sat down.

He got up immediately.

At first, it seemed as if she didn't recognize him again. He had gained a good deal of weight, but the scars were of course recognizable forever. He had changed, there was no doubt about that.

But not enough to raise doubts. When recognition flashed in the eyes of the woman, Godegisel ventured a smile.

"I'm back," he said.

"I see."

"You didn't expect it."

"No." She shook her head. "No."

They were silent for a moment.

Godegisel turned his head and nodded into the taproom.

"Now you work here."

"They took everything from me. I'm just a woman."

"I was there."

She said nothing for a moment, her expression a bit painful.

"You're on your way somewhere?" she asked.

"No, I'm here for you."

The slight hint of a smile hushed over Pina's slightly haggard face, as if she had heard something she liked but didn't quite believe.

"What do you want?" she asked.

"Much, but above all, pay a debt."

She frowned. "You don't owe me anything."

"I see that quite differently."

She looked a little confused now, found no reply, so Godegisel continued.

"You don't like working here," he said. She nodded.

"Do you want to leave?" he asked. She nodded again.

"I'll buy you a house wherever you want to live," he said.

She stared at him, eyes wide, seriously disbelieving, seriously hoping but fortunately not unwilling, offended, or disapproving, as he had feared.

"Are you … going to live in this house, too?" She asked.

Godegisel swallowed the lump in his throat, which had suddenly formed.

"I … really would like to do that," he said. He reached for her right hand, letting it slide into his hands, almost by itself.

Alewar grinned, got up and waved to the landlord. Iavus came running up to see the strange scene, a man of nobility and wealth, and a seedy coaler's daughter, and opened his mouth. But before he could say anything, he found three *solidi* in his hand, handed over by Alewar, who also led his index finger to his mouth.

Iavus wasn't stupid. He understood. He would have to find a replacement for Pina. Of course, the bitch would plunder the rich jerk and then run away, but that was his problem.

He saw the three leave the tavern and shrugged.

* * *

Neumann sat behind the newly-carpeted desk and repeatedly asked himself why the incapable cabinetmakers were always the ones who were assigned to him. Sighing, he leaned to one side and pushed the piece of wood back under the too short table leg, since he had once again removed it by a careless movement. Naval engineer Dahms watched the process with quiet amusement, then he looked devoutly at the cup in front of him. It not only steamed auspiciously out of the container, it also smelled like it had expected.

Coffee.

Not that he had made a significant contribution to that. Köhler and Behrens had dealt with the problem of coffee roasting, as soon as they all safely arrived in Ravenna, and their partially rebuilt settlement had taken possession again. The enthusiasm of their approach dealing with wild coffee beans was comparable to the energy with which they had established their first still. Dahms had wanted to give them a few tips, but after a short time he had to realize that he had more than enough of his own work on the table, and that he shouldn't annoy the two innovators longer than necessary. And it was amazing that a short time after their first experiments this cup stood in front of him. The coffee was very, very bitter. He had sweetened it with honey, which produced a very unique aftertaste that he usually favored with tea. But sugar was very rare and expensive, and the only alternative was *defrutum*, a cooked grape commonly used as a sweetener, but which made nasty clots in coffee and diminished the enjoyment of drinking. So honey.

Neumann had reappeared and looked at Dahms' cup. His eyes were a little envious. Dahms caught his eye and grinned.

"Have you had your ration today?"

Neumann grunted something. Their very limited stock of experimental coffee was already as good as used up. It would take quite some time until Aksum would deliver more. Furthermore, they had used many beans as seeds, so the yield would be greater in the future. A volunteer detachment from the *Saarbrücken* had taken over the sponsorship of their small plantation, had protected the plants by high hedges and walls, and visited the field regularly to cut back the shoots and loosen up the soil. The men showed a remarkable dedication and discipline in this work, so that Neumann felt the need to look after it only once a month. The dry spell was soon over anyway. From Aksum, they heard that the local cultivation had already begun, on state plantations, with really large fields and many workers. But even there, the first significant harvest was not expected before next year, and until the first major delivery arrived in Rome ... After all, the great coffee roasting company of Ravenna would be ready. Köhler and Behrens had planned and built oversized, so they had been accused of hubris in their planning. Neumann found that the two men had planned wisely.

"The quackery production is running again, I've heard," Dahms said, making a spectacle of taking a sip of coffee, smiling pleasantly, rolling his eyeballs delightfully. Neumann looked at the demonstration with a sour expression before answering.

"If you're implying that I resumed the first courses at our Medical-Pharmaceutical School, that is true. I have set the curriculum for two years. Then we should have proper local doctors as graduates who deserve that name. The bigger problem is the medicines. I have to reinvent the whole chemistry here. Sometimes I don't know where my head is."

Dahms dismissed his friend's complaint with a wave of his hand.

"I try the same – in mathematics, mechanics, geometry and related fields. Do you hear me whining?"

"You have coffee too."

"The last."

"Then you'll cry soon too."

Dahms frowned and then nodded slowly. "You might be right."

He emptied the cup and set it down on the tray, which a servile spirit would soon clear. He went to the window and looked out. The lights of the *Saarbrücken* were easily recognizable. The cruiser was moored at its old place, and Dahms knew it would be there for long. The coal stocks were running out. The machines showed signs of failure. He would still be able to keep the cruiser functioning, but soon ...

He felt Neumann step beside him and nod in the direction of the *Saarbrücken's* on-board lights.

"How much longer?" he asked.

"I'll give her a year, after that she won't go anywhere anymore," Dahms replied. "If we take great care of her, then maybe two. But what is a weapon worth that your enemies know to be motionless in the harbor and nowhere to be seen? Our new Emperor already spoke of a round trip in the coming year, up to Britain. And he isn't wrong. We have to show ourselves. He has to show himself. For that the old lady is very well suited. But I'm not worried."

He turned away and looked at Neumann.

"If we shut down the *Saarbrücken* for good, I'll make an academy out of the ship, with a lot of illustrative material. Until then, our fleet building program will have come a long way. We will have many steamers, and they will all carry cannons. The oceans are ours until the technology gets around and the others catch up. But for the coming years, maybe even decades, our lead won't diminish much. We have to use this time properly. Maybe fate has even given us the ideal Emperor for that. The young Volkert is sensible and has experienced a lot for his age. He listens to people who give him advice and is moderate. He's not a friend of senseless wars, and he thinks a lot about the important reforms that are coming up. We just have to keep him alive, protect him and help him. Then the future doesn't look so bad."

Neumann nodded. "I can only agree with you. But sometimes I'm very afraid of the pile of work that lies ahead. I don't know if we can ever handle this."

"But we don't have to, old friend," Dahms replied softly, looking back at the lights of the cruiser. "None of us expects that. We do what we can to initiate things and confront as many people as possible with new knowledge and thinking. The rest – that'll go by itself. Not always as we want it. But I don't expect that either. After all, I'm not an emperor."

Neumann grinned. "Neither am I … And I'm damned happy about that."

Dahms didn't contradict him.

* * *

"I don't like the pomp surrounding the title."

"Belongs to the job."

Volkert looked down at himself, raised a hand, scratched at a sauce patch on the noble tunic. It was late evening. In the study a pleasant log fire flickered. Although both men were tired, they didn't think about sleeping. A long day full of meetings had ended, and Rheinberg had finally declared his resignation as Magister Militium. Volkert had accepted this decision with a laughing and a crying eye – crying because he felt he was losing a trusted guide and supporter, which of course wasn't true. Rheinberg took over the civil and military administration of the "German village," would take the newly founded university under his wing, and, together with Neumann, Dahms and others, help organize the transfer of scientific knowledge from the future into the new present. He certainly had his hands full.

He laughed because it had proved to be increasingly unsustainable that the two highest offices of the state were occupied by time-wanderers. Rheinberg had to leave in order to create a decent balance. This balance was all the more important as the conflict between the Empire and the Trinitarians was not over. Ambrosius had been put on the defensive with an official investigation into his role in the assassination attempt on Maximus and was currently subdued in his influence. But that wouldn't last forever. The fact that Volkert had confirmed the Edict of Tolerance as one of his first official acts, which had only recently been suspended by Maximus, had certainly also burdened the atmosphere. After all, at least the Bishop of Rome was pragmatic enough not to oppose the new Emperor openly. This gave Volkert a respite in which he could work on all the endless list of other pressing issues he had to deal with.

"Renna has agreed, of course," Rheinberg muttered, looking into his goblet. He wanted to drink some more wine, but he knew that Aurelia didn't appreciate being drunk when he got home. This had little to do with the general irritability of a pregnant woman, but more with certain principles according to which his wife sought to educate him. Since the rebukes were repeatedly relaxed by loving devotion and wise support, Rheinberg had submitted to this regime with a certain serenity. Here he was, in a sense, in the same shoes as the young Emperor, whose now quite official wife also did everything to exert a formative influence on her husband – and who obviously didn't want to accept the title of "Empress" purely as a title of honor.

"Renna will be a good Magister Militium," Volkert said. "He has the experience, and he is loyal. He is respected in fleet and army alike. I'm confident that we will do good with him."

"There are other challenges," Rheinberg added, and an ironic smile began to play around his lips. "What happened to Julia's ex-husband? What was his name?"

"Martinus Caius. When he heard that I became Emperor and Julia was to be my wife, he was hiding in the deepest hole he could find." The amused tone of the statement barely concealed Volkert's true feelings. The anger behind it was serious. It was Caius, after all, who almost had killed his daughter. But with Volkert in office, a different kind of response to such problems had emerged. He was no one who wanted to be characterized by blind vindictiveness.

"I punished him hard," Volkert explained.

"How?"

"He has been appointed administrative official, in a deserted Asian patch. It's not only far away from all possible amusements, he also has to work hard. I gave him a very dutiful and pedantic supervisor. Caius now either turns a faithful and diligent servant of the Empire, or he soon will commit suicide. But I figured some honest and disciplined work would be the biggest punishment that man can suffer. Even his family thought that my decision was quite wise and didn't protest."

Rheinberg smiled and bowed his head to pay respect to the Emperor for his wisdom.

Volkert waved his hand, scratching on the sauce patch, which was only rubbed deeper into the fabric by his efforts. He sighed and gave up. Then, musing, he looked into the fire, cleared his throat, and said, "Captain, there's a story I want to tell you."

Rheinberg raised his eyebrows. The undertone of the young man's voice had turned exceptionally serious. All the lightness was gone. "If it has anything to do with your life after your desertion, forget it," Rheinberg said. "It was my fault, and I can only ask for forgiveness."

"No, that's not it. Something happened during my passage from Italy to Africa, before the battle against Maximus."

Rheinberg frowned. "This action with the pirates? I already heard the story."

"That too is not the point. It's about what I encountered after our victory …"

Volkert closed his mouth when someone knocked and then entered the room. Rheinberg looked up. It was Bertius, the Emperor's servant, a former legionary who had once saved Volkert's life, and now, when he was not serving his master with more or less diligence, enjoyed a good life at court. In any case, his belly had noticeably increased in recent months, and Rheinberg didn't have the impression that this process would soon come to an end.

"My Lord!" Bertius exclaimed, indicating a bow. "Sir, a messenger with a letter from the eastern border. He probably arrived here some time ago but wasn't admitted for a long time. He insisted now and, well, you have ordered that no one who has a legitimate cause be rejected. The letter bears an official seal of the border troops. It was sent about four months ago …"

"Will you just let him in, Bertius?" Volkert interrupted, decorating his words with a slightly angry glance. "You can finish for today. We don't need anything anymore."

"Yes, my lord," Bertius replied eagerly and, perhaps, too hastily for hiding his relief. "I'll let the man in."

It was not long before the messenger arrived, a simple legionary, a man of stately stature, clutching the scroll with the letter like a weapon. He bowed deeply in front of the high gentlemen, nearly dropped to his knees, and was only made to stand up when both men specifically requested him to do so.

"What's your name?" Volkert asked.

"Quintus Virilius, sir," the man said, quite awed.

"Why have you been sent?"

"I was given this letter. There's another one from my commander, explaining everything."

"You received a letter? From whom?"

Virilius shrugged. "I don't know from whom. I was on the border guard when that Hun appeared, handed over the letter, addressed to ..." He glanced at them both as if he realized only now who he was talking to. "... to the time-wanderers and to Magister Militium Rheinberg."

Rheinberg opened the parchment, leafed through a letter from a border officer, whose content he briefly digested. The second roll, which had been inside the parchment, consisted of animal skin.

Volkert leaned over. "Virilius, when you were given that message, was there no conversation?"

"Nothing, sir. I immediately took it to my superior, sir. I felt it could be important."

Volkert nodded. He smiled weakly. The good Virilius had made a long journey to see that his light was not put under the bushel.

"You did it right, my friend," Rheinberg said. "You'll return to your post and receive a letter from me for your commander, in which I will commend you. You should also receive plenty of travel money. The way is long."

Virilius smiled gratefully. "Yes, sir. Thank you, sir."

"You can go now."

The legionary bowed again before leaving the room.

Volkert looked at the animal hide, recognized the language and the writing. "This fits in well with the story I wanted to tell you, Captain."

Rheinberg raised a hand and read aloud:

"Dear sir. I hope this message will find you in good health and in full command of your destiny. I, unfortunately, cannot say so, and although I will try to postpone the inevitable, I propose that you remain alert and attentive to matters beyond your eastern borders ..."

They read the text together. It wasn't long. It warned Rheinberg about the Huns. It informed him of the sender's efforts to postpone an attack on the Roman Empire. The author also made it clear that the Huns suspected that Rome was so rich in spoils because he and his men couldn't avoid pointing that fact out in order to prove their usefulness.

The letter was signed: "Jonathan G. Hailey, First Mate, *HMS King Henry*, Royal Navy."

They looked at the fine, neat handwriting, thinking about the concise words that had been laid down without self-pity and with no prospect of help or rescue. There had been no request for support. Neither had they learned why a British sailor had landed with the Huns.

"The same thing must have happened to them as we did," Volkert came to the inevitable conclusion. "I met one of their men. He must have escaped the Huns."

Now, finally, he could tell the story of the rowing slave he had discovered shortly before his death in the belly of a pirate ship – someone who addressed him in English, only to die completely exhausted shortly thereafter.

Rheinberg listened to the details of this experience in silence. He raised the animal skin, scanned the words again and sighed.

"What are the consequences, Emperor?"

Volkert frowned. "For one thing, the Huns imprisoned British sailors – even though one seems to have gained their confidence enough so that he has been able to send this message –, and, secondly, that the reason for their early appearance is the presence of the same British. Third, this man, Hailey, seems to have so much influence that he can delay the big rush of the Huns, at least he believes that. Our victory over one of their larger divisions might have helped him to prevail."

242

"How long will that last? We can hardly rely on that."

"That's true."

"There is something else to consider."

Volkert looked at Rheinberg attentively.

"If a British ship – from whatever time – suffered the same fate as the *Saarbrücken* and the crew could get into the hands of this enemy ..."

"Which obviously didn't have as significant consequences as our appearance here," Volkert added.

The Captain nodded.

"The Huns in the East were in any case completely surprised by our weapons," Volkert concluded, recalling his fact-finding mission, which had degenerated into a battle. "Either the British come from a time when firearms were not that widespread, or they successfully hid them from the Huns."

"We will not find out until we meet one of them," Rheinberg said. "But the point I wanted to make is this: If this happened to us and an unknown British ship ..."

"Who else? And where?" Volkert completed the sentence.

Nobody knew the answer. For the Huns, a primitive people in their view, the potential transfer of knowledge and technology wouldn't fall on very fertile ground. The chance was great that no damage was done.

"I'm just imagining China," Rheinberg muttered. "I don't know much about the history of Far Asia, but what I know is that there are developed empires with tight governmental organization. When the right constellation arises and a smart Chinese leader realizes the potential of time travelers, as Gratian and Theodosius have done, we aren't the only ones who are changing the course of history."

"Provided that all that has happened to us happened to others at a similar time."

"The British are apparently still alive, at least for now. So they landed here around the same time. A little earlier perhaps, as they are already familiar with the Huns and one could end up as a slave to pirates. One year earlier? Maybe two?"

Volkert frowned.

"There can be only one reaction to this problem for us."

Rheinberg looked expectantly at the young Emperor.

"We have to explore the world," Volkert continued. "We have to send expeditions across the seas. We know our neighbors and know that either nobody has arrived there or the arrivals have gained no influence. But that doesn't have to apply to the rest of the world. Your example worries me, Captain."

Rheinberg nodded, sighed softly and got up. He stretched his body.

"Another pressing issue, Your Majesty."

"This job is no fun."

Rheinberg grinned. "I see that as an order to build an exploration fleet."

"And me?" Volkert asked bleakly. "I have to sit here and ..."

"Find the means," Rheinberg said sunnily and waved to the Emperor. "Have fun. Anyway, I'll be leaving for today."

Volkert looked after Rheinberg as he walked out, and decided that it was high time to finally go to bed.

His life would prove exhausting enough, he was sure of that.

* * *

Clodius looked up as the big cart, accompanied by three riders, came to a stop in front of his modest dwelling. He felt a bit unsure about the unannounced visit, but as it should be he got up from his bench, stretched out his old limbs, reached for the stick, and walked slowly towards the newcomers. There were four men, if you counted the coachman, and one of them was very well-dressed, indicating that he was in the service of an important man. The other three were plain servants, but by no means run-down.

Clodius looked questioningly at the leader of the group, then bowed his head slowly – he couldn't do much more without much effort.

"Greetings, gentlemen. If you are looking for the right way, I will gladly give you information!"

"No, old man. Are you Clodius and this is your house?"

"That's me. You are looking for me?"

Before Clodius could become worried, a friendly smile crossed the man's face. He half turned and said to his companions, "We are where we are supposed to be. You can unload!"

Clodius watched in confusion as the other three men immediately went to work and took the cover from the cart, which had been stretched over several boxes. A big cage was also visible.

"My name is Alewar, servant to Knight and Senator Godegisel."

Clodius needed a moment to process the words. He had hoped to hear something from his former protégé once again, but hearing the name in connection with the words Knight and Senator came a bit unexpected. "Godegisel ... so he's fine?" he asked helplessly.

"He has a villa not too far from here, in the settlement of the Goths. His wife and himself invite you to visit him anytime."

"Villa?"

"The noble Godegisel is a man of rank and dignity, and a representative of his people to the Emperor and Senate."

Clodius scratched his head. This information was a bit difficult to reconcile with the Godegisel he had nurtured so that he could survive his ailment. Many others from the area had not had this luck. The last half year had been pretty tough. Clodius had been spared the disease, as he had expected. But the times weren't easy. Many fields were not tended. The trade had come to a standstill. Clodius got along just fine, but yes, it wasn't easy. "Then ... I'll follow this kind invitation one day ..."

"My master sends you presents as well, Clodius!" Alewar interrupted him, pointing to the boxes and cage that had been unloaded. He wandered over with the old man and opened the containers. In the cage, Clodius saw a somewhat tired-looking cock and three well-fed hens, which immediately led to a knowing smile. In the boxes were all sorts of utensils, household goods, but also food, cereals, flour, spices, some fresh fruit and vegetables. Clodius's eyes widened as he saw his menu suddenly and radically expand in quality and quantity. Then there were matching clothes, for winter and summer, and new footwear. Alewar presented him with a particularly skillfully carved walking stick. The grip felt smooth in Clodius's hand, as if it never had another owner.

Clodius was overwhelmed. He lacked the words. Before he could say his thanks, Alewar brought out a smaller box he had not opened yet.

"This gift is presented to you with special regards by my Lord," Alewar said solemnly, and made a ceremony to open the box and reveal its contents.

Clodius looked in, holding the air for a moment, then, shakily, he stretched out his hands and stroked the treasures offered to him. It was, as he could easily ascertain, a collection of scrolls on fine parchment, and copies of the Scriptures, some of which he already called his own, but in poorer quality. His greatest treasure, now as complete as it could be – Clodius had to get an overview – and copied by master craftsmen and, as he was now allowed to determine after rolling up, also decorated with wonderful drawings and ornaments. A treasure, a true, an immeasurably valuable, a comprehensive, an overwhelming treasure.

The old man became very dizzy. A little awkwardly, he wiped moisture from the corner of his eye.

"My lord gives you this too, noble Clodius," Alewar said, handing the old man something. A bag of clicking coin, heavy and well-filled. "In addition, I should like to tell you the following: If you feel one day no longer able to live alone in your house, you will be granted shelter and care in my lord's mansion until the last of your days. Until then, I – or one of my comrades – will travel to you twice a year, at the beginning of spring and at the beginning of autumn, to deliver you an alimentation sent by my lord and to inquire about your well-being." He paused for a moment, adding in an almost apologetic tone, "If that's alright with you."

Clodius cleared his throat. For a moment he searched for words, feeling overwhelmed in his old days. "I'm fine with it," he replied, his voice cracking and then he made a sweeping gesture with his hand. "But did I earn all this?"

"My lord is of this opinion." For Alewar, that was enough to know because he didn't say more and looked quite friendly.

Clodius cleared his throat. "I would like to visit him. I would also like to meet his wife."

That was not said out of courtesy. He really meant it that way. And the servant of Godegisel seemed to interpret his words exactly the same way as he nodded. "Should you express this wish, my master gave me the order to drive you with the cart and take you along. One of my men stays in your house, stashes all presents, and guards your belongings until your return."

Clodius ran a hand over his hair. For a moment, he recoiled from his own zeal. "I have to pack something, it will …"

"We have time. Do not hurry. My men are helping you. Give us only instructions, and we will faithfully carry them out."

Clodius saw only friendly readiness in the eyes of his visitors and relaxed. He spread his arms.

"I can offer you some chicken soup!"

Alewar laughed. "I heard it is incomparable."

Clodius was quite flattered. "I will hurry."

"No need. It will be several months before your grandchild is born."

Clodius had already turned away when he realized what Alewar had said … and what Godegisel, the Goth, clearly carried in his heart for him, the old freedman. Clodius shook his head, had to wipe his eyes again.

Chicken soup.

He still had some in the pot.

He just had to find some clean plates.

He stumbled a little as he stepped into his hut, a little overwhelmed by the emotions that flooded him.

Then he thanked the Lord for this day and for his new son.

* * *

It was said that gardening has something meditative. Working with your bare hands in the ground, planting roots in the small, carefully dug holes, or sprinkling seeds that would someday sprout new plants – all of this connects one to God, who had prepared everything so wonderfully for his chosen people of this earth, so that they could receive all they needed for their survival.

Meditative, indeed. That might be true for a while. Surely it was good to seek peace, to move away from the confusion of the world and to seek strength in silence. There were certainly others who were willing to devote their entire existence to this way of life, who, in the quiet dignity of the simplest activity, saw the highest praise they could sing to the Lord.

Ambrosius sighed. Some quickly began to get very bored.

He straightened from his crouched posture, perched on his knees beside the long patch of kitchen herbs. The bed was almost ten meters long and one meter deep. The different plants, neatly arranged, were separated by thin wooden plates, which had been pushed vertically into the soft earth. Ambrosius, former bishop and at this time no more than a simple priest, was not even finished with half of the work he had been asked to do and his back ached. No one resented him for allowing himself a break. He wasn't in a dungeon. He was no slave and no servant, the latter at least not in the immediate sense of the word.

In search of a suitable way to get rid of the annoying bishop, without wantonly provoking his followers in the church, the new Emperor Thomasius had invented a tradition that was later to have a significant impact on church life: the monastery. The Emperor himself had founded it, far from any major city, in the middle of Gaul, in such a remote area that even a Christian like Ambrosius was sometimes inclined to call it godforsaken.

He wasn't alone in this.

Also Petronius, who had survived the confusion in North Africa, had been sent here to "think things over," as the Emperor had said, until the end of his days. The property wasn't small at all. A stone church had been built, lodgings, a stable, a well drilled, fields laid out. In addition to Ambrosius and Petronius, twenty-six other priests lived in the community, and they were all here voluntarily. That all their roommates belonged to the Arian heresy, Ambrosius was not surprised to discover. The Arians had a great interest in keeping him under surveillance. And so there were always some of his brothers in his vicinity. His mail was read. He wasn't allowed to cross beyond the fencing of the sprawling complex. It wasn't a prison in the traditional sense. Nobody was tortured. He wasn't hungry – the meals were even quite varied. He could do more or less what he thought was right as long as he participated in the community tasks and didn't cause any trouble. Ambrosius was still trying to figure out what exactly qualified as "trouble." So far, he had met with tolerant friendliness among his brothers.

It was almost as hard to endure as the monotonous work on the field.

Petronius, who was busy planting herbal seeds not far from him, mumbled something to himself. Ambrosius couldn't help but smile. The poor guy was suffering from the aftermath of their defeat especially hard. He saw his lifelong dream destroyed, the desire to once hold an episcopal ministry. Sure, Ambrosius had quietly been exiled from his position, but at least he could boast of having once reached the height of his career. In addition, the former bishop continued to make a name for himself as a scholar. Nobody prevented him from writing witty religious treatises and memoranda. There were even enough people who wanted to read them. Perhaps Ambrosius wouldn't be recorded, in this version of history, as a particularly successful politician, but he was still able to work on his image as a clerical teacher.

This was no consolation for the good Petronius, whose qualities lay more in the realm of intrigue and subtle whispering, and not so much in learning and spiritual contemplation. Sure, he knew the scriptures – but more because it was expected of someone like him and less because his religious zeal drove him to study hard. His ambition had been different, and so he now suffered more under the exile than Ambrosius himself did.

The former bishop looked around, nodding to the two brothers who happened to be busy nearby, setting up a hedge of berries that would make a wonderful source of compote. They returned his silent greeting with friendly restraint.

Ambrosius was lucky to have all his limbs. The new Emperor was different from the previous brood, he had to acknowledge that.

249

Politically blinded, yes, and not filled with the fire of the true faith. But nobody who seemed to be particularly vindictive. And he had smart advisors. Even the Bishop of Rome he was said to have pulled on his side.

Ambrosius wondered where and when he had failed. This was an important question. Did one not learn from mistakes? And even if this lesson couldn't be of much use to him anymore, the knowledge itself was valuable enough. After careful consideration, he concluded that he had made two mistakes. For one thing, he had let Theodosius drift too easily into the spell of the time-wanderers. On the other hand, he had too hastily planned the end of Maximus.

Ambrosius looked at the small shovel in his dirty hands and sighed. Both mistakes were forgivable because they were based on human fallibility, the size of the task that had overwhelmed him. He had been premature and too optimistic about the outcome of the plan. The Lord put always big stones in the way of the Faithful, no matter how much he thought their way was right. Ambrosius had sunned himself in the blessing of God, forgetting that the blessing always included trials with the risk of failure.

He was ready to accept these mistakes.

Indeed, as he thought of it, a third, a fatal, indeed unforgivable mistake was responsible for his failure.

Ambrosius pressed his lips on each other and rammed the shovel into the ground as if to stab the dirt. He took a deep breath, trying to get his emotions under control. Yes. Unforgivable. All his life he would regret that. And this monastery was a wonderful place to deal with his self-reproach intensively. Perhaps the Emperor had sensed that and deliberately exposed him to this torture.

Ambrosius, he was convinced, had not shown enough fanaticism and radicalism. Deep in his heart, he knew that God had expected more from him. He should have punished more Arians. He would have had to persecute other heretics just as intensely, the Mithras followers, the Jews – especially the Jews! – and the followers of Jupiter and Mars, the friends of the Egyptian cults and the oriental ones. Here he had proved too hesitant. And so, he was sure, the Lord had turned away from him and given his enemies victory.

Ambrosius hoped that someday someone would arise who was stronger in faith and had the grace and gift of wielding the cleansing sword of the true gospel with greater fervor than the former bishop of Milan.

His prayers concentrated around this hope.

List of characters

Aurelius Africanus: Roman Trierarch

Ambrosius of Milan: Roman bishop

Aurelia: companion of Rheinberg

Peter Behrens: infantry sergeant

Bertius: Roman legionary

Charamadoye: King of Nobatia

Claudia: servant of Julia

Clodius: a freedman

Johann Dahms: Chief Engineer of the *Saarbrücken*

Flavia: a thief

Gaudentius: prefect in Africa

Godegisel: gothic nobleman

Dietrich Joergensen: Officer of the *Saarbrücken*

Julia: daughter of Marcus Gaius Michellus

Harald Köhler: NCO of the *Saarbrücken*

Klaus Langenhagen: Officer of the *Saarbrücken*

Magnus Maximus: usurper and emperor

Modestus: Praetorian prefect of Constantinople

Dr. Hans Neumann: Medical doctor of the *Saarbrücken*

Petronius: a priest

Marcus Flovius Renna: Roman military prefect

Jan Rheinberg: Captain of the *Saarbrücken* and Magister Militium of Theodosius

Richomer: Roman officer

Marcus Tullius Salius: Roman centurion with a special mission

Sassmann: German infantryman and sharpshooter

Lucius Sempronus: Roman officer

Theodosius: Roman Emperor

Quintus Virilius: Roman legionary

Thomas Volkert: Ensign of the *Saarbrücken* and Roman officer

Klaus von Geeren: Infantry officer and company commander

Johann Freiherr von Klasewitz: former First Officer of the *Saarbrücken* and officer in the service of Maximus

Wazeba: an envoy of Aksum

Preview

The Emperor's Men #7 "Rising Sun," will open a new chapter in this exciting Alternative History-universe.

The new submarine flotilla is the pride of the Japanese Navy. The maiden voyage of the newest boat not only attracts the attention of the Imperial family yet is at the same time a test for the selected crew. But shortly after departure, something mysterious happens: The submarine seems to sink, and all crew members lose consciousness. When they awaken, they realize with horror that their boat has left its element. It rests on the top of a gigantic tomb for the King of Mutal, lord of the largest metropolis of the Maya, in the middle of the Central American mainland, some 1500 years in the past. The confused crew goes straight into war and faces the crucial question of where their path will lead them now – to an empire or straight into disaster?

Made in the USA
San Bernardino, CA
04 March 2020